Children of Earth
Part 2

Princess of Luna

Machine Mind of Ceres

Henry Melton

Children of Earth
Part 2
Princess of Luna
Machine Mind of Ceres

Henry Melton

Wire Rim Books
Hutto, Texas

WRB

Printing History
First Edition: November 2025
ISBN 978-1-935236-95-5

ePub ISBN 978-1-935236-96-2

Website of Henry Melton
www.HenryMelton.com

Printed in the United States of America

Wire Rim Books
www.wirerimbooks.com

Acknowledgements

As I bring the Project Saga to its conclusion with this Children of Earth trilogy, I'm grateful for the special early readers, some of which have been helping me from the beginning, decades ago. This time, it was a big ask, seeking help with three books at once.

Jim Dunn, Linda Elliott, Todd Hartman, Mike Lynch, Scott McNay, Tom Stock

Contents

Princess of Luna

Machine Mind of Ceres

The 48–Hour Lunar Day

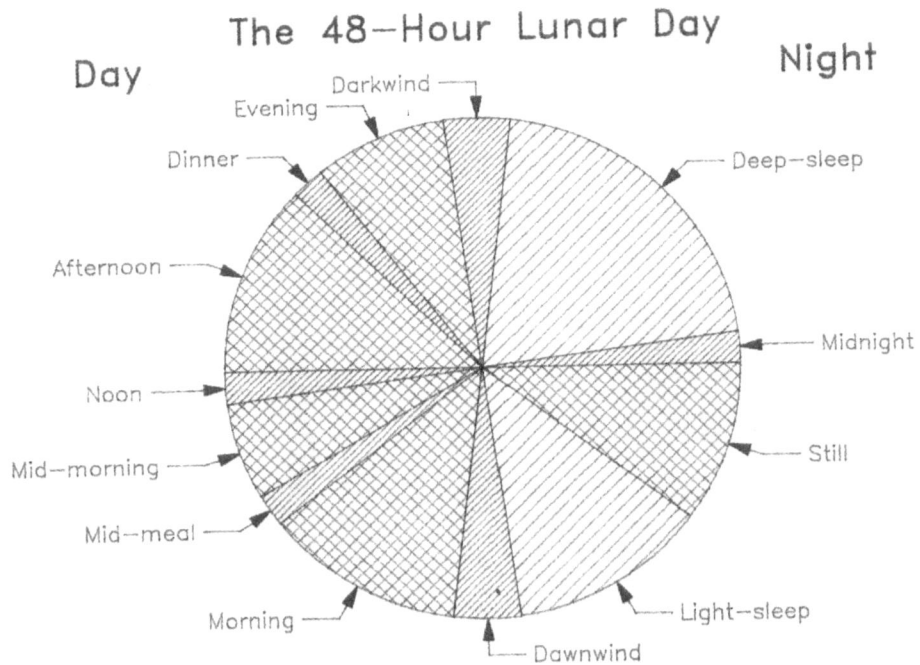

Day

Night

Evening — Darkwind

Dinner

Afternoon

Noon

Mid–morning

Mid–meal

Morning

Dawnwind

Light–sleep

Still

Midnight

Deep–sleep

Northeastern Luna

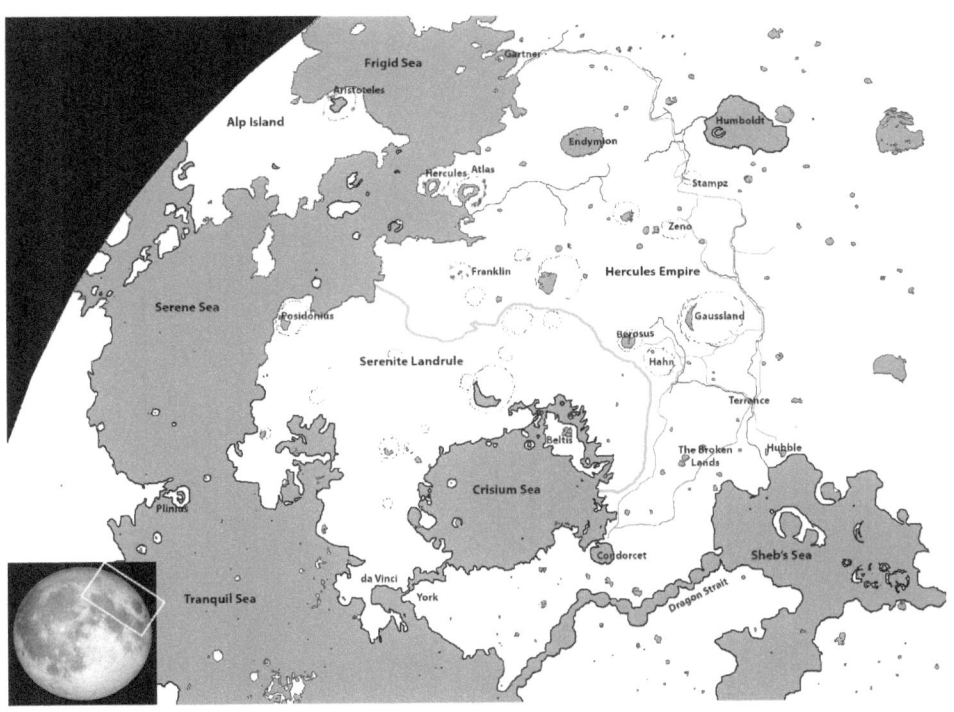

Cis-Terran Space

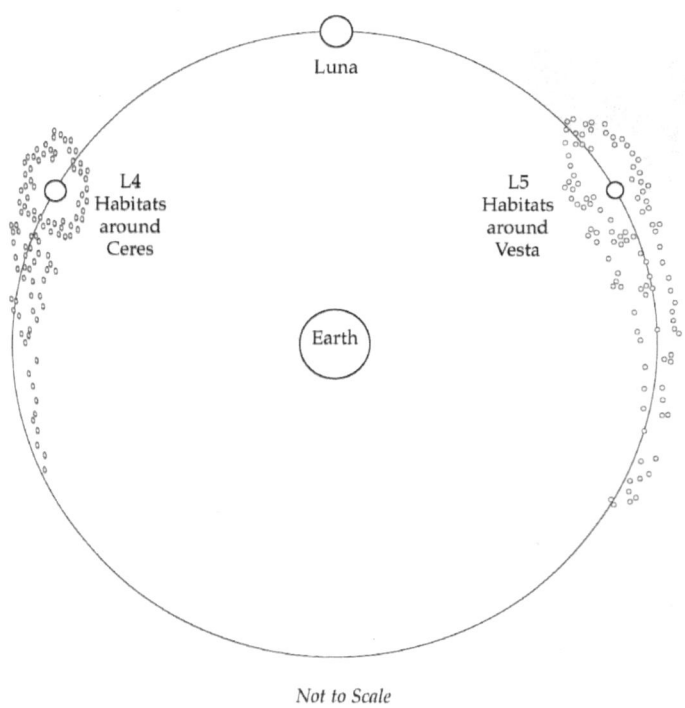

Not to Scale

Princess of Luna

After the system-wide collapse of civilization known as the Plague, survivors were left on Earth, Mars, and the Space Cities—the Lagrangian habitats clustered around Ceres and Vesta in Earth orbit. Most of those habitats were no longer self-sustaining and many people migrated to the partially terraformed Luna, since Earth and Mars were off limits to space travel.

It was not surprising that even on Luna, people had trouble getting along in peace.

Message Goodbye

I'm going to die!

Ohen bar Clay of Chase-on-Ha felt the panic thoughts surging through his new traveling companion, Lord Casey, third son of Baron of Chimbote, Xanthe, Mars. Casey had only been appointed Ambassador to Luna just this morning. It was a big job for a young noble, only a couple of years younger than Ohen was, although Ohen had to convert the thirteen Mars years into twenty-six Earth years or thirty-three U'tanse years just to get a better feel for how mature he might be.

Ohen said, "Just calm down. That strap on the seat will hold you in place, but it's not really necessary. Down is toward your feet, just like always."

Casey nodded, but his eyes were locked on the display. "But the window…."

On the display screen, the rough surface of Phobos was visibly moving, covering a third of the frame. The hazy expanse of the Martian atmosphere showed in the background. Casey felt like they were falling, ready to crash.

Ohen blanked the screen. He knew their orbit was safe, but the visuals were too upsetting to the man who had never flown anywhere, much less into space.

"Just close your eyes, Casey. Think about the floor under your feet and the cushion of your chair. We're safe. The artificial weight you feel is close to what you've felt all your life."

The young noble gentleman tried. He'd bravely accepted King Harmon's charter to go on this historic mission to represent Mars to the emperor of Luna, but from the moment they had lifted off, his life-long position as a noble of the Kingdom of Xanthe now meant nothing. He was at the mercy of this giant of a man who controlled powers he'd never dreamed of. And it was far too late to turn back.

Ohen could read all of Casey's thoughts. *And you'd even be more upset if you realized my psychic abilities. I need to hide what I shouldn't know.*

Ohen said, "Are you feeling better now? I have one more task to take care of before we leave Martian orbit."

Casey tried to calm himself and opened his eyes. The room seemed just like before. They could be back on the ground for all he could tell.

"What's an orbit?"

Ohen adjusted the gravity back to Mars normal. He'd attempted to raise it a little so that they could get some exercise on the trip to Luna, but maybe that was a little too much too soon for Casey.

"Oh, an orbit is just a path through space. It's special. Not so slow that we go back down to the ground." *Don't say crash!* "But it's not so fast that we fly off into space either."

Ohen looked at Casey and it appeared he was calming down.

"I will need to look out the 'window' again. You can just close your eyes if it's too stressful."

"I'll be okay." Casey said confidently. He'd done that all his life, charged ahead when he didn't really know what he was doing. Mostly it had worked out okay.

The screen lit up and Ohen marked the position of the beacon he'd left in orbit when he'd first arrived on Mars. It was still squawking out it's radio signal, awaiting for the rescue mission. He needed to change what it said, but to do that, he needed to bring it back inside.

"What is that cross in the stars?" asked Casey.

"It's just a marker, as if I'd marked on the window with a grease pen. It just shows me where I left a device. I need to pick it back up."

Casey nodded, not really understanding.

Quickly, the tractor beam pulled the small device back to the boat and with a little care, he sucked it back into the airlock with a utility beam.

"Do you want to look at it?"

Casey nodded and stood up. Ohen opened the inner hatch and picked up the gadget. He had to be careful. The side that had been in the sun was hot to the touch.

"It's got spikes," Casey said.

"Those are radio antennae. This device sends a message to the U'tanse, my people, when they come to rescue me. Right now it's saying that I'm going down to the surface of Mars. I need to change that."

He put it on his work bench and switched into recording mode.

"Urgent: Under no circumstances should any tractor/pressor beam be directed toward Earth! There is a powerful, active protection around the planet and it can drain the power cells of any craft that attempts to send any beam or object toward Earth.

"This is indeed the home system of humanity. Not only Earth but also Mars and Luna have been settled."

He went on for a couple of minutes giving a summary of what he'd learned.

"At this point, I am traveling to Luna, in order to learn more. I don't advise landing on Mars yet because they are at war. Explosive-powered projectiles are commonly used. Extreme caution should be used. The king of Xanthe is aware of the U'tanse and might be open to diplomatic contact, but things can always change."

He turned off the recording. Casey had listened to it all. He'd known most of the details, but was most impressed that Owen Barclay hadn't tried to hide any of it from him.

Ohen nodded. "That ought to do it. I'll now put it back into a stable orbit where my people can hear it if they're looking for me."

He put it back into the airlock and a puff of air launched it back out.

Casey saw the package dwindle in the window. "You're just leaving it out here."

"Yes, circling the planet for years, until someone hears it."

Ohen paused for a moment. "Do you want to leave a message for someone before we leave the area of Mars?"

Casey considered it. "Like a computer message?"

"Yes. We're close enough to Phobos so that likely it would relay a message. I just don't know how strong the radio is in your computer. It'll certainly reach from the ground up to Phobos, but when we're half-way to Luna, I really don't know if it's strong enough."

"But didn't the king talk to the emperor of Luna?"

"Yes, but Phobos was relaying that message. It probably has very powerful radios, in addition to sensitive receivers. I just don't know what the computer on Luna is capable of. We might be out of contact for a while until we reach Luna."

"How strong is the radio on this spaceship?"

Ohen shook his head. "My people use a different kind of radio. I really don't think computers and my ship can exchange messages."

Casey nodded. "So I'll be cut off for a while. Maybe I should send a message to Luthe."

Ohen coached him how to set up his little canister radio and then Casey addressed a message to Lady Luthe at Orson.

"Hello, Sis. I just thought I'd let you know that I'm on my way to Luna. I'm sorry that I took this position without giving you time to yell at me, but when the king asked, I had to jump. The king has promised that you'll be taken care of financially."

He talked some more, and Ohen tried not to listen in, but they were in the same room, and would be for the remainder of the trip. He wondered how the message would make it to Lady Luthe. She certainly didn't have a computer of her own. Probably some military officer would have to copy it down on paper and a courier would deliver it.

But Casey was grateful for the chance to send the message and tell his sister about seeing Mars from above the atmosphere.

· · ·

Ohen was just a little nervous after learning about the powerful Project Control which could disable him and leave his boat, the B3, stranded in space if he accidentally violated one of its rules. It had happened before, when he was approaching the inner planets and attempted to use Earth as an anchor point to drain some energy. It was possible to keep the boat alive with batteries as he'd done before, but he never wanted it to make that mistake again.

This time, he'd asked his Martian computer to suggest potential flight paths from Mars to Luna. Once he'd answered a few questions about his boat's capabilities, the computer suggested several, all guaranteed to be free of conflicts with Project Control.

Ohen chose one that would give Casey a good view of his departing home planet and, once they arrived, a good view of Earth and Luna. It wasn't the fastest route, but Casey probably needed some time to adapt to space flight before dropping him suddenly into the role of the Ambassador from Mars.

"Barclay, why did you come to Mars all alone. This spaceship is big enough for more people. It's more like the parlor at my house than the inside of a carriage."

Ohen spread his hands. "It was a miscalculation. The real starship that can travel between the U'tanse home and Earth was almost out of power. There was only energy to return home. When we were on the far outreaches of this star, when it was only a small dot in the sky, we were uncertain whether this was Earth's system or not. Most of the crew wanted to return home quickly and were skeptical that this was Earth's sun.

"However, I was hopeful that it was really the right place. I volunteered to get closer in this small boat, so that I could confirm whether we had found Earth or not. Sadly, it was a journey of many months and there was only room for me and my supplies.

"When we confirmed that Mars had an atmosphere and that Earth had three moons, then there was strong doubt that we had found the right place. The starship returned home and I was left alone to find a way to survive until they could return for me."

Ohen smiled. "Then, when I saw farmland and cities on Mars, I knew people could live there, so I landed. And then I was captured and caught up in the Xanthe-Candorian war."

Casey nodded. "So this 'starship' is a bigger craft then?"

"Oh, yes! We had four of these boats docked inside of it. There was a crew of fifty, although there was really room for hundreds of people if we had needed them. The starship can leap instantly between stars. It's not like this boat, where we have to travel days or weeks to get from one planet to another."

"So they will come back for you?"

"Hopefully. The starships are very rare and valuable. It might take years before they return. I have to plan for my own survival in case they never make it back."

. . .

Ohen made Casey train his muscles and get used to space travel. When he wasn't watching Mars dwindle in size out the screen, he made Casey walk around in the cabin. He explained what the airlock was, and the dangers of the vacuum outside the outer door. He even exposed half an apple to vacuum and let Casey feel it and imagine what would happen to a human body in the same circumstances.

But the "window" was an endless fascination to the man who had never traveled more than a few hundred kloms from his family's estate on Mars, usually by horse-drawn carriage. Ohen even set up some quick-aim buttons so Casey could switch the outside view from Mars to Earth and Luna on a whim. It took a bit for him to accept that the viewport wasn't a real piece of glass to the outside and could be aimed at will.

"Phobos and Deimos are just rocks, aren't they?"

"Very big rocks, but essentially yes. But that's true of Mars as well, and Luna and Earth. The difference is that when a rock gets big enough, its gravity is strong enough to pull itself into a ball."

Casey accepted that Barclay knew what he was talking about, even if it didn't make any sense. A lot of what was going on didn't make any sense. But he had to believe his own eyes.

. . .

"Computer," Ohen asked on the second day, "it doesn't appear that Casey's most recent message was sent. Are you out of radio range?"

"Yes."

"Is there anything I can do to increase that range?"

"Radio signal strength is reduced by distance and any barrier between sender and receiver. Moving the computer outside the hull and positioning it on the same side as the most sensitive receiver would help some, but there will still be a period of time on this transit that no reliable communication is possible."

"How about if I set up a radio booster so that I could transmit your signal with my radios?"

"There exist such booster devices. It is possible that there is one in the Orson Welles warehouse."

Ohen winced. It would have been nice to know that earlier.

"I have more technical knowledge that most people. What are the specifications necessary to make one of those boosters?"

"The core is a computer specially programmed to handle communication transfers and two broadband transmitters and two sensitive receivers."

Ohen was hesitant to give up just because he didn't have the computer. "What is broadband in this situation?"

"Three kloms through three centimeters should be adequate for a mobile installation."

Ohen sagged. That was everything he considered radio. The entire spectrum. Could one radio even handle that range? Certainly not U'tanse technology.

"A smaller range won't do?"

The computer hesitated, and Ohen knew it wasn't because it was calling for help from Phobos. It must be attempting to calculate possibilities.

It spoke, "For an emergency situation, simple transmissions can be monitored by the larger Project installations, however normal messages using the standard Net protocols are not possible."

Ohen sighed. The computer was giving up on the idea. The computers had their standard system and hacking into it with his alien technology was not possible. At least without an in-depth understanding of those protocols. It was hardly likely the simple utility computer he'd brought back to life had that information loaded in its public memory. It would be like explaining to a Ba how a human brain worked. The Ba had never been able to explain themselves—how a collection of small tile-like creatures yet appeared to be a single individual. They didn't even understand the question.

"Hey, Casey. I'm giving up. We'll just be out of contact until we get closer to Luna."

Arrival at Luna

"Luna doesn't have a moon." Casey was staring at the cloudy atmosphere. "No rocks."

Ohen nodded. "Luna is a moon. Back before spaceflight, that's what people on Earth called it—the Moon. But I really don't know anything about it. The only things I know come from a book written back at the time of the Star—the Betelgeuse supernova. That's when my ancestors were kidnapped.

"Back then, Luna didn't have any atmosphere. Things have obviously changed."

Casey munched on rattle beans, a U'tanse snack food that he'd fallen in love with. "You can see the ocean, over there, and down there." He stared at the image. "It's a lot different than Earth. A lot more clouds."

Ohen nodded. "The atmosphere is deeper. It makes sense. You can't change the gravity on that scale, so the only way to get enough oxygen in your lungs is to have enough weight of the air above you to make it happen. It was the same as the air on Mars."

"What do you mean?"

"On Ko, and on Earth, the atmosphere is just about a hundred kloms deep. That's all it takes to make enough air pressure to breathe. On Mars it's a lot deeper, and on Luna it must be a thousand kloms deep to make the pressure work."

Ohen reached for the display controls. "You can see it here. He adjusted the magnification and pointed to the thin line of Earth's atmosphere against the blackness of space. "Compare that with the atmosphere of Luna. It's a big difference."

Casey nodded, but he wasn't actually curious about the science of it all. He was just overwhelmed by new things.

...

The computer spoke. "Message has been transferred."

Ohen, who was reading at the time, reviewing the few paragraphs that had been written about Luna in the Book, stood up and walked the two steps over to the computer.

"Computer, send a message to the Emperor of Luna: The ship from Mars is approaching Luna. On board is Lord Casey, Ambassador from Mars and Owen Barclay, representative of the U'tanse people. We should arrive within a day, however we would appreciate landing directions. Neither of us have maps of Luna. We can see the features on the ground when the clouds cooperate, but have no more information than that."

"Message sent."

Casey pulled out his canister computer and sent his own message back to King Harmon telling of their arrival at Luna, but giving no real detailed information. It also went through with no problems.

Ohen nodded. There had to be something with a sensitive radio receiver and a strong transmitter for Luna, just as Phobos had served that duty for Mars. Maybe Luna didn't have a moon of its own, but there was something, somewhere.

It was over an hour before a message came back from Luna.

"Greetings from John Fasail, technical advisor in the court of Emperor Neeley. I have been given the task of providing your directions. I do have the latitude and longitude of the landing area at the court, but if you don't have a map, then that's not enough. My computer tells me that with three landmarks, your computer could establish that coordinate system for your use. Does this make sense to you?"

Ohen replied, "Yes, however we will have to be coached through the process. I am familiar with latitude and longitude and that would be most useful. From our current position above the atmosphere, I can make out perhaps ten percent of the surface. I will put our ship into an orbit until we can identify the necessary landmarks."

The conversation was sluggish, as there were relay delays, just like there had been with Phobos. And even when the first landmark was identified, Ohen was made painfully aware that the Martian computers were effectively blind and landmarks visible on the ship's display weren't available to them. Just because a human could see the peninsula below didn't mean that the computer was even aware of which direction the ship's display was showing.

Deeper questioning revealed that Casey's canister computer could sense the position of a nearby person and could actually identify a face, but didn't have the resolution to be of any help. Ohen's computer had a better camera, hidden as a little dot above the keyboard. When they moved a table and positioned the computer before the ship display, the computer could identify the markings. Ohen then had to adjust the orbit and orientation of the display so that the window to the land below was pointed straight down toward the center of the globe.

It took hours. Ohen and Casey watched the land appear through the clouds below, and when there was something distinctive, Ohen tried to describe what they saw to John Fasail. It then took long minutes before the technical assistant found something similar in the maps at his disposal and relayed the latitude and longitude back to the ship. Even after a half-dozen landmarks were described and identified, the computer still hadn't found an unambiguous solution.

Ohen said, "I'm going to change the orbit of the ship, so that we'll get a greater range of surface features." That took another hour, and then they had to start the process all over again.

Finally, the computer declared that they had a minimal map of Luna with its coordinate overlay. They had still never seen more than a fraction of the surface, but they could head in the right direction.

. . .

"Casey, you should sit down and use the lap belt. We're going into the atmosphere."

Ohen had adjusted the orbit again to aim them for a straight approach but when they encountered the atmosphere, he had to constantly make corrections. The Lunar atmosphere was not only deep, but it had many layers, often with different wind currents.

They were also flying blind. The boat, B3, was never really designed for flying with no visible references. In space, there were always the stars and planets. Even flying on Mars, there had been the sun and the landmarks below. In the technical literature back on Ha, he'd heard of experiments with inertial orientation, but when he was designing the boat series, it had never seemed that useful. He chose to wait until the technology matured.

I could use something like that now. They were getting lost all over again. They had a map, but now they had no idea where they were on that map.

I should have stayed above the atmosphere until I was at the correct position and then killed my orbital velocity and settled straight down.

But maybe he could pull through. He just had to rely on his own sense of where the winds were blowing him and try to compensate.

Casey asked, "How long is this going to take?"

"Never done it before."

The boat was slowing down. They'd killed much of the forward velocity and they ought to be within a thousand kloms of the Stampz crater that had been identified as their destination.

But the winds kept increasing in intensity.

"Computer, message to John Fasail: We are into the thicker parts of the atmosphere, fighting severe winds. We will probably need more help with landmarks once we get in visible sight of the land."

A minute later came the reply: "Are you caught in the dawnwind? I never thought to warn you. Luna has devastating winds every sunrise and every sunset. You can never attempt to land in the winds. It will calm down during the middle of the day and the middle of the night. Don't even try to fight the winds!"

Ohen had about made that decision on his own. Fighting the winds up high was bad enough. Getting close to the ground and being thrown about by storm winds higher than he'd ever experienced was just suicide.

He had been traveling northeast and had dropped into the night shadow shortly before the winds had gotten bad. He needed to travel eastward to advance into the daylight, if that's what it took to ease the turbulence.

But am I sure this is east?

He could sense thoughts. There were many people living on Luna, but it didn't feel as populated as Mars had been. Still, both of these worlds were more densely populated than the U'tanse settlements. He wished he could navigate by those thoughts, but that wasn't his skill. Unless someone was visualizing their position and he could make sense of that, the thoughts were just a general presence, with no pointer to the mind behind them.

Suddenly, a gust caught the square, wing-shaped boat and flipped it.

"Hey!" Casey shouted, gripping the belt on his chair. In spite of the floor gravity, the tumble could be felt strongly as the lunar gravity was added and then rapidly subtracted from the artificial pull of the beams in the floor.

"Just hang on!" Ohen worked the controls, fighting the end-over-end tumble and then easing them into a slight flat spin to give the boat more stability.

He laughed. "Well, if I wasn't lost before, that one scrambled my sense of direction."

Casey's hands were white-knuckled. "Not a laughing matter!"

"We're in no danger. It'll just take longer to get there."

Ohen's clairvoyance was a help. He could sense the ground a dozen kloms below and it helped him keep the boat flying straight and level. He decided to push up higher, for now.

A few minutes later, Casey pointed at the display. "Hey, clear skies... no, I lost it."

Ohen paid more attention to the screen and when the gap in the clouds reappeared, he cancelled the lateral spin. With the ground below and the sunlight showing the sky above, he was able to fight the winds successfully and fly into the clear air.

The sun was coming up. The clouds around him were lit, and in places on the ground, mountain tops and crater rims were standing in bright contrast to the land below. Isolated clouds were racing past, a very visible indicator of these sunrise and sunset winds.

People live with this every day? John "just forgot" about these winds? It appeared Luna was a very different environment than Mars.

Ohen set a course in the direction of the sun, generally, staying in clear sky as much as possible.

After a few more minutes, he called his guide again.

"Advisor Fasail, we have found a patch of clear sky. We are in daylight and the winds appear to be easing somewhat. We are over open waters, I don't see land. The sun is about twenty degrees above the horizon. I've totally lost our sense of position. I could use your advice."

There was a fifteen-minute delay, then came the reply: "Good to hear you made it through the dawnwind. I apologize again for not warning you. If you can't see land, and the sun is at twenty degrees, you are probably over the Crisium Sea. You can expect a large island at the northeast edge of the it. If so, then from that point, you need a northerly bearing, just slightly easterly. And from that point I have very good maps, so you'd need to fly low enough so we can compare landmarks. There are only three laser cannon left on Luna, and none are anywhere near your location, so there should be no danger flying in visible sight of the ground."

Ohen was shocked at the revelation that Luna even had energy weapons of that power. His own lasers were hardly powerful enough to scorch wood. They were just ranging and communication instruments and no one ever considered making laser cannons.

And it appeared Luna had a history of warfare, just like Mars. Probably Casey wasn't surprised, but any U'tanse would be.

Ohen adjusted his course northward. When they passed over the large island, he was disturbed to be able to make out ruins, buildings long ago flattened by some large explosion. He couldn't sense any current inhabitants on the place. He adjusted his course north-northeastward.

They continually updated their guide with their position. "Just call me John." His replies were sometimes immediate; sometimes there were delays. Maybe he needed time to consult his maps. Maybe it was a relay delay, like with Phobos on Mars.

Flying at an altitude of just a couple of kloms above the landscape, Ohen could see the ground clearly now, even when the sun was obscured by high-level clouds.

John sent a final route. "Keep following the river until it branches to the east. Follow that eastern branch until you see a crater wall with an entrance gap. That is Stampz. Your landing field is at the center of the crater, next to our ship. It is well marked."

They were getting close enough that Ohen was beginning to get a telepathic sense of John Fasail during some of the calls. He was starting to pick up a sense of conflict.

John was eager to have them land, excited to meet people from another world. But he was also charged with keeping the pilot of the other spaceship up to date on their location.

It would be a crime if this turns into another battle between ships. I hope these Martians know that blowing up a beamship would destroy us both.

Ohen caught a flicker of history. Something the guide had read as a child. Apparently that island in the Crisium Sea had been flattened by an exploding ship.

Ohen could certainly understand. Any interplanetary vessel like his had enough energy stored in its power cells to be dangerous. If the B3 were destroyed, it would easily destroy this whole cratered settlement.

And it was a very enchanting place, visible on the screen as they sailed over the crater wall and saw the patchwork agricultural lands and the city in the center.

John's thoughts intruded as he saw them in the distance. **What kind of a ship is that?** The pilot in the cylindrical ship parked near the tall stone castle was watching them through his ship's telescopic camera, puzzled as well.

Ohen quickly got on the computer.

"I am in sight of the Stampz central city. My ship is U'tanse design, and probably not what you're used to. I see a green patch next to the tall Project-style ship. Is that our landing site?"

"Yes, that is where you should land. Do you use cirrance, as our ship does?"

"We use rapid cycling of tractor beams to produce downward winds. I assume that's what cirrance means?"

His reply was immediate. "Yes, that's it. People have been warned to avoid the area as you land."

Ohen had his mind wide open, trying to catch every thought of John and Curtis, the beamship pilot. Curtis was hearing every word, echoing in his ship. There must be a secondary radio link between John in the castle and the pilot's station. Curtis had a powerful weapon aimed at them, just in case it the strangers were planning an attack.

Ohen was relieved it didn't appear to be a laser. But it was critical that he made no threatening moves.

"Okay, I intend to hover over the landing patch and settle down gently. I'm not really sure how Project beamships land, but the U'tanse design is very agile in the air. I'm just a little nervous about your winds."

John sounded relieved. "It's okay. Inside the crater walls, the winds are tame for the most part. Plus it's hours since dawnwind and there's hardly a breeze out."

Ohen was glad he'd had the chance to fly up the river from the sea. It had given him a better feel of how the B3 handled in lunar gravity and the lunar atmosphere. His instruments showed that the air pressure was about half of the U'tanse standard. The oxygen percentage was much higher to make up the difference.

When he centered the boat above the landing patch, he could see ripples in the grass. He hadn't really paid much attention when he'd landed on Mars the first time, and the only other time was on the roof of a building. He went through the same steps, but this landing was prettier.

"I'm down," he told Casey. "I'll be adjusting the gravity to lunar standard, so be careful."

Casey jumped up from his chair. "I need to change into my court dress." His mind was abruptly centered on his ambassador role. He rushed to the bin where he'd stored his luggage.

Ohen called John. "We're powered down. It'll take us a little bit to adjust our air and gravity to Luna standards. Please be patient."

"Take your time. We'll have a greeting party down there before too long. It's an historic occasion."

John was quite an actor. His voice was friendly, but like most of the officials of Stampz he was anxious over having another spaceship here. Their history was highlighted by battles won or lost by the presence of a beamship to tip the balance. A peaceful diplomatic mission was known in theory, but it had never worked out in practice.

Lord Casey was quickly dressed in his trimmed finery, and it made him look at least a few years older. Ohen didn't have anything fancy, but he did have his dark blue uniform he'd used when he was a military advisor for the Kingdom of Xanthe. It was good enough and didn't have any decorations he'd have to explain away.

"I've been adjusting the air to Luna's composition and pressure over the past few minutes. Have you felt any difference?"

Casey took a deep breath. "Maybe a little. I hadn't noticed anything until you mentioned it."

"As we walk out the door, be careful. Gravity will be half of what you expect, so you could trip and fall. People will be watching, so don't give them something to laugh about."

Casey took it to heart. He went first, resting his hand on the doorsill as he stepped out. He couldn't help but grin as his step had an extra bounce to it.

Ohen paused to set the door to lock behind him. If their hosts were considering attacking them, then they'd certainly consider sending in a sneak thief when he wasn't looking.

Still, the people watching as they came out were more friendly than not. The officials were just being cautious, and given their history, being prudent.

A man twice his age and dressed just slightly better than Casey stepped forward from the crowd.

"Greetings, travelers. I am Richard Neely, Emperor of Luna."

Banquet

Ambassador Casey bowed, and Ohen followed his cue. All of a sudden, Casey was the expert in diplomacy and he was just an engineer out of his depth. He'd just follow along.

Casey introduced himself and the Kingdom of Xanthe he served.

"And my traveling companion is Owen Barclay, representative of the U'tanse people."

Ohen bowed again. "I am a traveler, a scout. My people have been lost from Earth since the time of the Star. It is only recently that we have rediscovered the rest of humanity."

The emperor nodded. "Seeing your strange ship, I can well believe that you are not from here." He waved at one of his attendants. "Harris will set you up with rooms in the castle. We've been looking forward to your arrival and the cooks have been planning a banquet for noon. I hope you're up for it."

Ambassador Casey chuckled. "Barclay here has a legendary appetite. I hope your cooks are up for it."

. . .

It was an hour or so later when a casual remark by one of the maids caught Ohen by surprise.

"What do you mean? Isn't it already nearly noon?"

"Oh, no, sir! It's barely mid-morning. Just look at the sun."

He went to the window and looked out over the courtyard where there were still a cluster of people gathered around the strange looking new ship. The sun didn't look like it had moved much.

"Miss, how many hours are there in a day?"

She shrugged as she unpacked his sparse clothing into a free-standing cabinet. "I've been told there are forty-eight hours to the day; dawnwind, morning, mid-meal, mid-morning, noon, afternoon, dinner, evening, dark-wind, deep-sleep, midnight, the still, light-sleep, and then dawnwind again. I personally sleep through the afternoon and the deep-sleep, but other people have their own schedules."

Ohen nodded. "I guess I'll have to adapt. I've been used to twenty-four hour days."

She smiled. "You must be rushed all the time to get through a day like that."

He chuckled. "Perhaps you're right."

. . .

At the banquet table, Casey was seated close enough to Ohen so that they could hear each other, but Ohen was surrounded by new faces. In his close circle, Ohen could feel the thoughts of the pilot of the cylindrical ship. The man was burning with questions, but had been told to wait his turn.

Ohen had questions of his own.

"Why do you have a forty-eight hour day? Earth has twenty-four, and so does Mars. Even the planet where my people were taken has a twenty-hour day. As you can imagine, this long day feels … excessive to me."

A thin, gray-haired man, Chancellor Folken, said, "I'll have a great deal to ask about your people's history, later. However, Luna's day is well documented. The powerful spin-beams that were spinning Luna up from a one-month-long day to a planned twenty-four hour period were interrupted at the time of the Plague. Everything fell apart in that chaos and the Project controllers decided to cancel the beams while they could be shut down under careful control. The result was this double-length day of ours."

The old scholar shook his head. "It was certainly a mistake, but as the Project collapsed, it was one that couldn't be corrected."

"A mistake?"

Folken nodded. "Definitely. Humans still haven't adapted to the longer day. Some people can sleep the whole night through and stay awake all day, but most don't. Culturally, we have made our adjustments, but our biology hasn't. And then there are the sun winds."

Ohen chuckled. "I've had experience, flying in."

"Our long day gives the sun ample time to heat the atmosphere and the winds blow from the day side to the night side constantly. The result here at ground level are fierce winds at sunrise and sunset. If your ship wasn't parked here in the protection of the crater and shielded by the castle, then it would likely be flipped at sunset."

"Perhaps I should take preventive measures."

"Ordinarily, yes. But like I say, here in the crater, it should be safe."

Ohen shook his head. "I have so many questions—after I finish this wonderful food!"

The conversations were wide-ranging. Merchants had their own tales of wagons being overturned by the winds, but were also curious if there might be possibility of trade with Mars. And who were the U'tanse?

Ohen was picking up many thoughts from the people around him, but he had to be very careful not to reveal what he knew. He didn't even want the idea of psychic gifts to cross their minds. If people didn't speak the words, he had to pretend he didn't know.

The pilot, Abraham Chung, introduced himself. "I've got to ask, your ship is TP-based?"

Ohen nodded, "Tractor/pressor beams, yes. Four main units at each corner, steerable in all directions in three dimensions. Originally designed to be a transport between the moon of Ha and the planet Ko, which is much like Earth, this design was chosen to be the landing craft for the starship, since we hoped to investigate planets with atmospheres."

"You fly through the air edge on?"

"Right. Flying like a wing with reduced wind resistance. With the beams aimed vertically, I can land in no more space than the dimensions of the boat."

"Boat?"

"Yes, I tend to call these landing craft 'boats'. The starship, which is much larger, is the ship. But that's just words. My boat can travel the whole system. I had to travel from far beyond the gas giants before I reached Mars."

The pilot shook his head. "I've never traveled farther than the space cities—all in the close neighborhood to Earth and Luna. I'm not sure which planets exist, to be honest. I'd love to get a look at your ship—boat."

"And I'd love to see the insides of yours. There are hundreds of cylinder ships on Mars, but they're all locked off. I've never been inside one."

"Hundreds of ships?" He shook his head, amazed. "I can't imagine that."

Chancellor Folken had been listening. "If Mars has that many ships, why haven't we been visited before now?"

Ohen said, "It's the quarantine. During the Plague, when Mars was first hit, the Project controllers declared a quarantine, and no ship could leave Mars until it was lifted."

Then Chung mused, "And then the controllers all died."

Folken frowned, "The Plague is gone, isn't it?"

"That's what everyone on Mars thinks. No cases for centuries."

"But what about those ships?" Chung asked. "Are they alive?"

"That's the first thing I asked, when I realized all those decorative columns were actually spaceships." Ohen shrugged. "People didn't know, but I asked the computer and it wasn't optimistic. The ships weren't properly shut down and are now drained of energy. They are mostly in good shape, although sometimes people build walls right up to the hull of a ship and that might cause problems."

Chung leaned forward. "That's very interesting. I'd love to tell you the tale of Ship and Brilliant Morning."

Two people down, a man said, "No more Kimmer Ballads at the banquet table!" There was laughter all around. Ohen recognized his voice. He was John Fasail, the man who had guided them across Luna.

The pilot sighed. "Sorry, just the short version then. These cylinder ships have the capability of beaming power back and forth between them. In our history, our first ship brought a dead ship back to life and that became my ship, named Brilliant Morning."

"You have another ship?" Ohen asked.

Chung shook his head. "That ship was destroyed at Beltis Island, in the Crisium Sea. It totally wiped out the place when the power cells vaporized."

Ohen gasped, "I think I saw that place. Nothing but rubble."

Chung nodded. "Every new pilot is taken there. The ground has been melted into glass. It used to be forested land, but nothing much can take root, even after all this time. We visit as part of our training, so we can understand how dangerous our power cells can be."

Ohen had a feeling that the cylinder ships were much more powerful than the boat. His boats were more personnel transports and exploration craft than cargo ships. That cylinder configuration seemed to be designed more for bulk cargo.

Chung was excited. "So if I took Brilliant Morning to Mars and beamed power into one of those dead ships, then maybe I could bring it back to life."

"Except for one thing. That quarantine is still in effect. If your ship is controlled by a computer, like all those Project ships were, then it would land on Mars and never take off again."

Chung frowned. "Oh. But your ship ...."

Ohen nodded. "Yes, my boat isn't under control of the computers. Not a Project ship. That's why I was able to land on Mars and leave with no problem."

There were other conversations around the table, but Ohen was well aware that every word that he or Casey was saying was followed closely. Pilot Chung's idea of rejuvenating and capturing a Martian ship was very exciting to many of them.

Casey was asking a lot of questions about the political situation on Luna and revealing the fact that Mars had a great number of countries and that, although he was confident King Harmon would soon be the most powerful leader on the planet, Mars was a planet in conflict.

Ohen asked, "Chancellor, I'm unfamiliar with the title. What does it mean?"

The man smiled, "Well, in my case, it means I am the spokesman for the Alpine Society, an educational group promoting literacy and scholarship on Luna. Our headquarters are here at Stampz. We're not officially part of the government, but we have close ties with the imperial family and I get invited to many of these banquets. I'm very glad to be here when you showed up. You claim to be from a world not part of the Solar system?"

"That's correct. The U'tanse are a fragment of humanity captured by an alien race back at the time of the Betelgeuse supernova. We barely survived, but over time, we bought our way out of slavery and took over the technology of our captors. For all this time, Earth was a place of myth and legend and we had no idea that humanity had spread to Mars and Luna."

"That's amazing. I've been taught all my life that the stars are so far away that any practical star travel would require faster-than-light travel, and the best minds of humanity had decided that such a thing was impossible."

Ohen nodded. "Exactly. Our physicists believe the same thing. Starship travel is impossible. And yet, the U'tanse have inherited a small number of craft that can travel between stars in an instantaneous leap. We know how to use them, but we don't understand the technology."

"So you didn't invent this?"

"No. The U'tanse use a mix of human technology preserved from the time of our capture plus the technology of the Delense, which we learned."

"The Delense were your captors?"

Ohen chuckled. "No, they were extinct when we were captured. The Cerik were the masters, and they had enslaved the Delense, before they exterminated them."

It was well into the apple cake when Ohen pointed up to the chandeliers above the table. "Those are electric lights?"

Chung nodded. "Space premium ones. These bulbs have lasted over thirty years."

It turned out that Stampz had been using electricity for several decades.

"Do you tap into the electricity of your spaceship?"

Chung hesitated. "While we can do that, we have wind turbines at the Gate. Power is generated during the sunwinds."

Ohen nodded, "And now? Isn't this the 'Still'?"

"Right. We produce power during the winds and use the excess to pump water up to reservoirs on the crater wall. The water spins turbines during quiet times as it returns to the basin near the Gate."

"Fascinating. Mars has been without electricity since the Plague. I had introduced it in the Kingdom of Xanthe, but only for limited use, reactivating equipment left over from the collapse. I had wondered how to store electricity. Batteries were impractical."

A thought intruded. **The tall one sounds well educated.** It was a woman's thought. He glanced up the table a moment later and noticed a young woman seated next to the emperor.

Is she a young wife?

She turned and listened in to the emperor's conversation with Casey. Quickly, Ohen changed his first opinion. She was the daughter. The princess of Luna.

It's a shame Mom can't make it down the stairs anymore. She would have loved to listen to them.

Ohen frowned. He caught just a hint of her worries. The empress had some kind of wasting disease and could no longer be in public.

Some day, when the U'tanse came back for him, would it even be possible for the expert healers like Kerry on the starship to help the people of Mars and Luna? The prohibition against magic and witchcraft was far too real a danger to ignore.

Library

When he walked back to B3's landing site, Ohen deliberately paid no attention to the pair of guards shadowing him. He was not even surprised when the door lock showed signs that someone had been testing it while he was at the banquet. It was obviously a combination lock and they had forgotten to return it to its initial starting position.

Once he entered the airlock and was out of sight of the guards, he opened up the lock and changed it so that no combination would work. He could open it easily with psychokinesis, just like he had on Mars when the batteries ran out, but no one else could, not without damaging the airlock door itself.

His hosts were friendly enough, but getting access to another ship was a really big deal with the Lunarians. It hadn't been spelled out in his conversations, but he'd picked up enough thoughts to make it clear. Stampz was the capital of the combined empire, with an imperial family officially in charge, but Stampz really had no army to speak of. The Hercs and the Serenites, the two major cultural groups, both had historical ties with the imperial family, but either of them could swallow up Stampz easily, if it wasn't for Chung's Brilliant Morning ship. In the past, a beamship had defeated armies easily. Owning the lone ship gave Stampz an unrivaled position of strength.

I really need them to understand that B3 has no military power. I don't have a laser cannon, and I doubt there's anything I could do against their ship or troops on the ground either.

I need to make it clear that they'll gain a lot more by respecting diplomacy than by trying to steal my boat.

He went to the computer. "Send a message to Raymond Wills at Orson on Mars."

He explained to his blacksmith friend how the Stampz people had built a power system using windmills and by pumping water back and forth from a high point to a low point. Raymond was probably the electricity expert on Mars, now that Ohen had left. Maybe he could make a version of the system that would work for the Xanthe Kingdom. He certainly didn't owe Raymond that report, but it wouldn't hurt to help out Xanthe a little more. Eventually, he wanted everyone to be grateful to the U'tanse for making their lives better.

. . .

Chancellor Folken waved at him from down a long hallway and almost broke into a run, before he realized his running days were long past.

"Ambassador Barclay! I've been looking for you."

Ohen raised his hand. "And I'm happy to talk with you, but I'm really not an ambassador. Just Ohen or Barclay is fine."

He nodded. "Ah, yes. Owen. I'm so used to everyone having a title around this place that I'll probably make mistakes.

"I was hoping to talk a bit more about your people. I've never heard any tale of visitors from another planet, and certainly nothing was mentioned during the time of the Star. I thought we could go to the library and see if there are any reference books we could check."

Ohen tilted his head. "You have a library?"

Folken laughed. "Oh, yes. The best library in the world. Perhaps on any world. Are there libraries on Mars?"

Ohen told the chancellor of the military library at Orson, but it was almost exclusively historical records of the kingdom and of course the extensive maps collection.

Folken nodded and listened carefully. "I wish we had good maps of Luna."

They were walking on the basement level of the castle when they entered a well-lit office chamber, with many reading chairs arranged in clusters.

A woman's voice called out, "Don't disparage our maps, Chancellor."

It was the woman Ohen had identified as the princess. Only this time she was dressed in a floor-length, plain white robe.

Folken gave a gentle bow. "Owen Barclay, I'd like you to meet Alice Neeley, the Head Librarian. Alice, this is Owen Barclay, a traveler from another star."

She nodded. "It's good to meet you Sir Barclay. I overheard some of what you said at the banquet."

Ohen nodded to her. "As I was telling the chancellor, I have no real title. I don't seek one either. As I introduce myself, people assume I am named Owen Barclay, but that's not quite accurate either. My people are named with a reference to the father's name, but tracked on the official family trees based on a matrilineal structure. My clan, so to speak, are the descendants of Omelia, wife of Samson the Giant. My name is Ohen bar Clay, Ohen son of Clay. The given name of Ohen, O-H-E-N, is only three generations old and presumably made up at the time. The name Owen, which is what everyone on Mars called me is a much older name, I assume."

Alice nodded. "I can barely hear the difference between Owen and Ohen."

"And I'm content to be called Owen Barclay the rest of my life. I only brought it up because the two of you sound like scholars and might be interested."

She nodded. "I'll probably make mistakes from time to time. But yes, I would like to know everything about your culture. You certainly look like a normal man, other than your height. You say your ancestor was a giant?"

"Yes, are you familiar with a book called the Bible? A religious text?"

That brought a large smile to the librarian. "You must come see the books. I'll show you our Bibles."

She hesitated with her hand on the door, looking at him closely. "We have strict rules about dust and other contaminants." She pulled on gloves from her pocket. "I don't think I have gloves in your size."

He sighed. "That's a problem I've faced all my life. The only gloves I have are my spacesuit gloves back on my boat."

She nodded. "I'll have a set made for you, if you wish."

"I would be grateful."

She led the way inside, and Ohen stopped in his tracks as he saw the row upon row of bookshelves.

"How many books do you have?"

Alice said, "That's one of my ongoing chores. Every few decades, a new chamber is carved into the rocks below and Brilliant Morning heads for the space city Alexandria, where the master library resides, to fill its holds with more books. Classifying the books that come back is something I hope to achieve before I'm done."

She told him the tale of the huge library of books that had been assembled in a space warehouse, destined for the colonies on the newly terraformed Mars.

"And then the ability for the new settlements to print their own copies from a database happened sooner than expected and the giant warehouse was abandoned. The warehouse settlement renamed itself Alexandria and tried to become a tourist attraction. Then when the Plague triggered the universal collapse, the electronic records of all those books effectively vanished. The only books left were a few isolated volumes and the invaluable Alexandrian library."

Ohen nodded. "I can see it. My people were left with only about a hundred books, mostly childrens' picture books, a few novels and cookbooks that the Cerik, our captors, had collected incidentally when preparing to attack Earth. The Father of us all, Abe, spent his life composing the Book, all of his recollections of Earth history and technology.

"The Book is a hefty volume, but one I can hold in one hand. It's just one man's summary of all of that!" He waved at the countless books on the shelves. "I can't imagine what might be there."

. . .

The three of them toured parts of the library with Alice handling the books with her gloves. She showed off the Atlas of Luna, with its extensive map engravings of the current land and oceans of Luna and compared them with an ancient tome that showed the bare landscape before the terraforming began.

Ohen nodded. "These are excellent, but let me tell you of the map room at Orson in the Kingdom of Xanthe." He described the tables as wide as the banquet table and three meters long, with glass covered photographs of the land from space.

"On such a map, the crater of Stampz would be about this big," he said, holding his hands to describe the circle. "You could clearly see the larger buildings and the roads. Probably the ships might be visible, but that's at the limit. Sadly, they are all hundreds of years old, probably photos taken from the moon Phobos on a cloudless day. And even if a spaceship could take fresh ones, there are no printers capable of printing such an image."

Alice looked thoughtful. "Abraham has described a large screen that Brilliant Morning can use to display images. I suppose he might be able to display such a map. Sadly, I haven't managed to find an adequate excuse to take a ride on the ship myself."

Ohen smiled. "I would have thought an imperial princess could have dazzled the pilot."

She gave a slight smile and dismissed the idea with a one-handed gesture. "He's known me all my life, and there are really too many rules restricting access to the ship. We lost the original ship when a crown prince thought too much of his own power and ordered the ship into a trap. It was his last order."

"Hmm. I had hoped to get a look at it, in exchange for a tour of my boat. Maybe you should come along as well—just to provide a third-party comparison of the vehicle designs."

They laughed. The chancellor sighed. "I'd love to come along, too. However, I've been warned you have to climb ladders and that's enough to dissuade me."

Ohen wondered just how frail the man was. In one-sixth gravity, a ladder would hardly be a handicap. The castle had staircases to navigate the floors. Was that a difficulty for him?

They moved on to a section highlighting books printed locally on Luna. It was clear that the Atlas of Luna was one of them.

"Your local printers make larger books than the old ones."

"Yes, I've been told it was because it was difficult to print smaller text. The technology is improving each year. There has even been some experiments with colored inks, although that's still rare. Sadly, many of the older printing presses have been sold to the gossips."

"What's that?"

The chancellor chuckled. "A few years back, one of the printing presses was acquired by a small company in Franklin. The owner specialized in writing single sheets, often just a few paragraphs on a single topic. When he began gossiping about the lives and scandals of the nobles, he began selling a lot of them. They're called gossip sheets. Of course scholars like us were sad to see it. Those sheets were passed around for a day or so and then discarded. Better to write a book that would last, I say."

Alice smiled. "Of course there's the argument that having more things to read, some with a timely urgency to them, has increased the literacy among the population. Not all places have any library at all. Most cities are still hungry for anything to read. The scandal sheets serve a purpose, although I probably wouldn't buy one."

Ohen asked, "You implied there were other temporary publications?"

Alice nodded. "Oh, yes. Once people saw that there was money to be made with the gossip sheets, other operations began in other cities. Some of the more famous scandals have made their way here over time. I have a small collection of them. I doubt you'd know any of the people mentioned, but it does give a hermit like me a taste of cosmopolitan life."

Folken mumbled, "Don't let your father hear you talk about them like that."

She laughed. "I've shown a couple of them to him. My brother Allen was mentioned in one of them."

"You have a brother?"

She nodded. "Two. Allen is working as an imperial representative in Hercules. My younger brother Dalton does the same in the Serenite court in Posidonius. *They* get to see the world. I have to be content with my books."

When they encountered the shelf of Bibles, Ohen begged Alice to thumb through the pages of one. With several false tries, they located the story of Samson.

"They're so big," he said. "Part of Abe's Book is his memories of the Bible, but it has many fewer pages than this! It was only the stories he remembered from his childhood and a summary of the main themes. He always made a point that his memory was incomplete and imperfect and that no one should ever take his summary as infallible. I guess he was right."

Alice said, "I would love to get a chance to read your Book. It sounds like a fascinating volume."

"I'll see what I can do."

Ohen instantly regretted talking about the Book. Of course these scholars would want to read it for themselves. But there had never been any attempt to hide the U'tanse psychic gifts in those pages. *How am I going to explain why I can't let them read it?*

There was a rap on the door. Alice spoke louder. "Enter."

A maid, by her uniform, bowed. "Miss, your mother needs your attendance." The maid's thoughts were more urgent than her words.

A surge of fear flickered from Alice, quickly stifled.

Ohen wondered what was going on.

Alice smiled to the men. "I'm sorry, but I'm needed elsewhere right now. Chancellor, do you wish to finish the tour?"

Ohen raised his hand. "It's okay. I'll come back to the library another time. I have a big list of other things to do as well."

She nodded and hurried out, trusting Folken to protect her books.

Learning Stampz

The chancellor was worried about the empress as well. As they walked out of the library, Ohen said, "I didn't see the empress at the banquet."

Folken's thoughts were easy to read. Catherine Neeley, Alice's mother, had been wasting away from some disease for some time now. He feared she wouldn't last the month.

But his words were less dire. "Oh, she hasn't been feeling well lately. She was sorry to miss your welcome party." His thoughts made it plain he was just making it up. Nobody but close family and her personal servants had been able to speak with her for some time.

As they parted, Ohen sought a secluded parlor where he could use his full senses. He settled into a high-backed chair that was the most comfortable he'd ever used, and one that was out of sight of the door.

Alice was still racing up the steps to her mother's quarters. She was actively avoiding thinking about the worst possibilities. When she entered the bedroom, Alice and the attending maid locked eyes. It was almost telepathic. The attendant didn't know what to think, but Catherine wasn't on her deathbed, yet.

Alice allowed herself to breathe deeply and let her nerves settle. She sat next to her mother's bed and held her hand.

It helped. Ohen would like to be able to get skin to skin touch with the lady himself to use his psychokinesis to better analyze her condition, but that wasn't likely.

Still, he had gotten used to Alice's thoughts and her mother's touch was a partial gateway for his psychic sight. Just like the time before when he'd had to analyze the spore infection of his crewman Martin, back when they were still hunting for Earth's star system, he began seeking out her condition.

Empress Catherine had the markings of a healthy body from earlier times, but it looked as if she'd been slowly starving to death. She had no body fat, and her muscles were wasting away as they were being consumed to keep the rest of her body alive. Alice was aware of her mother's hand as just skin and bones.

Something had interrupted the lady's digestive system. Ohen strained to detect the problem, but he had never been trained as a healer. He was better at it now than before the expedition, but he had his limits. He just couldn't use his psychokinesis at this distance to make changes in her body, and he wasn't sensitive enough to detect microscopic defects under these conditions either.

And if I could heal her psychically, that would reveal the U'tanse secret, something I could never do.

. . .

Where is Barclay?

That thought kept hammering away from various people, not just the guards that were shadowing him. It was plain he'd never get much time alone, out of sight. Not here in the castle.

One person was worth his attention, he decided. He got out of his chair and waited near the staircase, just stepping out into view at the right moment.

Casey looked up with a smile. "There you are? Do you have a moment?"

Ohen chuckled. "I thought you'd be right at home among all these titled people."

"Well, perhaps. This court does feel familiar, but…" he glanced around, "I'm really out of my depth." He lowered his voice. "I was just riding on my father's name, doing a favor for the duke by spying on you. I wasn't really an official of the court—not until I was abruptly named an ambassador and shipped off into space. I haven't been trained for this."

Ohen gestured him to a comfortable seat nearby, one visible where the guards could see them. "So you think talking to an untitled commoner will help?"

Casey sighed. "Well, you've been in the court at Orson. You probably have some idea what I should be doing."

"What *have* you been doing?"

He shook his head. "Just talking to people. I keep getting the feeling they're waiting for me to say something profound."

Ohen rubbed his forehead. "Okay, so nobody knows what we're trying to do. Not even us. What is this ambassador thing, anyway? What does the word mean? U'tanse aren't familiar with the term."

Casey nodded. "Okay, in my history, ambassadors were sent to other countries to work out conflicts. The ambassador was supposed to explain away conflicts and be a high priority messenger between the kings. I don't see anything like that here."

Ohen nodded. "Right now, there's not even a realistic way Mars and Luna could fight. So, lets just work toward the future. Someday, there might be regular spaceship travel between the two worlds. When that happens, we want everyone to start out as friends. To be honest, people fear the unknown. I've been trying very hard to make people understand that the U'tanse, while strangers, are really useful people to have around. When my people show up, I don't want them to be feared as monsters likely to destroy the local people."

Casey nodded. "So I should do the same. Be a friendly example of a person from Mars?"

"That's part of it. But you also have your canister. Tell the Emperor and his people all about Mars, and also tell King Harmon and his court all about Luna."

"I shouldn't keep secrets?"

"Have you been ordered to keep something secret?"

"Not really. No."

"Then I would be as open as possible. Talk to everyone, courtiers, merchants, and anyone you greet in the city. Be an upstanding, honorable man anyone would be happy to invite to dinner. But... be careful not to charm too many young women."

Casey chuckled. "My mother said something like that before I went off to Orson."

Ohen felt the echo of his words, not only in Casey's thoughts, but from someone just around the corner. Their shadows were listening in.

"Casey, one last thing. If you can somehow make everyone rich, then they'll love you. Obviously, trade of goods between the planets is years in the future. We may never see it. But there are other things we can exchange—ideas. If you can think of something Mars knows that will make a local businessman some money, then you should tell him. Make it a trade in ideas if at all possible, but be the person who helps others."

Casey nodded. "If I can think of anything."

Footsteps on the stairs, and then, "Oh, there you are!" John Fasail came up to join them. "I was wondering if you had talked Abraham into showing you Brilliant Morning yet."

Ohen sighed. "Not yet. Honestly, the long day is getting to me. I haven't slept in a very long time. How do you people handle this?"

Casey nodded. "I fell asleep in a chair a while ago, myself. I'd hate to do that when talking to someone."

The technical support guy grinned. "Nobody stays awake all day long. Everybody's got their own sleep schedule."

Ohen's stomach growled. "And what's the meal schedule?"

. . .

They started with a table for four in the dining hall, but shortly another table was scooted up to join them.

John said, "This isn't an official meal time, but you'll always find someone here and the kitchen is staffed forty-eight hours a day. If you're like me, with a job here, you just flash this token and they feed you." He showed his metal fob on a string.

"You are official guests of the court so you should have no problems either. However, the court's dining hall is popular even with other people in town so they've had to charge anyone who just drops in for a meal."

Across the table, a man with a stripped vest raised his finger. "That's me. I'm a steam engineer just in town for a day. I saw the strange ship outside and when I heard there were visitors from Mars here, I couldn't believe it. You guys are really from Mars?"

Casey introduced himself. "What's a steam engineer?"

The man smiled broadly and expanded his chest. "You don't have steam engines on Mars?"

The Book had mentioned steam engines and given a couple of paragraphs describing how they worked, but with the U'tanse relying on inherited Delense technology, they'd never needed to go down the steam engine path.

Ohen listened as Casey puzzled out Hank Russel's descriptions of his steam engine-powered vehicle, learning more than he'd ever gleaned from the Book.

"My engine, Number 33, is a Franklin Hybrid. I can run on rails from Stampz to Mercurius, but I need to switch to road wheels to continue on to Hooke."

Ohen was getting visual memories from the engineer and it was fascinating big-iron engineering—a steam-powered engine that towed a dozen trailers behind it. He wondered silently why, if Stampz had an electrical system, did they needed steam engines? Certainly they had electric motors, he'd sensed them in the castle's ventilation system. Did they not scale up to enough power to haul freight?

It was also fascinating that one of the other strangers who had invited himself to the table was tense, ready to jump into the conversation if the Hank the engineer started to reveal any sensitive topics. Ohen wondered if the worrier was one of those shadows who had been following him around.

"I'll be heading out the Gate after dawnwind, so if you'd like to take a look at Number 33, it'll have to be before that."

Ohen asked, "Where is it? It'll probably be . . . 'still' before I can make it. I need to spend the darkwind in my ship, just to make sure that it is safe in the winds."

Hank gave him directions.

John asked, "Is there any chance I could take a look at your ship?"

Ohen nodded. "Soon. I think as soon as we can set up exchange visits, you would be welcome to come along. Maybe you, Abraham Chung, and also the librarian, Alice. I'd rather make it a party where I can only have to explain things to a group rather than one at a time."

He sighed, "But until then, I need to check on a few things by myself. My ship's security has alerted me that someone has been poking at the door." He chuckled. "There are a lot of people hoping to get a peek, I guess."

The man he suspected was shadowing him reacted. He urgently needed to alert his superior that the visitor's ship had some kind of security system.

After the meal, and another hour of talking, Ohen made his exit and walked toward the landing area. He had the shadow's name, Luke Gonzales, and could now recognize his face. However, the shadow's thoughts indicated that now that he was identified, someone else would have to take his place.

Ohen was coming to view the imperial guards as a fairly professional organization, and from some of the history he'd picked up, they had to be. The major kingdoms that made up the empire were always testing the imperial family for weaknesses. There were factions that would like to take over that top position, and others that just wanted the empire to split up into their historical power centers. And long ago, there had even been an attack from an asteroid orbiting Luna. The Neeley family never felt totally safe.

And here he was, another wild card from space. The Emperor was friendly and open, and Ohen could sense that in his thoughts as well, but his guards were ever suspicious.

As he walked up to the door of the B3, he could feel people watching him. One had a scope trained on the combination lock, hoping to see his fingers in action. However, all he had to do was shift his position a little until no one could see what he was doing. He opened the mechanism with his psychokineses, leaving the lock untouched.

Inside, with the door closed behind him, he felt himself relax. He was always acting with other people. He could never be himself. With the airlock doors closed, he could finally let everything go. He was comfortable being a hermit, but he'd get very little time alone for awhile.

I'm going to be having visitors. He needed to clean the place up. There were chores to be done.

But maybe after a little nap. He estimated when the darkwind would arrive and set an alarm and stretched out on his bed. He was out within seconds.

. . .

After a tense darkwind, where he hovered near the controls in case the winds ever threatened to do more than shake the boat, and after a little cleanup, Ohen had a nice long sleep.

When he opened the door, still a little surprised it was dark, Ohen appreciated the quiet night. *It's the still.* If he wanted to go look at that steam engine, now was the time.

He went through the motions of locking the door behind him, just for the spies watching him, then he walked out under the faint light of the street lamps. There were other people out as well. The lunar night was just a different kind of workday for some.

He had sensed the location of the engine earlier, so he walked the streets, allowing himself to ease into a faster stroll with several meter-long steps, once he saw other people doing it. He'd been hiding his strength, but the human body had been designed for one Earth gravity and simple steps only made sense when walking inside buildings.

There were several street lamps clustered near an intersection, and he saw why. There were iron rails crossing the stone-paved main road, with warning signs warning of possible engine crossings. Ohen turned to the right and followed the rails.

The rails split into two branches, allowing the lead engine to turn around by taking one branch and then backing up onto the other. There were a dozen ox-drawn carts lined up near the cargo wagons on the rails. People were still in the process of loading Stampz agricultural produce onto the wagons.

He looked at the wheels, trying to see how the hybrid system worked, but other than noticing that there were built-in jacks for lifting the engine and the wagons, he couldn't see the other style of wheels. Maybe they were just warehoused at the end of the rail system.

The engine itself was much like he imagined—water tanks, steam boilers, a special wagon filled with chopped lumber, and the driving pistons. It was big and heavy. Wouldn't an electric motor be more efficient? Was it just the problem of supplying enough electricity over long distances? Couldn't they use the iron rails for transferring power?

He shook his head. Someone had already worked this out. Fortunes were spent on this. It wasn't likely, that with all those books in the library, that they hadn't considered the alternative options.

It just might be the issue of enough power. Stampz wind power system just might not have the excess capacity to drive a heavy cargo transport like this.

He walked closer to the engine and felt the heat radiating from it. It was already fired up. There was a warning whistle, and the drive shafts moved. The train of connected wagons lurched as it moved slowly away from the loading area and then stopped again. Water was poured into the tank and probably Hank Russel was doing his last minute checks, preparing for his next journey.

Ohen walked away, not willing to track the man down and disturb him at his workplace. He had a lot more to see in the capital, and he'd rather just walk around and observe, rather than be escorted. If he needed directions, he could just ask. The men following him wouldn't let him get too lost.

Seeing the Empress

The librarian was the last to arrive. She hurried across the field in the morning light as fast as she could move in her long gown.

"Are you waiting for me? I'm sorry. I got held up."

Abraham Chung, the pilot, said, "No problem. We were just chatting."

John Fasail just smiled. "I knew you'd be late. What book was it this time?"

She shook her head. "Just paperwork."

Ohen knew the truth. She'd been up at her mother's side since the dawnwind came through. Paperwork was on her mind because she was getting behind in her official duties, as caught up with her family troubles as she was.

He gestured to the boat. "We're all here, so let me introduce you to B3, the third of four boats that we brought along on the starship Leonardo."

Alice asked, "Named for Leonardo da Vinci?"

Ohen smiled. "Yes. Some sort of scientist/artist from ancient times."

She nodded. "I know. I've got a book that talks about him and his work."

He chuckled. "Then you're ahead of me. The Book only mentions him a bit. No real details."

John said, "So the U'tanse really are just a branch off of humanity. Your story is sometimes hard to believe."

Ohen nodded. "As is this castle on Luna. I've always known that Luna was an airless, uninhabited moon."

He led them to the airlock. "Let me open both doors. There's not much room inside the airlock."

Abraham paused to look over the airlock controls. "I could use this. The design is all different from what I'm used to, but the principle is the same."

John looked around. "There's more space inside than I assumed. Project-designed ships have more cargo volume, but you have enough floor space."

Ohen nodded. "And I have to be careful how I use it. All those cabinets over there are my food stores. Water, wastewater and air recycling are under the floor."

Abraham went to the pilot seat. His eyes darted over the unfamiliar controls. "Do you have computer control?"

Ohen shook his head. "Not like Project ships. There are over a dozen computer-controlled systems, but all are under my manual control. I rely on them to control my air and floor gravity and such, but the boat won't fly without a trained pilot at the controls."

He glanced over at Alice. She seemed a little overwhelmed.

"Let me get you some seats." He tapped on a wall switch and his bed extended out of the wall. Another switch brought out the bench seat that Casey had used as a bed on the flight from Mars.

John chuckled. "That's a big bed."

Ohen smiled. "I designed this boat. I was an industrial designer before coming on the starship voyage. Of course I was going to include a bed long enough for me. It's really adjustable. The bed extrudes from a roll inside the wall. I can make it any length, but I'd hardly make it tiny."

They laughed.

Ohen went around the walls, showing off the various controls. He turned on the display screen and showed images of the castle and the people wandering by outside. There appeared to be several guards posted to keep others away.

Abraham nodded. His thoughts showed that his Project ship had a much bigger and more flexible display.

Alice asked, "So you lived in this space for your trip?"

"The starship had much more walking around space. It is probably larger than your castle. But yes, once I took the B3 to come get a closer look at the inner planets, I've been living in this room."

"How could you survive? Especially how you eat."

He smiled. "Oh, I packed well. I love the meals at the castle because the ones I can prepare here are bland in comparison."

John said, "Don't tell me you've been living on trail bread."

Ohen laughed. "Hardly that. The U'tanse have been focused on making nutrient-rich foods from the very beginning. We were trapped on an alien world with just a few Earth-native plants. We have studied and experimented, finding alien plants and animals that can be eaten or altered to be edible. Even if I ran short on my normal supplies, I have nutrient supplements that could keep me alive for quite a while. I'd hate it, but I'd survive."

Alice's mind was racing. Could those U'tanse supplements help her mother? How could she ask him for help without revealing her need? The bad health of the empress was a state secret.

After answering everyone's questions, Ohen hinted that he was ready to take a look at Abraham's ship. They all filed out and Ohen secured the boat.

Abraham called out, "Brilliant Morning! I'm bringing some guests to visit."

A strong woman's voice echoed from the ship. "Challenge: A trickle from a mountain creek."

The pilot said, "The stripped salamander ducked under the rock."

The outer airlock door opened. Abraham gestured for them to enter.

Ohen asked, "That was a security code?"

"Right, and it's different every time, so I don't have to worry about being overheard."

Ohen smiled. "Lots of memory work."

Abraham shrugged. "I'm used to it."

Once they all entered, Ohen nodded. "I'm impressed. You could haul lots of cargo in this space."

"And there's another one just like it on the upper side of the cylinder. However, it's harder to load and unload from there. I tend to keep all my long-term supplies there. I actually haul some cargo from Stampz when there is an urgent need for speed."

Ohen nodded. "There is a nearby star system that the U'tanse discovered before we came here. We arrived in the middle of an asteroid belt and we struggled to collect as much metal as we could with our boats. It would have been so much easier with a ship like this."

John said, "Yes, we—" Abraham had elbowed him. They had been collecting metals from asteroids long ago parked in the Lagrangian clusters L4 and L5, but it was a state secret. Much of the wealth of Stampz and the imperial family came from the metal trade. Stampz had more gold than the rest of Luna combined. Ohen pretended he didn't notice the leaked thoughts.

Abraham said, "Are you ready to see the command deck? We'll have to take the ladder."

Alice said, "If you don't mind, I'll go last."

Abraham led the way. Ohen was quickly up behind him, then John. Ohen didn't look, but he sensed that Alice just climbed with her hands. Her long gown made it difficult to use her feet on the ladder's rungs.

Ohen said, "That's a big display." Abraham nodded and showed off its features, verbally giving commands to the computer.

John asked, "When you contacted the emperor, we were surprised when the message came through the computer system. We use radio, but it's short range—line of sight. We didn't know such long distance communication was possible."

Ohen looked thoughtful, "But you talked to us when we arrived at Luna, giving us directions."

"We had to figure it out. Since you called us, we could simply reply. Brilliant coached us on how to use your code number, but nobody had done that before."

Ohen nodded. "Mars uses computer messaging frequently, but they only have a few computers that have survived since the Plague. Nobody uses simple radio. The U'tanse only have simple radio systems, but I'm not really sure if my boat's radios are compatible with yours. That's something we could check on later.

"As far as the computer system, it appears to be an encrypted radio-based system, but not at all compatible with my boat's radios. As long as you know the code number, the computers somehow manage to route the messages, either text or voice, through relays. On Mars, the moon Phobos was the main relay. Messages were delayed until Phobos was in the sky."

John asked, "So you have a computer like Brilliant Morning's brain?"

Ohen tilted his head. "I have a computer that's related to it. There are some small computers left on Mars, slowly running out of power. Probably it's not as capable as yours, but it does transfer messages and I have used it for math problems. It's not connected to my boat in any way."

They talked some more. Ohen avoided asking about the weapon system that had been mentioned before and they weren't volunteering that information. Still, with his clairvoyance, he could see much more about the ship than they described. It was plain that the ship could be voice controlled, but only by someone with the right security clearance.

Ohen thanked Abraham for the tour and they left, Alice sliding down the ladder first. Once out on the landing field, she hesitated as they split up to their own tasks.

"Mr. Barclay. Ohen. Could we talk a bit more about the U'tanse?"

"Of course. Is it about our health training?"

She reacted. "What do you mean?"

"Oh, it just seemed to me that you were very interested when I talked about my food stores. You appeared to have something on your mind."

She sighed, looking around to see if anyone was listening. "Maybe. I do know someone who is suffering from a wasting disease. I was wondering if your supplements might be useful."

"I don't know. How advanced are your healing skills?"

She shook her head. "Stampz has always had a reputation for our excellent doctors, but in this case, she seems beyond their skills."

He nodded. "In U'tanse society, we have highly trained healers. It was necessary to develop those skills early, even to survive. I was never in that class. For one thing, I'm male and the Healers are almost exclusively female.

"However, there is a lesser tier of training that I took, mostly since I would be on my own and have to deal with any injuries by myself. I know the principles of health care, but I don't have the skill. Still, I would be happy to examine your patient. Maybe just looking at the problem from the perspective of a different culture might give you some insight."

Alice was nervous. A number of problems raced through her thoughts so quickly that Ohen couldn't follow.

"Perhaps," she said, "just using your nutrient supplement might be enough."

Ohen shook his head. "That's not advisable. There are several types, and some can even react poisonously with others if not taken properly. Now, I've been trained on how to make that kind of judgement, and I would be willing to share my stocks, but only if I'm sure I'm not going to kill your patient.

"I really need to examine the person myself. Is it because the patient is female? You and the doctors could be there as well."

Alice closed her eyes tightly. "It's urgent. Could I come back to your boat in a little while? I need to confer with someone before I can make that call."

"Of course."

She raced off. Her thoughts were plain to read. She needed to talk to her father to get permission.

He went back to the B3 and pulled out his supplements and reviewed the instructions. He'd been trained, but Kerry, the healer on the Leonardo who tried to refresh his skills before he left, had been more concerned with how he treated himself should his food supplies run out, not how the supplements could be used on a third party. He prepared a little bundle of items he'd mostly likely need.

It was only a few minutes after that when there was a knock on the outer airlock door.

She was there. "I've gotten limited permission. Can you come soon?"

He held up his bag. "I'm ready now."

They went to the castle and up the staircase. There were people watching, but no one spoke. Alice led him to a door and gestured him in.

Someone had hurriedly taken down some wall hangings and draped the cabinets with plain cloth. Probably it was an attempt to disguise the lady's identity, although Ohen would have known even without his previous clairvoyant visit. Even in her current condition, the empress was very obviously Alice's mother.

There were two attendants, one was the maid he'd sensed before. Another was probably a doctor. She was a little skeptical of this stranger who had come to visit.

Ohen knelt down beside the bed. He reached for her hand.

Alice said, "No! I'm sorry, but there's a ... cultural restriction, a taboo. You can't touch her."

He frowned. He looked at Alice, and the doctor. "I really need to check things like her heart rate and her breathing, and things like that."

Alice looked at the doctor. They appeared stymied.

Ohen asked, "Is it skin to skin? If I had a gloved hand, or a scarf, could I touch her that way?"

Alice looked at her mother. The lady gasped, "Let him."

The maid hurriedly went to a drawer and pulled out a finely woven blue sash and handed it to Ohen.

He wrapped it around his right hand so there was only one layer between his fingertips and her skin, and then took her wrist. He closed his eyes and listened to her breathing.

His clairvoyance probed deeper. It was only a moment before he finally located the problem. There was a tumor on her small intestine wall, almost completely closing off the duodenum and pressed against the pancreas.

He asked, "How long have you had difficulty eating?"

She whispered, "Several months."

The maid said, "Four months."

Ohen wished he knew what their medical level was. Kerry or any of the real healers could shrink that tumor quickly. Alternately, a surgeon could cut it out, but he certainly didn't have that skill.

Ohen asked, "May I have permission to feel your abdomen?"

Alice said, "Carefully, please. She's in pain."

He knew. He could feel the lady's queasiness.

Gently he felt the area. He nodded, as if he were doing something wise.

Then, he concentrated on using his psychokinesis to kill as many of the tumor cells as he could manage. He kept at it for a few minutes.

Alice asked, "What can you feel?"

He sighed and pulled his hand free. "There's an obstruction," he looked at the doctor, "but you probably already know that."

He reached for his bag. "I can do a little to help the patient absorb more nutrients, but until that obstruction goes away, she will still have problems. Can we talk about what needs to be done?"

The empress whispered, "Talk where I can hear. I need to know."

Ohen looked at Alice for permission. She nodded.

He saw all eyes on him, looking for hope.

"I wish I were a fully trained healer, but I'm not. One of my people's healers could remove the obstruction, possibly with surgery, and when the wound healed, that would be the cure."

The doctor introduced herself. "I'm Healer Kristin. Our medical experts are only now experimenting with body cavity surgery. It's there in the books, but while I'll remove a bullet in a leg, or even amputate a limb if there's a bad infection, the kind of surgery you suggest is much too risky for … this patient. Maybe in another few decades, we'll have that skill, but not yet."

Ohen nodded. "Okay, then." He opened his bag. "Here's what I suggest. I can prepare a layered approach. The first is an anesthetic to deaden the nerves in her digestive tract just enough to allow her to keep down two other potions. One will attempt to dissolve the obstruction—kill off the bad cells. The other will be nutrition supplements, so that she can gain strength with a minimal impact on her digestion."

The doctor nodded, not really understanding how he could kill off the tumor with a potion, but taking it on faith that he could. Not that Ohen had such a potion. He'd need to use his psychokinesis for that task, which meant several visits to do the job.

The empress said, "I haven't been able to keep anything down."

Ohen nodded. "I understand. That's why the first dose is to quiet your nausea."

He went to a nearby table and carefully measured and mixed his potions. The first was just as he promised, to give her more tolerance for the others. The second and third were both nutrient supplements, but they looked different.

He gave instructions. "Let her sleep when she can, but repeat these dosages every four hours otherwise. And I must come back to make the followup potions based on how she is doing. Do I have that permission?"

He got the promises and watched as she took the initial dosages. They were tiny dosages, small enough that she could keep them down. He spent every moment when he wasn't talking, trying to kill more tumor cells. That would be the real cure, and he hoped they wouldn't change their minds about letting him return to finish the job.

I hope this will work. Medicines are common. Nobody will mistake this for psychic healing.

He left on his own, leaving Alice to assist with her mother.

Someday, the U'tanse would return for him. The healers would be valued, as long as no one thought it was witchcraft.

Stampz Day

"So you knew?" asked Emperor Richard a few long days later.

Ohen took a pastry from the tray and nodded. "Nobody said anything, and they tried to hide it, but your daughter and her mother look quite a bit alike."

"And I'm glad Alice asked for your help. Nobody thought Jane would pull out of it. You say it was a cancer? I've always been told that's incurable."

"She was lucky. I wouldn't have been able to help at all if it had spread. And only some cancers can be killed with chemicals that attack the bad cells and leave the good cells to survive. Don't think I'm some medical miracle worker. I'm not. It was just very lucky I had the right supplies at the right time. And I still think I need to check on her for a few more days, just to be sure it doesn't come back."

"Alice told me that. It was just a whim that I replied to that message from King Harmon. Your people will be welcome here when they come for you."

Ohen sighed. "Whenever that might be. And please don't spread the word that I'm a healer. I'm really not."

The emperor nodded. "Officially, Jane was never sick in the first place, so I can't very well brag about her miraculous recovery now."

Ohen asked, "Why the secrecy?"

He shrugged. "Everyone is always probing for weakness. My ancestor James, the first emperor, came to power when both major nations had suffered massive destruction due to spaceships and then, when it reached its worst, he was the only one with a heritable claim to power and the only person with a spaceship at his command. Currently, we have some military power, but it's still that lone spaceship and our economic might that keeps the crown on my head."

They talked for an hour, but then the emperor's chief secretary intruded, reminding him of his next appointment.

. . .

Alice was pushing her mother's wheeled chair in the hallway. She waved. "Do you have a moment?"

They moved to a nearby parlor.

Ohen smiled at the empress, "You've regained a little more color."

June cleared her throat. "Thanks to you. I'm still as weak as a newborn, but it's so much better now." Sitting upright and dressed for the day, she had much more presence than she had as a patient.

He'd been back several times over the past quad, eight real days, but only four lunar days. As he had before, he smiled and chatted, while underneath it all, he probed for any remaining cancer cells. He was nearly sure they were all gone, but he'd still check whenever he had the chance. She still had a long way to go to heal and recover her strength.

"I'm sure everyone in the castle is happy to see you out and about."

Alice looked worried. Ohen waved his hand. "Don't worry, I've always known that my patient was the librarian's mother."

June chuckled. "Alice the librarian. That's my fault. When I was pregnant with her, I had discovered several novels which I loved. The author's page talked about the famous author and librarian who was born Alice but changed her name to André for her pen name. I decided if my child was a boy, I'd call him André and if a girl, Alice."

Alice smiled, "And my mother told me all about her. I learned to read using her books. Sadly, I haven't learned how to write fiction, but I'm a good librarian."

Ohen sighed. "Still more books I need to read. Thanks again for the gloves."

Alice nodded. "And you still need to let me read your U'tanse Book!"

He nodded, stalling. "I was wondering if you could help me with an experiment, if you have permission to use Brilliant Morning's computer to send messages."

Alice frowned. "Maybe. I'll need to ask and get a little training from Abraham. What is this experiment?"

He shrugged. "Computer messages can travel great distances, even from world to world, but they need relays to capture and forward the text from place to place. On Mars, this was the moon Phobos. I don't know how it's done on Luna. I want to send several messages back and forth from the computer I have on my boat to the computer built into your ship. I can time the delays and discover information about the lunar relays."

She nodded. "So we just talk back and forth? I can do that. I'll let you know when I get the permissions."

. . .

John Fasail waved him down at the midnight meal. Ohen took his box and sat at the table. "What's up?"

John smiled, but it was an act. He'd been coached by the security guards to mention metals in their conversation.

John said, "I've heard you're planning a trip in your boat in the morning."

"Hardly a trip. I'm just going to be testing the range of messaging using the computers."

"And you've recruited Alice to help?"

"That's right. She has a lot of questions about the U'tanse and my radio test needs a lot of back and forth conversation, so we can do both at the same time."

John nodded. "Well, I've got a lot of questions, too. Maybe I can help."

Ohen chuckled. "Not that I have any ulterior motives here, but I think the conversation will be quicker and flow more easily with just the two of us."

John grinned, "So I'd be a third wheel?"

Ohen shrugged, "Not sure of the metaphor, but I do want a two-person conversation rather than a dinner party. But I'm here now. What do you want to ask me?"

John waved his hand. "Oh, lots of things. I do remember something from our tour of Brilliant Morning. You mentioned some star system nearby where you harvested metals?"

Ohen nodded. "Yes, when our starship leaps, makes its faster-than-light transfers, we don't really know where we will appear. That time, we arrived in the middle of an asteroid belt and when we checked out a nearby one, it was just a pile of metal rubble, much of it valuable. Using our boats, we transferred a much as we could back to the starship. Likely it will be well received at home."

Ohen pushed on. "I assume you've done the same with Brilliant Morning, but I could be wrong."

"What do you mean?" John was sensitive to the others in the dining area, but there wasn't really anyone else listening in.

Ohen shrugged. "I keep my eyes open. Stampz is a wealthy community here, and yet when I looked around at the shipping containers loading up on Hank Russel's steam train, they were all agriculture produce. There could be other sources of income for the capital city, perhaps even taxes from other regions, but I haven't seen any signs of that, like I did in the city of Orson, the capital of the Xanthe kingdom on Mars.

"It occurred to me that just as your spaceship has gone to the Lagrangian colonies to collect books for the library, there were likely abandoned mining colonies there as well. Just looking around the city here, Stampz has easy access to metals, and yet, Hank Russel's steam train has more distant portions of its route where it has to ride on roads, rather than rails. I wondered if mining for metals was difficult here on Luna, just as it is on Mars.

"I gather that the process is energy intensive and on terraformed worlds, there are no deposits of coal and petroleum that were important when Earth developed their high-energy industries like iron smelting and long distance transport.

"If you aren't already doing so, then harvesting metals from those asteroids nearby and selling them could bring the Stampz economy a great deal of money."

John sighed and brushed his hair back. "So you just puzzled that out on your own? It's supposed to be a secret."

"Oh, sorry. I'll not mention it again, then. The emperor talked about preserving your secrets. It's part of your security policy."

John nodded. "Sorry. But while we're on the subject, you say Mars has an iron problem as well?"

"Oh, yes. There is a pre-Plague factory in Tempe that manufactures iron pipes and sells them to other nations, and that's the primary source of iron for firearms and farm tools, but as far as I can tell, there's nothing like iron rail transport or even steam engines on Mars. You really ought to have a conversation with Ambassador Casey about seeing if there's a market on

Mars for your steam engine designs. It might be hard for them to duplicate, but it's worth the conversation."

John then steered the conversation to a sporting contest to be held after dawnwind.

Ohen frowned. "So you jump off the peak of the castle? How does that work?"

John explained about the Kimmer sailsuits. "Kimmer were the original lunar inhabitants, descendants from the original terraforming engineers. There were a few scientific outposts working on the ecology when the Plague happened. The Project shut down the spin beams that were trying to spin Luna up to a twenty-four hour day when everything fell apart. When settlers from the Lagrangian cities came to settle on Luna, they considered the Kimmer just forest savages, but they had skills of their own, like the sailsuits."

John smiled, "One of my ancestors was the first to puzzle out the Kimmer history. Abraham is half-Kimmer. Most of the chief pilots have been Kimmer." He laughed. "They always claim special expertise due to their flying history."

"So after dawnwind?"

"Actually, make that an hour after sunrise. It will still be windy."

. . .

Ohen had kept up a pattern of sleeping every darkwind and deep-sleep in B3 and then napping during light-sleep and during the afternoon in his room in the castle. He went down to the dining area for a breakfast during the dawnwind and found Alice talking with one of the cooks. She looked more festive than usual, dressed in a light blue dress rather than her usual long white robe.

He waved and she came to join him. "Don't order breakfast," she said.

"What? Why?"

She smiled, "It's Stampz Day. Nearly the biggest holiday of the year. Don't worry, you'll have plenty to eat. Follow me."

It was breezy outside, and Ohen was surprised to see rows of canopied wagons set up alongside the main road with people cooking over outdoor firecages.

"Those are to prevent the fires from getting out of hand?"

She nodded. "No open flames, ever."

He understood. Luna's atmosphere had a much higher percentage of oxygen than he was used to. He could image it would be a problem.

But the sizzling meat and freshly cooked pastries forced him onward.

"Princess Alice!" A vendor called out and waved. She fixed a wrap brimming with savory stuffing. And then one for the tall guy.

She thanked the lady and they ate, looking at all the food and craft goods. Ohen tried to limit what he ate, and turned down the offer of knitted flowers and quilted blankets. Nobody was going to charge the princess anything, but he didn't want to take anything he wasn't going to use.

He pointed to the jewelry vendor, expecting to see more home crafted items, and was surprised to see a number of silver, gold, and copper wire items. Little cages with tiny flowers inside, pendants made to look like animals and flowers.

"Very nice work," he said to the smiling young girl. She offered him a wristband.

"Is this copper?" he asked.

"Yes, Dad got a deal on metal wire from the last shipment. The copper turns color pretty fast, however. I have another one here in silver."

Alice said, "Do you want it?"

Ohen said, "I'm just curious. Besides, I don't have any of the local currency. I neglected to bring any trade goods."

Alice turned to the girl. "We'll take it. The ambassador needs a keepsake from his first Stampz Day. I'll pay." She pulled a coin from a pocket in her sleeve.

The young vendor blushed. "I couldn't …."

Alice put the coin in her hand. "What's your name? I might want something come Freeday."

They'd barely finished the transaction when there was a long blast of a horn from the castle.

Alice snatched at his sleeve. "It's starting. We need to get to a good viewing place."

"What is?"

"It's the Race for Freedom!" She pulled him to the edge of the crowd. "You can see them up at the top."

Up at the peak of the castle, under the fluttering banners, he could see four little figures in white suits.

"Those are the sailsuits?"

"Yes. It's Abraham, John, Perry Quill, and someone named Otto. I forgot the last name. He works with John. Perry is Abraham's apprentice pilot."

"What are they going to do?"

"When the horn sounds three blasts, they will all jump off from the castle and head for Brilliant Morning. It's in commemoration of a famous escape when the Kimmer pilot named Darkwind jumped out of the castle when the Crown Prince of Hercules tried to hold him and the Duke of Stampz captive.

"They'll race to see who gets the farthest from the castle. Two years ago, John had a crash landing on top of one of the pastry vendor's wagon. Nobody was hurt, but people still joke about it."

Closer to the castle, someone was shouting at the top of their lungs, probably explaining what was going on, but Ohen had noticed that in the lunar atmosphere, sound didn't travel as well as on Ha, or even on Mars.

The horn sounded its blasts and four figures jumped, spreading out from the peak.

The sailsuits caught the wind, with the wing-like sleeves and capes that seemed affixed to the feet. One flyer twisted his path to the side. The crowd cheered and Ohen was able to pick up some hints as experienced watchers were following the event.

Some flyers were trying to get free of the castle's wind shadow. Others were trying to stretch their glide path to gain extra distance. Second by second, they were getting closer to where Alice and Ohen stood.

For a brief instant, the flyers were sailing overhead and Ohen got a good view of how John held his arms and legs.

The crowd started to move, chasing the racers to the finish. The first came to land on his feet. The second stumbled and rolled, with people there to help him up.

Abraham Chung was the winner. He sailed well past the towering spaceship. All of them got close.

"That looks fun."

Alice smiled, "Yes, I've always thought so, but I can't get anyone to make me a sailsuit. They all think I'm too fragile."

Ohen sniffed. "I'd probably be too heavy."

"Charles Fasail, John's ancestor, used a sailsuit and he was heavy. Not as tall as you, however."

As they walked toward the spaceships. Alice told him the historical story of Darkwind's escape in more detail. Ohen was getting a little worried about the crowds, hoping that none of the vendors had parked their wagon too close to B3.

He was finally relieved to see that the landing field had been roped off, whether to protect the ships or to have a safe landing zone for the sailsuited contestants, he didn't know.

John waved in the distance, surrounded by well-wishers. Each of the men in white suits had their own little crowd. Children asked if they could fly too. Some the adults were thinking the same thing.

Virtual Roadtrip

A stocky woman in cook's garb was standing there in the field, holding two picnic baskets. She held them a little higher when Alice approached.

She smiled at Alice. "This one is for you."

Looking up at the tall man, she frowned slightly, "And this one is yours."

Ohen smiled broadly. "Thank you! I really appreciate it."

She cracked a little smile and gave a slight nod.

Alice said, "Mary, I'm sorry for having you trek all the way out here."

"Oh, there's no problem, dear."

Ohen could feel the questions boiling off of her. Was her darling princess getting too close to this stranger? Why two picnic baskets? Should she tell someone what was going on?

Ohen turned to Alice. "What's the plan? Do you have a password for Brilliant Morning?"

She chuckled. "Abraham really didn't like it, but he did give me a one-time access code, and I'll be on my own. I really didn't know how long you'd be off in your ship, so I had Mary here fix us up something nice so we won't starve."

"That's thoughtful of you. I have food on my ship, but it's getting a little old."

Alice picked up her basket. "You have to keep your distance. I'm not supposed to let anyone overhear me talking to the ship."

Ohen and the cook watched as she went up to the ship and whispered something. The door opened and she waved and then went inside.

"Well, thanks again, Mary. I'll appreciate every bite."

He hurried off to the B3 and entered. He sat in the pilot seat and pulled his computer out of the cabinet just in range.

"Computer, make a voice connection to the ship Brilliant Morning."

"There is an incoming voice message from Alice Neeley—"

"Take that message instead."

"Connected."

"Hello, Alice. You're ahead of me. I was just about to call."

"Oh! It works! I was wondering if I did it right."

"Yes, and the message came in under your name. I didn't know if you had an identification code or not."

"Well, I didn't before, but when Abraham coached me on how to send messages, he said I needed one. I hope I can remember all those numbers."

"Write it down, I guess."

"I did."

Ohen smiled, and looked around the boat. "I guess I have a few things to take care of before I take off. How about you?"

"Oh, yes! I left my basket down at the airlock, racing to get up here. It's kind of spooky being here alone."

"I'm starting a log for the test. Item one is that there doesn't appear to be any delay in messages when we're just parked a few dozen meters apart."

"What are you going to log?"

"Time, distance apart, and any delay in the messages."

A few minutes later, Ohen announced to the crowd outside, "I will be lifting off shortly. Please keep your distance."

He didn't really think there would be any problem. Landing in tight quarters had been a problem he had foreseen during the boat's design phase. He started the beams and launched the boat a dozen meters into the air with a sharp pressor pulse, transitioning instantly into using tractor beams to pull volumes of air downward for thrust. B3 was quickly rising, with the crowd below cheering.

"Alice, I think I need to circle just for a minute."

"Oh, why?"

"They think I'm flying as part of the celebration."

She laughed. "Go for it. I'm going to ask Brilliant if I have permission to look through the viewer."

He put B3 through a set of maneuvers, swooping around and even flipping end over end—all part of the training exercises boat pilots were supposed to master.

"Hey, Ohen, I can see you! Don't you get sick doing that?"

"No, I've got the floor gravity on. I barely feel it. I'll do one last pass and then head west. I want to see Stampz Gate again."

"Oh! I wish I were with you. I barely get out of the castle. I've never traveled anywhere."

He leveled out and said, "When John was guiding us in the first time, I managed to let him view my screen through the computer. Would you like to try that?"

"Look through your viewpoint? Yes. What do I need to do?"

Since the computers had done it before, it was easy to set up. Ohen positioned his computer where the camera looked at his display and soon she could see the results.

"Hi there!" He ducked into the frame and waved.

"Don't block my view! I'm enjoying this."

The crater wall with the huge crack, forming an exit canyon where the river drained out was fast approaching. Ohen held an altitude just a little higher than the canyon walls.

Alice squealed with glee. "I've only seen the Gate once, when I was little, and I was riding in a wagon down at the bottom. See that wagon there, next to the tracks? It's barely a dot from this high."

Ohen had his attention focused on the row of windmills at the top of the crater wall, spinning like the tops he'd played with as a child. He hadn't even realized what they were when he'd first arrived. He wondered if they were designed that way to resist the high speed winds.

Alice sighed. "And this is as far as I've ever seen. They took me straight back to the castle after that."

"You sound like a prisoner."

"In a way, I am."

"Why is that? Don't your brothers travel?"

She didn't answer. Ohen felt her thoughts, even as they kept getting farther apart, but it was an old issue with her and not something she wanted to share.

"Alice, we're reaching the point where we're no longer in direct contact. With the radio waves being blocked by the crater wall, voice and the video are being relayed somehow. You might see a flicker in the video, and it might stop altogether for a bit. I need you to keep me informed when that happens."

"Oh, I saw that. It was like you said, the image of the forest outside the crater froze for just an instant. Sorry I didn't mention it."

"No problem. Is the video still flowing smoothly, or is it choppy?"

"It's smooth now. There sure are a lot of trees out there. Those are trees, right?"

"Yes, most of Luna is like this. I've only seen the agricultural fields inside the craters."

Ohen tried to sense whether there was a delay in their speech. If there was, then it was slight. The relay had to be relatively close, at least in terms of the speed of light. It couldn't be on Mars or Earth. Those Lagrangian colonies were nearly as far away as the Earth, so it couldn't be them, either.

None of that was surprising. The Brilliant Morning might have powerful radios, but his little computer didn't. He'd proved that on the trip from Mars when they moved out of radio range.

"Alice, you're a lot more familiar with the maps of Luna than I am. Give me directions unless you just want to watch random trees and craters as I travel west."

"Oh, I wish I'd prepared. Let me think. Zeno is to the south and Mercurius is southwest of here."

"Hmm. If I can locate the train tracks, then I could follow them to Mercurius."

It took a little while and he had to fly at a lower altitude to keep them from vanishing in the forests, but soon he picked up the trace, paralleling a river.

"How many steam engines are there? How much traffic should I see?"

"Sorry, I haven't really paid that much attention to it."

He nodded. "That's okay. I'm always asking questions and sometimes there's no quick answers."

"I'm supposed to talk a lot, and I'm running out of things to say. Can you tell me more about your people?"

"How about this? I'll read some of the Book, and you can ask questions. If you can't then just make a noise."

"Hmm. How about this?"

He heard a metallic tap.

"Is that a spoon?"

"Right!"

He pulled out the Book. "Okay, I'll be skipping around. It's not really a chronological narrative."

"Sounds like you have it at hand."

"Oh, yes." He had worked out his excuse for not letting her read it herself.

"The Book is pretty important to the U'tanse. Obviously, I was going to bring my personal copy along on this trip to search for Earth."

He thumbed through the early passages. "This is a good place to start.

"My name is Abe Whiting. I come from Austin, Texas in the United States, on the planet Earth. Although, probably Texas and the United States no longer exist. Austin is a city. But when the red giant star Betelgeuse in the constellation Orion went supernova, there was a burst of electromagnetic pulses that wiped out our semiconductor-based technology, followed by a flood of radiation that killed many."

Ohen read on, listening for her clicks and keeping an eye on the railroad tracks below. He kept the boat moving slowly. There was no need to cover lots of ground.

In the reading, he told of Abe's encounter with Sharon, skipping over the passages where he realized she was a telepath and could open locks with her mind. He was barely into the paragraphs where they were captured by the Cerik when the clicks stopped.

"Alice?"

There was no reply.

The computer's voice said, "I am unable to maintain a live connection. Transcribe your voice to text?"

"No. Send the voice and re-establish the voice connection when you are able."

He brought the boat to a hover, logging the time when the clicks ended. He stopped the reading and prepared to wait.

"Alice, the relay has gone out of range, so when you hear my voice start up again, tell me immediately."

There was a small crater with a meadow inside, relatively near the tracks. He quickly brought the boat down for a landing. Ohen really didn't have any idea how long he'd have to wait. Something orbiting Luna just outside the atmosphere would have about a four-hour orbit. He just might have to wait that long.

He just hoped Alice wouldn't give up on the test and go home.

But it was only fifteen minutes later when her voice startled him. "Ohen? The image on the screen just froze and you're not talking. Ohen? Ohen?"

"Oh! I just got your message. Can you hear me?"

"Alice, I am getting your voice again. Please reply instantly."

There was just a couple of seconds. "Ohen? You're back! I knew you said this would happen, but I was worried."

"Good. I'm really surprised the connection came back this soon. How is the video?"

"It looks like you're on the ground, somewhere."

"Right. I just parked in a little crater in the middle of nowhere while I waited. I had just opened the picnic basket when your voice came back. I like the egg sandwich."

"Well, you can eat, but I'd really like to hear some more from your Book. What happened to Abe and Sharon?"

He chuckled. "Okay. If you don't mind I'll just stay parked for a bit and read."

"That's great. But expect some questions."

Ohen was noticing that there was a bit of delay in their conversation. Still only a fraction of a second, barely perceptible, but not as instantaneous as it had been at the first.

He read some more. She had questions.

"Do you mean to tell me that it was just Abe and Sharon? No others. All the U'tanse came from them?"

"Yes. Just like Adam and Eve. They were the progenitors of us all. When people talk about Abe, more often than not, they say 'Abe, the father of us all.' After all, there are plenty of U'tanse named Abe these days."

She sounded disturbed. "Well, I'm not a farmer, but I've been told you can't really start out a herd of cattle with just a bull and a cow. They get inbred and feeble."

"Well, yes. Even Abe and Sharon knew that from the very beginning. That's why they developed lots of skill in genetics and health. It was struggle in the first generations to look out for recessive genes that would cause problems."

"Ohen. Um. You shouldn't really talk about this with other people."

"Okay. Why?"

She hesitated. "When you get back, there's a history book I need you to read. For now, don't talk about … the mechanics of … heritability."

He got the sense it was something cultural that he had missed. The topic never came up when he was on Mars. Maybe it was a Luna thing.

He shifted on to read about the Cerik and how the U'tanse lived in underground burrows to protect them against the poisons in the atmosphere.

They had another communications blackout after less than an hour. It lasted nearly thirty minutes.

"Ohen? I'm back, I think."

"Good. I've finished off my picnic basket. I think I'll start heading back to Stampz. I've got a good idea about what's going on, I think."

"Oh, tell me. The blackouts seem pretty random to me."

He lifted off and started back.

"Alice, I think there are several Project stations in orbit around Luna. At least two or three of them. They act as relays for the computer messages, but they probably have other purposes."

"Oh, that sounds like the Angel stations! There's a Kimmer song about them. The Alpine Society knows about them as well. They help maintain the atmosphere."

The Emperor's Need

John nodded. "Here in the notes Charles Fasail left, he describes the flight where he and Darkwind discovered one of the Angel stations. It orbits just above the atmosphere and uses wide pressor beams to catch escaping hydrogen gas molecules and sends them back down into the air to recombine. There are wide wings which he assumes are solar power collectors.

"There used to be more of them, but several sacrificed themselves to divert an incoming block of ice that would have destroyed much of this continent."

Chancellor Folken nodded. "Part of the charter of the Alpine Society is to educate the population sufficiently so that we can go back into space and rebuild the lost Angel stations. With a full compliment of stations, and the occasional addition of asteroidal ice chunks dropped into the ocean, our atmosphere could last indefinitely. Without them, gradual loss of gas will cause the oceans to drop and the atmospheric pressure to decay within ten thousand years or so.

"We wouldn't live to see it, but unless we act, our world will be doomed. We have to regain the technology of the Project, somehow."

The emperor had joined their meeting. "Sadly, while the Alpine Society's goals are absolutely important, my duties are more urgent in the current day. I am fascinated by your communications test. You say that with the help of the Angel stations, the message system used by Brilliant Morning and your little computer could allow me to, perhaps, communicate with my sons in a matter of minutes?"

"Theoretically, if we had more computers, yes. When an Angel station is in the correct position, one can talk as if you were in the same room. When they're not, just wait a few minutes and another one will move into position. Messages can be sent at any time, but some will be delayed."

Ohen tapped his finger on the wooden table. "The critical question is this: have any computers survived on Luna from the time of the Plague? On Mars, where it was already settled, there were many thousands of them, but gradually they all ran out of power. Only recently the method of recharging them has become available.

"Here on Luna, you say there were a few research stations at that time. There likely were some computers, but have they survived?

"It's important because no one has the technology to make new ones. It's like your Angel stations."

The emperor frowned, "I'm not above asking for favors from you and Ambassador Casey. What is the possibility we could trade with Mars for some of their recharged computers?"

Ohen shrugged. "I can't speak for King Harmon, but computers on Mars are critical military resources. There would be strong objections to such a trade, I'm sure."

Alice was shifting in her seat, unwilling to speak up, but with something to say. When Ohen turned his eyes to her, so did her father.

"Alice? You know something?"

She faced her father. "When mother went to Franklin for the Centennial of the Rebuilding, she stayed at Baron West's mansion. Didn't she say something about the baron's collection of Plague-era artifacts? Might he have some derelict computer?"

"Maybe, we should ask her."

. . .

Empress June's social calendar was still limited to a private tea party or two with her favorite friends, but Ohen was always welcomed. She was usually relying on her walker to regain stability when she was on her feet. This time she greeted her guests standing with an elegant cane. Alice stood at her side, but didn't attempt to help.

Chancellor Folken, and a couple who were only introduced as Lord and Lady Lemas made up the rest of the party. Everyone entered and sat. Ohen waited until June and Lady Lemas caught up with the family gossip.

Alice asked her mother about her visit to Franklin and the Centennial celebration.

Ohen was happy that June had wonderfully vivid visual memories. The celebration events were informative, especially when they reviewed the devastation caused by the bomb dropped from orbit that had flattened the ducal castle and burned most of the city surrounding it. Most of the royal family were killed in that war, leaving the then Duke of Stampz as the last remaining survivor to take over the throne.

Mt. Ural, the attacking asteroidal settlement, had been defeated in battle by Brilliant Morning, the much smaller but vastly more agile attacker, piloted by Darkwind. Supposedly it had been chased off, but still existed somewhere in the Lagrangian clusters. With its own ship lost, the asteroid could still move itself, but not risk another attack from Luna.

When June mentioned the collection of artifacts owned by Baron West, Ohen spoke up.

"Did you get to see these artifacts? I was able to look through the archives stored on Mars. I wonder if they had similar devices."

Using June's memories, he prompted her to talk about what she saw, giving names to some of the devices.

When the party was over, he nodded to Alice. "The baron has at least two devices that might be computers. They're obviously dead and out of power, but that might be remedied."

She nodded. "Then the next task is getting the both of us an invitation to see his collection."

"The both of us?"

She nodded with determination. "If I'm ever to leave Stampz, this is my best opportunity."

. . .

Emperor Richard frowned at his daughter. "We had this conversation before."

Alice nodded. "Yes, back when I was twelve. Things have changed. We can't get you what you need without me. Ohen needs to go because he has the experience to know which devices are undamaged and which are just decorative junk. You're stuck here in Stampz. Mom hasn't recovered enough to attempt a trip like this. I'm the only one who can sign the promissory note for whatever Baron West wants to charge for it."

Ohen could sense the unspoken thoughts. There was an issue. They were both so familiar with it that they didn't even dwell on it, but it was important. So important that the princess could never travel.

Alice wasn't done with her arguments. "Ohen can travel to Franklin and back very fast, so with luck, we could be back the same day. His ship will certainly attract the baron's attention. My position will insure we get an invitation to look at his collection."

She paused and then said, "I won't be there long enough for some local noble to try to romance me."

Ohen made a mental checkmark. It was part of the puzzle.

Richard was trying not to say the obvious. How trustworthy was this visitor from other worlds?

Not that he could answer the man's unspoken thoughts.

Alice continued. "Of course, my maid Selena will come with us."

"Perhaps the chancellor—"

Alice cut him off. "No. You may not have noticed, but Folken is not up to the trip. He's been weakening of late." She sighed. "He's over a hundred and I'm afraid his age is catching up with him."

The emperor nodded. "I'm aware."

"Barclay, you don't happen to have anything in your bag of tricks for old age, do you?"

Ohen shook his head. "Sorry. It's not unusual for U'tanse to live over a hundred, but twenty-five of our years equals twenty of yours, so that doesn't mean much."

He wasn't about to mention that "over a hundred" was a very loose term. If a healer had sufficient skill, a normal lifespan could be doubled. It was rare, but he'd heard of determined individuals who lived past two hundred, if they could afford the effort.

He stood. "Your Majesty, if it would help, I'll step outside for a moment so that Alice can make her plea. From my perspective, I support her idea. You've trained a very brilliant daughter and her ideas are worth consideration." He bowed and left.

From outside, he could still follow their thoughts. Alice was making the argument that Ohen had never made any advances on her and he showed no sign that he was hunting for a title. Then she turned her arguments on the advantages of instant communication with her brothers in the remote capitals.

Ohen's mind wandered, and as he tended to do from time to time, he clairvoyantly checked on B3. There was a blinking light on the computer. Someone had left him a message. He'd need to check on that. General Jonah sometimes sent him a question, but since he wasn't really in a position to monitor what was happening on Mars, he couldn't really help.

He searched the area around the boat as well. There were two of the security guards keeping watch. He thought there was another, but the third guy was watching the first two. A quick sampling of his thoughts was disturbing.

I wish those two idiots would find something else to do. I'll never get a chance at the stranger's ship if I can't even get close to it.

Ohen frowned. The third guy wasn't from Stampz. *I need to put better protective measures in place, in case he somehow gets through the airlock.* His greatest worry was that someone would cause damage to the door that he couldn't fix with the local technology. He'd really be stuck here if that was the case.

Alice came out of the private meeting room, interrupting his dark thoughts. She smiled. "I got permission."

He smiled. "That's great. How soon can we leave?"

She put her hand to her chin. "Maybe two days. I have to get a new dress to play the part. A courier on horseback will be sent ahead to notify Baron West that I'll be arriving."

He chuckled. "You don't wear your librarian's robe all the time?"

"Not *all* the time!"

"Maybe I should do some more cleaning myself. Especially if you're bringing a maid. I'd hate to be labeled a slob in her eyes."

"So I don't count?"

He shrugged. "You've already seen me at my worst."

She frowned. "Speaking of that, do you have any fancier clothes? You look like a workman, not a diplomat."

"Well, that's what I am. No. Nothing fancy in your eyes."

She nodded. "Then follow me. We'll need to get something made."

He was tempted to take her hand as she led the way, but that was prohibited. He hadn't understood the taboo, but maybe she'd explain it sometime.

. . .

Later, back on the boat, Ohen tapped the keyboard on his Martian computer. The waiting message was from Raymond Wills, the blacksmith apprentice back on Mars who had risen to become the best electrical expert on the planet.

"Barclay, I hope you're listening to this. I've gotten permission to set up a wireforming die machine to spin new copper wire for my windings. I'm just wondering if I should make smaller diameter wire. I could make greater lengths with the same source material that way. Is there any reason I should stay with the diameter that was used originally to wire buildings?"

Ohen took his time to compose his answer. Raymond was very bright, but there was much he didn't know about physics and beyond his limited experience with electromagnetism and battery chemistry, there was much that could trip him up.

Carefully explaining how the resistance of the copper would climb as the wire diameter decreased and the dangers of making a generator that would burn out in use, Ohen gave him some simple rules for calculating what would work best. He spelled out the very simple equations that explained the relationship between voltage, current and resistance. It was impractical to quote a whole textbook over the computer's messaging system, but he hoped he could help.

With the message being relayed from Luna, to an Angel station, then off to Phobos and then down to whatever computer Raymond was using, they could hardly have a back-and-forth conversation. But he trusted Raymond could figure out the technical issues.

I need to talk to John about the level of technology Stampz is using. They have a wind power station and many kloms of wire to distribute the electricity. Did they get that all from the library books? How much did they have to re-invent? It might be fun to get Raymond and the Stampz engineers talking together.

. . .

Emperor Richard had him sit. It was just the two of them this time.

Ohen noticed the wire-wound rheostat at the emperor's fingers as he adjusted the overhead light. The windings looked too dark to be copper, probably a resistive alloy, but the contacts looked gold. Someone in Stampz had some technical expertise. It was another puzzle he'd need to figure out sometime.

The emperor tapped his fingers on his armrest. "I'm against letting my daughter travel to Franklin, but the stakes are high. If you could get me just one computer so that I could have instant communication with my sons ...." He shook his head in thought. "I just have to say that the empire hasn't been this close to a fracture in my lifetime. There are so many factions tugging in so many directions. Many would rejoice if things fell apart.

"And yet, it is very important that Alice is protected. And that falls on you."

Ohen nodded. "I have every intention of being at her side the whole time."

"There are issues. She is my daughter, and that alone makes many want to get closer to her."

Ohen chuckled. "On Mars, I had a couple of unexpected offers that had nothing to do with my mind or my sparkling personality. I understand the situation."

Richard nodded. "And I worry about you, as well. Nothing against you personally, but there are some things you don't know, and that exclude you as a potential suitor as well."

Ohen nodded solemnly. "I have suspected as much. I have begun to treasure my conversations with Alice, but there is a certain distance that she always preserves. Perhaps someday I'll understand, but with cultural taboos, such as her gloves, I hesitate to even ask."

Her father took a breath. "You are playing your role as the representative of the U'tanse. Our family has our role as well, and yes, some things can't be explained.

"I just want your promise to return Alice safely and untouched as soon as you possibly can."

"You have my promise."

...

Lord Casey waved Ohen down in the dining hall during the dawnwind and looked him over. "Fancy. They finally talked you into court dress."

Ohen waved his arm. "Yes. I guess. I'm not used to the puffy sleeves, but I guess I could get used to it."

"You got used to your military uniform back in Orson. This is really no different."

"It's more colorful. The uniform was darker."

Casey leaned closer. "I hear you're taking a trip to Franklin. Is there any chance I could go along with you?"

Ohen frowned. "It's tricky this time. The princess is going and everyone is afraid she'll be harmed. Maybe next time, but I can't make changes this late."

Casey nodded. "I understand. It's just that I'd like to go see the world as well."

Ohen looked toward the stairs. "Speak of her highness, there she is."

The Imperial Princess Travels

Alice, Princess of Luna, was dressed in a flowing gown in Stampz signature colors, white and light blue, but her hair was an architectural design all its own, with gold sunflare spikes and something that almost looked like the emperor's crown carved from something white. As he stepped closer, he noticed that gold thread was woven all through her gown, giving it a sparkle as she moved.

The maid beside her, holding a travel case, seemed almost invisible in contrast.

Alice smiled as he came in range. "There you are. I see the suit came out okay."

"Not quite as spectacular as your gown. Are you trying to blind Baron West?"

She laughed. "Perhaps. It's just a reminder of the imperial status. He just might have ignored me in my librarian garb." She turned to her side. "And this is Selena, my maid coming with us."

The girl's eyes were wide and she had to crane her neck up to see his eyes. She looked frightened.

Ohen nodded. "I was wondering when the winds would subside. I hesitate to think what would happen to your hair."

Alice laughed. "Did you know that court ladies use a closed cabriolet for that very reason? I have one on the ground floor waiting for us. If you can have your ship's door open for me, I can slip in quickly and Selena can take care of any mishap. We shouldn't have any wind issues by the time we get to Franklin."

He nodded. She was on top of everything. This was her project, after all. She had to prove to her family that she was competent.

He escorted the ladies to the closed carriage, drawn by a horse. Once the outside doors opened, he raced on foot to get the B3 ready for them.

The driver of the carriage edged the door so close together that the carriage wouldn't open all the way, but it was perfect for Alice, bending down to protect her hair to duck inside. Selena's cap was almost blown away, but soon they were all inside, and the maid's combs came out to repair any loose locks.

Ohen watched the carriage pull away on the display screen.

"Alice, I've got one more thing to do outside and then we can take off."

She nodded, concentrating on her hand-held mirror.

Ohen ducked through the airlock and strode over to the men standing nearby.

"Roger Mills!"

One of the guards jerked at having his name called. Ohen came close and lowered his voice. "You guys may not be aware that my ship can record sounds… voices around it. I know who you are and the job you do. That's fine with me. But I also wanted you to know that a man in a red knitted shirt and wearing a brown cap has been waiting for you to slack off so he can get a chance to test my door lock himself—and I'm not fine with that."

Mills nodded slowly. "That's good to know."

Ohen gestured to the boat. "I'll be lifting off in a couple of minutes. I'll probably be back before darkwind. Watch the dust."

. . .

Selena shrieked as the boat lifted off. Alice took her hand.

Ohen concentrated on the controls, making sure the boat stayed stable and level. He raised the floor gravity a little to make everyone feel secure.

But Alice's thoughts were ecstatic. **I'm really flying!**

Ohen said, "I'll put the front image on the display. I assume you want to go out over Stampz Gate canyon again?"

Alice said, "Yes, please."

By the time they had cleared the crater, Ohen realized he'd never felt the thoughts of someone so overjoyed in his life. Part of Alice's surge of joy was seeing things she'd heard about all her life, but part was her realization that for the first time, she was getting to go beyond the ring of Stampz crater.

Ohen was comparing the landscape below with the map that showed the route to Franklin. He pointed out the landmarks, partly to keep Selena from panicking again, but just to talk with Alice.

"Is that the Spanish River?" Alice asked.

"Yes, but we won't be following it. We need to cross the Mercurius highlands and then on past Hooke. Can you see the trail tracks? I'd like to follow those for a while if we're not too high. Features on the ground get obscured by the sky haze and the clouds."

A little later, Selena pointed, "What's that? It moved!"

Ohen hunted for a second, and then saw it. "Good eyesight. I'm going to zoom in." He slowly adjusted the magnification until they could make it out.

Alice said, "That's a herd of animals. Are they deer?"

Ohen said, "I wouldn't know a deer if you put one in front of me. We didn't have them on my world. You're the expert."

Alice chuckled. "Then let's just say it's a herd of deer, then. I've seen pictures and occasionally we've had venison at a banquet, but I've never been close to the live animals either. Selena?"

The maid was surprised to have her input sought. "My father hunted on the crater slopes. We occasionally had venison, too."

When they passed over Mercurius, they lost sight of the rail tracks and Ohen paid closer attention to the minor craters on the map, matching them to the details he could make out. Often the forest totally obscured some features that might be more visible from the ground.

By the time they passed Hooke and began to anticipate Franklin in the distance, Alice started checking the papers in her travel bag and memorizing opening phrases to use when they greeted Baron West.

Franklin was a sight to behold. A castle, much more elaborate than the Imperial castle at Stampz, crested the central peak of the crater. A large city surrounded it, and black clouds streamed from an industrial complex off to the side. He'd heard that Franklin was the center of the iron industry.

Ohen nodded to himself. It explained the large swaths of deforested lands he'd seen coming in.

The city even showed some remaining ruins from the meteor impact during the Hercules-Serenite war of long ago, although most of it was rebuilt.

Ohen checked his notes. Brilliant Morning had visited Franklin a few times in the past and he had the landing field marked on a map. It was parkland close to the castle. Ohen just hoped that the courier on horseback had arrived and given the message that they were visiting. He'd hate to land in the middle of a bunch of palace guards with guns. The hull was pretty tough, but he'd rather avoid any dents.

But there was a fancy carriage waiting for them, with six soldiers in ornamental uniforms waiting at the edge of the landing field. A gray-haired man in finery stepped out of the carriage as B3 hovered into place above the grass. Ohen landed as smoothly as possible.

"We're down." He turned off the floor gravity so everyone would feel normal again.

Alice was on her feet. "Ohen, you stand just a pace behind me on my right side. Selena will follow."

"I'll have to secure the airlock door immediately after we step out." He opened the inner door and bypassed the safety that ensured that there would always be one door closed at all time. They needed to step out as a party.

"Okay, I'll pause while you do that, but try to be discrete about it."

It was a little clumsy as they exited, but he was in position just a few seconds late.

Alice was in her haughtiest princess mode as she graciously allowed the baron to entertain her for the day. Ohen was introduced as a traveling ambassador from Mars, interested in his collection of pre-Plague artifacts.

Baron West was excited to get on the good side of anyone from the imperial family, and just a little frustrated, not that he let that show on his face. **Why did Amos have to be in Atlas today? I'd love to have this girl as a daughter-in-law.**

He was also suspicious of Ohen. **Who is he really? Why is the famously reclusive princess traveling alone with him?**

Ohen was pleasantly quiet, standing so close to Alice that no one could ignore him, yet never taking the lead in the conversation. The people's thoughts were interesting enough.

There was a tea party to greet the baron's family, and a couple of wealthy neighbors who were close enough when the call came out about the surprise visit.

Alice waved off the apologies for the lack of pomp, her ornate white gloves showing. "This is just part of my education, before I begin … other duties. My mother's description of your collection made it an important stop on my tour."

The deliberately vague hints triggered a lot of speculation, and Alice was relishing the confusion. In reality, she knew she was likely to remain the librarian until someone safe enough was chosen to be her husband. A fancy tour of the great cities of the world had been a fantasy of hers for years and she couldn't resist playing the part, even if it was just for a single day.

Ohen nearly forgot about all the politics as they entered the room where the baron kept his collection.

The devices were arrayed along the walls, polished and dusted, not at all like the piles of discarded computers back on Mars. Forgetting the other people in the room, he went down the row, using his clairvoyance to see inside the devices. The first computer he saw, while looking pristine on the outside, was filled with mud and corroded internally.

Alice was explaining to the baron about Ohen's experience with pre-Plague devices from his time on Mars.

After a few minutes, he turned to them. "Baron, this device here is the jewel of your collection." He tapped a floor-standing metal cabinet with a darkened display that, when it was alive, had showed the status of the contents.

West frowned. "What is it? I've never known, other than it's heavy."

Ohen nodded. "With your permission, I believe I can open it up without damage and show you the interior."

The baron conferred with the man who maintained the collection, and the slight man in robes nodded, pulling out a bound notebook and began to take notes.

There was an electrically operated latch that Ohen could operate via his psychokinesis, but he couldn't tell them that. Instead, he rapped along the door's seam with his knuckles as he invisibly forced the mechanism. With a click, the front door, about two-thirds of the height below the display, came open a crack.

Ohen swung the slightly stiff door wide and opened the interior.

"As you can see, there are twenty-four canisters in here. Each is contained in its own sleeve. More than half have been opened and are empty." Ohen reached for one of the canisters that was still sealed, and began to unscrew the lid.

"I strongly suspect each chamber was temperature-controlled and was used to transfer animal specimens from the Earth to Luna."

The lid came open and there was just a whiff of long decayed flesh. He showed them what he found. "It looks to me like the bones of an embryo of some kind of mammal. Perhaps a deer or a goat or something. All life on Luna was originally transported to this world from Earth, or possibly some laboratory on a Lagrangian station. The engineers trapped on Luna during the Plague were turning specimens like these into the herds of animals that now roam your forests."

The curator of the collection was writing down his words at a frantic pace.

"The cabinet was computer controlled, designed to keep each sample carefully preserved. Since most were empty, likely those animals matured and became the ancestors of some animal that lives on Luna today. Those like this one that were never opened could be species that were intended to live on Luna, but never survived the Plague when the scientists were killed.

"Baron, you have, right here, the Garden of Eden of all life on Luna. Like I said, it's the jewel of the collection."

The curator carefully took the sample jar from Ohen and gently returned it to its position. "I'll have to examine all of these carefully and make individual glass jars to preserve them for display."

Alice said, "I have some books in the library that might help you identify which animal species they are."

The curator nodded. "Definitely. I'll need all the help I can get. This is most important to Luna's history."

Ohen pointed. "This device here is also interesting." The curator snatched up his notebook and the scratch of pen on paper continued.

In all, Ohen identified a half-dozen devices that had come from some biological laboratory, including some large computer that was probably dedicated to genetic analysis, from what he could guess. They were all definitely important historical artifacts.

There was a real puzzle in their thoughts, though. As excited as the baron was over the samples and the various laboratory devices, the instant he talked about the genetic analysis machine, everyone began to step away from it, as if it were hazardous—although it was most assuredly dead and long out of power.

The real treasures from the viewpoint of the imperial family were two "ordinary computers" that Ohen believed he could revive. There were also a couple of the hand-held devices that he'd seen on Mars but never attempted to revive. He told the baron those four were all "typical devices" that were common on Mars and when trade between planets was begun, they wouldn't be worth much.

Alice was well aware of what he was saying and began her pitch that she might want to take a few of the "low value" items off his hands to use as training examples at the Stampz library.

The baron wasn't dumb. He was thrilled that his collection of mystery devices were now solidly identified as important historical artifacts, but the idea that he might dislodge some of the imperial horde of gold was exciting as well. Just how savvy was this isolated princess when it came to negotiations?

Ohen left the process up to her, only reminding her that they needed to be back at Stampz before darkwind. It was just the incentive she needed to push the negotiations forward when the baron was inclined to think about it for another month or so.

Eventually, they ended up adding the totally dead, mud-contaminated computer, and taking only one of the little hand-held devices. Alice signed the promissory note for eight kilograms of gold and two of silver. They left Franklin after a rather more-elaborate meal in the banquet hall. Ohen talked about Mars and Alice waxed eloquent about the treasures in the Stampz library. So many people were paying close attention whenever Ohen looked her way and when she paid any attention to him. Alice was thrilled at the attention, no matter if the romance was all in people's heads.

When Ohen checked on Selena, hidden in the next room, he realized the servants were pestering her endlessly to give them the real gossip about the princess and the tall man from Mars. It was interesting to him to listen in on her guesswork as well.

By the time they said their goodbyes and Alice gave her promises to think about returning someday, it was in the afternoon. The B3 lifted off much earlier than he had scheduled. He offered to take an alternate route back to Stampz, just for the scenery, but Alice pointed to her maid.

"It looks like Selena is already asleep. We wore her out."

He nodded. "Then it's your call. Which route?"

She looked wistful. "I'd love to see the ocean. Do we have time to go north toward Hercules and Atlas before turning west?"

"I can make that work."

The Bad Word

Ohen pulled out a portable chair from storage and set it beside his command chair for Alice, while they let Selena sleep on the bench. They talked quietly, to keep from disturbing her.

Alice sighed as they left a forested area and swept rapidly north over a grassy plain. "I'm sorry if I pretended there was something romantic going on between us. It was just too much of a temptation."

He nodded. "I got that. You had to keep everyone guessing. The baron was really frustrated you wouldn't stay long enough to meet his son."

She shook her head. "There was that, of course, but there were three daughters of prominent families who were trying to catch your attention as well, and I was just relishing the idea that they were frustrated by my prior claim on you."

He shrugged. "I tend to disregard the attentions of women at banquets."

"Oh? If I recall, I first saw you at a banquet."

"Yes, but the lady in the librarian's robe was much more interesting."

She had a thought and frowned. "There's something I need to tell you."

"What's that?"

"Well… that word you used when describing the big computer. You need to avoid it."

"What word?"

"Um." She looked over at the still-sleeping maid. Then she whispered, "Genetics."

He frowned, "Why? Surely I've used it before."

"Well, yes, but only when the chancellor and I were present. We're a little more well-read than most. You shouldn't use it in public."

"Why? It's a straightforward science, and probably important in the history of Luna."

She sighed. "I'll give you a history book back when we're at Stampz. But for now, just avoid it, okay?"

"I guess."

He was grateful when the ocean appeared in the distance and they could change the subject. Ohen brought the boat down low to skim the ocean waves, and she got a great view of a fishing boat and cargo ships in the distance.

"Sorry, but I'll avoid the cities. I gather there are still some defensive laser cannon in place near the ports."

She nodded. "Yes, and we haven't warned them you would be here. People are very sensitive about spaceships. Hercules and Atlas were nearly wiped out during the Mt. Ural attacks."

He turned their course west and began the trip to Stampz. Alice was trying to contain her disappointment. Would she ever be able to take a trip like this again?

. . .

Alice was quick with her promise to give him a history book to read. She'd even put bookmarks in places for him.

He spent most of the next couple of days secured behind his airlock doors. His excuse was that he needed to carefully analyze the purchased computers, and he did spend some time at that. With so few devices to work with, he couldn't afford any mistakes. Within half a day, he had the two good computers recharged and using the one he brought from Mars, he tested them for performance. Both made solid connections to the relay in orbit and exchanged a couple of messages with Raymond Wills back on Mars just as well as his device.

Careful inspection with his clairvoyance confirmed that the bad one would never work. Too many internal components had been corroded in the mud beyond any hope of repair.

The little hand-held device was the one which took much more time to examine. From what he could tell with his sight, there did appear to be a smaller computer inside and a power cell scaled down smaller than any he'd ever seen before. If there were microphones or speakers, then they used technology he wasn't familiar with. The front face could be a display, but he wasn't sure. There was certainly no keyboard. None of it could work without power and it was much too small to cut holes for a wire like he did back on Mars.

His only chance was to charge the tiny power cell from B3's beams, but it would be very tricky. He'd need a very weak charging beam to avoid burning it out. Plus, even if the device worked, he wasn't sure what it did.

The Book mentioned cell phones, back before the Star. From the brief description it was a communicator people could carry in their pockets, but they were all destroyed by the Betelgeuse flare itself. This gadget had to be something else, but what, he didn't know.

There was a flash on his computer screen.

The voice said, "There is a voice message for Owen Barclay from Abraham Chung."

"Answer it. Hello, Abraham."

"Ah, you're there. I knocked on your door a few minutes ago and nobody answered."

"Sorry. I was deep in thought. What do you need?"

"Not much. It's just that the emperor is anxious about the computers Alice bought. Do they work?"

"Yes, I brought two of them back to life. I'm still struggling with the smallest one. I know that he'd really like three active computers and I'm not there yet."

"Well, why don't you tell him that, and turn over the two live ones. He's a kind man, but when he's anxious, he gets a little on edge, if you know what I mean."

"Sorry. When I dive into a technical problem, I sometimes get lost. I'll take the two good ones to him right away. Thanks for letting me know."

. . .

Alice joined him for the meeting. She beamed as she tapped on the keyboard and entered her identification code. "Oh, well, no messages for me, but nobody knows my code anyway."

Ohen chuckled, "Probably 'Princess Alice of Luna' would probably get through to you. When King Harmon of Xanthe on Mars sent a message to the 'Ruler of Luna' it reached the emperor."

Richard laughed, "And Abraham was terribly confused when Brilliant Morning told him about it, too. I had to climb up into the ship and set up an identification code of my own before it could play his message. Nobody knew computers had this messaging system."

The emperor nodded when Ohen turned on the second one and showed that it was active as well. "Well I had hoped for three of them, but I can always climb that ladder or get Abraham to relay it to me over the ordinary radio."

Alice asked, "That other computer ... it didn't work?"

"I never thought it would. I could tell just by holding it that there was something inside. In this case, it was mud. Probably someone discovered it at the bottom of a river or something. It's all silted in and corroded. Just like we told Baron West, it'll make a nice exhibit in your library, but it'll never work again."

"And I'll be glad to have it, but I'd really love to have a live one."

"I think your father has priority."

Richard said, "My sons have priority. I'll need to get these to them, secretly. They will need instructions on how to use them."

Alice said, "That's my job. I've been trained by Abraham and Ohen on how to use this type of computer and I can write up the instructions in the family code. The couriers will have to get the computers and the instructions to Allen and Dalton without attracting any attention."

Ohen ignored the family code reference. Of course they had to have codes if their important messages had to be carried via couriers.

Richard nodded. "Good. Make sure they understand that no one is to know that such messages exist."

Alice nodded. "I'll want your public code. We can't trust the computers to always get 'Ruler of Luna' correctly."

The emperor wrote down the string of characters and handed it to her. "Get on this now. I want to put the computers in their hands just as soon as possible."

She nodded and hurried out.

When they were alone, Richard looked at Ohen and asked, "Is there anything I could offer to buy the computer you use?"

Ohen sighed. "I wish there was, but it's just too important to my main goal. If I'm ever to visit Earth, then I will need to find a way to get permission from the Project computers that are protecting the planet. Even traveling through the Solar system is hazardous without a computer's help to avoid the restrictions enforced by the Project."

Richard nodded. Ohen was grateful that the emperor didn't just confiscate it. The man was sticking to the political rules.

"There were no other computers in Baron West's collection?"

"None that could be used as a messaging unit. You don't know of any other such collections, do you?"

"Not that I've heard of. The long-destroyed colony on Alp Island had some, but the place was incinerated by an asteroidal chunk of ice. There was a museum at Hercules, but it was destroyed during the Mt. Ural war. Luna has had its share of disasters."

Ohen nodded. Mars had millions of people when the Plague happened. Luna had just hundreds or thousands. There couldn't have been all that many general-purpose computers on the smaller globe when everything fell apart.

"What about the Lagrangian settlements?"

"The Space Cities? You think there might be computers there?"

"It's possible. You go there for metals and books, I know."

Richard nodded. "And other things. We haven't been looking for computers. Perhaps it's time for another expedition." Then he shook his head, thinking of problems that might happen if his military trump card was missing for too long.

Ohen asked, "When is your next scheduled trip?"

"There's nothing scheduled, and I'm always getting questions about it. You saw that sailsuit race on Stampz Day? Abraham always reminds me that it's zero-gravity training for the next trip."

Ohen chuckled, "And I bet Alice wants to visit the Alexandrian Library."

Richard nodded. "Now that she's made one trip out of Stampz, I bet I'll hear more from her." He gestured to the two computers on the table. "I hope these are worth it."

Ohen was playing a careful role. The emperor really needed quick communication with his two sons. They were the imperial ears monitoring the capitals of the two major power centers of the empire. Richard was asking himself time and again just how important it was to keep good relations with Mars and the U'tanse. His words were comforting, but his thoughts were closer to the edge.

Ohen said, "There are two possibilities to help you out.

"We acquired a small, hand-sized computer that might be able to be used as a communicator, but I haven't gotten it to work yet. It may not be usable at all, but I am hopeful. That's what I've been working on for the past day.

"Another option is to go to the 'Space Cities' and hunt for more general-purpose computers. I could go in my boat and you could keep Brilliant Morning here for you security purposes. It might take a while, since there are apparently hundreds of abandoned facilities in the Lagrangian orbits and there's always the danger that Project Control has some restrictive rules that I'd have to work around."

Richard nodded. "I'd appreciate if you could pursue both options. But the current political situation is such that I need to get something working for faster communications." He didn't say it, but there was the sense that someone was moving military forces closer to Stampz than the current imperial rules allowed. He was being boxed in. The imperial power was being tested.

Ohen nodded. "I'll get back to work then. If you or Alice need my help with the computers, just let me know."

. . .

Back at the boat, Ohen rechecked his sketch of the hand-sized computer. Mapping the internals with his clairvoyance, he'd identified a tiny figure that was probably the power cell. There wasn't any obvious chemical battery so he was pretty confident that the human technology of the Project era had managed to make some kind of TP power cell that small. The trick was getting it to charge. The danger was that the smaller the electronics, in his experience, the lower the voltage it used. If he tried to charge it the same way he'd charged the other computers, he might very well fry its circuits.

Nor could he sense when it was charged with his psychic abilities. The only way was to attempt a very low-power charging beam, and then test the gadget to see if it woke up. Since he didn't even know how to operate one of these things, that was a lot of trial and error in itself. If it still looked dead, then slightly increase his charging beam and repeat the whole process.

He started the charge and picked up the history text that Alice had loaned him.

He was ignoring the bookmarks for now. He wanted to understand humanity's history from the beginning. Much of it had been included in the Book, but the history text frequently had a different viewpoint from the version written by Abe. It was fascinating. Once he reached the time of the Betelgeuse supernova, it was all new. That was when Abe the Father and Sharon the Mother were kidnapped by the Cerik and the U'tanse began.

In the Emperor's Pocket

King Thomas's War was an eye opener. According to the text, at the time that the supernova flare wiped out the civilization based on semiconductors, genetic engineering had already begun and scientists on the island continent of Australia made huge strides in genetic alteration even with the crude electronics that had survived. A trade dispute between the northern nations and Australia broke out into a shooting war, and then someone unknown had created a fiercely infectious biological weapon that targeted every known genetic alteration.

The Die-Off, as it was called, destroyed every altered organism on the planet in horrible ways. Bioengineered weapons, improved crops and enhanced livestock, as well as any human that had any kind of genetic medical treatment—they all died. The widespread medical use of genetic alterations to cure cancer and other diseases meant that almost all of untouched humanity knew someone who died in agony because of that biological weapon. Many others died when food stocks collapsed.

Worldwide, public sentiment turned against any kind of biological engineering. Scientists were hunted down and killed. The terms "genetic" and even "hereditary" became vile terms to be avoided in everyday speech. While the technology survived, use of it became off limits without a special permit. According to the history text, the only remaining use was the tailoring of wildlife on terraformed Mars and Luna to allow them to survive the new air, water, and gravity.

Ohen understood why Alice had marked that chapter. It certainly explained why genetics was a taboo subject.

Ohen was also impressed that Baron West's computer, with its custom hardware to take biological samples and analyze them, was probably much rarer than he'd first assumed. It might be the only remaining computer designed for genetic analysis left in the system, if every world still considered the technology forbidden.

But, he shouldn't talk about what made it special, now. He'd never run into this taboo on Mars, but then again, the subject had never come up. Surely Mars had the same restrictions.

. . .

The computer spoke. "There is a message from Lord Casey of Chimbote."

"Go ahead."

"Hey, Barclay, could I talk with you a little?"

"A private conversation?"

"Yes, I'm in my room. No one can hear."

"Then go ahead. What do you want?"

Casey sighed. "I've gotten a request from the emperor. He'd like to buy my computer. I don't know what to think about it."

"I've had the same request. You have to ask yourself, where is your primary loyalty?"

Casey paused. "It has to be Mars, right? If I gave up my communications to Xanthe, then I couldn't be an ambassador. Still, I'm living here in the castle. The emperor is paying for everything."

"King Harmon gave you that computer to do your job."

"Right! I couldn't possibly give it up without the king's permission, and he'd never agree to that." He gave a sigh of relief. "I knew all this, but it helps to talk it out, you know?"

Ohen said, "I've told the emperor I'd be happy to relay messages for him, but what he really wants is a private computer all his own. He can always relay messages through his own spaceship."

"Right. I can make the same offer, but I have to keep the computer to myself for as long as I'm an ambassador."

"By the way, I know you're more in touch with Mars than I've been. How are things going back there?"

"I hear the war is going well. Xanthe is pushing the front westward and the Candorians are pulling back to the valley. The king is making claims on the Central Waterway, which he's never done before, and there's more talk about the navy. I don't understand that stuff. I'm concentrating on making more contacts, trying to find nobles close enough to military bases so I can get messages relayed to them. The nobles will know the merchants that might eventually want to trade with Luna."

He sighed. "It's like chess, only with a board so large I can't see the edges."

Ohen chuckled. "But it sounds like you're doing your job. Everyone should be pleased."

"I hope. But I can't give up my computer. Everything flows through that."

• • •

A few hours later, the little computer's screen lit up when he touched it. There was a decorative pattern, and then it blinked out, black once again. *It works! That screen display proves the computer is functional. It just needs more power.*

He charged it again at the same settings, only for twice as long. When it made a chirping noise and the screen requested his identification code, showing an image of a keyboard, he quickly typed his in.

"WARNING: Power is very low. Recharge soon."

He'd expected that. The little device continued with some questions, asking whether to use voice, text or both. Ohen barely started to answer when it gave a power failing warning and went dark again.

I need to risk a more powerful charging beam, but this is very encouraging.

• • •

Emperor Richard tapped on the screen, entering his identification code.

Ohen explained, "It is just a very tiny computer, suitable for carrying in your pocket. It has nearly all the capabilities of my computer, with a couple of exceptions."

The emperor nodded, meeting his eyes. "What exceptions?"

"One, it can only hold power for five years. Once I got it working I investigated the charging routines carefully. Brilliant Morning has been updated with all the details and Abraham can do it for you when the power gets low. You'll be warned a couple of months in advance when you'll need to worry about it."

"I take it your computer lasts longer?"

"Probably. I don't really know the details. Everything runs out of power eventually.

"However there's another restriction that will be more important to you. This little computer can't connect to the Angel station in orbit around Luna. Its radio is very weak. When I flew off yesterday for a few minutes, it was just to check the practical range.

"The pocket computer can reach my computer and Lord Casey's computer if they are within about ten kloms. It can reach Brilliant Morning for about fifty kloms."

Richard frowned, "So I can't talk to my sons with this?"

Ohen waved his hand. "No, that's not how it works. The computer messaging system can send messages from world to world even with weak radios because the messages hop from one computer to another. When you try to contact your son Allen, your pocket computer would send the voice or text to my computer or Casey's or Brilliant Morning's. That computer would send it to the closest Angel station. Perhaps that Angel would sent it to another Angel that would then send it you your son's computer in Hercules. Hardly any of these messages go directly to the person you address."

Richard nodded, "And no one can listen in?"

Ohen chuckled. "Definitely not. When I first encountered the system, I tried to understand how it worked and used my U'tanse technical knowledge and my own radios to see if I could interface with the computer's system and it proved to be well beyond my limits. Everything is encrypted and scattered across many different radio frequencies. I couldn't even detect if other messages have been relayed through my computer all this time. It's as secure as I can imagine. You'll be talking to you sons and no one can even know that it's happening."

The emperor raised the little computer in his hand. "But I need to be close to some other computer for it to work."

Ohen nodded. "Yes. If Casey and I left, and Brilliant Morning was off on a journey, then you could only use it for calculations and note-taking and all those other little tasks. If you tried to send a message, it would just wait in your pocket until some other computer came into range before it would send."

"I guess I can live with that, but it's a serious limitation, isn't it?"

Ohen shrugged. "When they were made, there were computers everywhere. No one could imagine a situation where they could be out of contact."

The emperor tapped on the screen several times, making notes to himself. "Sending you or Abraham off to find more computers in the Space Cities sounds more appealing by the minute. Are there more of these little ones on Mars?"

"Yes, there are. I saw hundreds of them in one warehouse. There are probably many more, and none of them are being used. I never got around to the attempt to revive this class of computer when I was working for King Harmon."

"Then I need to get trade with Mars on my urgent list as well." He smiled at Ohen. "Stampz would be a very different place if I could put one of these in the hands of all my people."

. . .

Alice slipped off her gloves as she smelled the aroma of her plate. Ohen's stomach growled. She smiled.

The communal dining area in the castle had various-sized tables, but Alice had chosen a small booth for just the two of them off in the corner. People could watch, but if they spoke quietly, no one could hear.

"How did you like the book?" she asked.

"It was very enlightening, especially the section about King Thomas's War. I can understand the cultural significance."

She savored her pasta, and then nodded. "It was very significant. Some blame the Plague on its aftereffects."

"How so? Do they think the Plague was ...?" He hesitated to say the words.

She nodded. "Some do. Humanity has had plagues of all kinds throughout its history, but nothing so severe, nothing so abrupt, and then ... it vanished."

She shrugged, "Then again, humanity has always wanted to blame natural disasters on other people. There were curses, witches, all sorts of psychic evil. The unknown sciences could be painted with the same brush."

Ohen nodded, not wanting to follow that trail. "I suppose we'll never know."

Alice ate slowly. "Father is pleased with his new toy."

"Did you make sure he credited you with buying it for him?"

"Perhaps a little. But he said you were planning on leaving?"

Suddenly a few little things, like this semi-private meal together, made more sense.

"Well... I've never made a secret of my long term plans. I'm just a scout for my people. We were hunting for Earth. I landed on Mars first, and then came to Luna when the opportunity arose. Eventually, I want to find a way to visit Earth, but it appears that visiting the 'Space Cities' will likely happen first."

She took another bite, the asked. "No long-term plans? After visiting Earth?"

He sighed. "I always thought that when my people came for me, I'd return to Ha with them. Now, I don't know. Humanity's home system seems to be more vibrant than where I came from. I had an offer to stay on Mars, but I turned that down. Luna has its appeal as well.

"However, I guess that while the opportunities to explore this system keep coming, I'm still compelled to be a scout. When that's done, I don't know what options will remain."

She nodded. "I understand duty. You might not have volunteered and you might not like your path, but you're still compelled to take those steps."

He took a breath. It was clear she was thinking more about her own situation than his.

"And my next step, I suppose, is to go to my local library and find out which of these 'Space Cities' I ought to search out first."

She smiled. "I actually have some records that could help. I probably shouldn't say this in public, but Stampz has already been doing a lot of that kind of research."

Ohen met her eyes. "Maybe that's supposed to be a big secret, but I already knew that."

She asked, thoughtfully, "Are you working for my father? What's your relationship, actually?"

He shrugged. "We haven't said. My position under King Harmon on Mars was much more defined, I started as a captured suspected spy and worked my way up. With your father, I'm more like a visiting ambassador. Yet I've done very much the same things for both, assisting by bringing old technology back to life.

"From my perspective, I'm just doing what I can to help. I really want the people in charge to have good thoughts about the U'tanse when my people arrive."

She smiled. "You'll have to tell me about this spy business sometime."

...

Ohen was surprised when he was allowed to carry the thick binder back to his boat. Alice was clearly reluctant to let it go but she had orders from her father.

It wasn't a bound book, rather a collection of papers—logs written by various pilots during their expeditions to the Lagrangian colonies. Ohen had a little difficulty reading the text. Each pilot wrote their logs in their own script and the collection had never been transcribed into printed text.

Still, Ohen was making progress. He was compiling a few notes for himself. He listed the colonies that were mines, asteroids that had been relocated from the primary asteroid belt into the Lagrangian clusters. There were others that had been looted farming colonies, and some that had been research facilities.

There was also a warning to steer clear of Mt. Ural, a heavily converted asteroid that still contained the people that had bombed the Lunar cities from orbit during the last war between Hercules and Serenity. It was still inhabited and its people would likely steal or destroy any ship that got too close.

There was also a list of Project facilities that were as off-limits as the Earth itself. Any ship that attempted to get too close, or to put a beam on them, was likely to lose its power. It was just like what had happened to B3 when he had ignorantly put a beam on Earth.

There was an interesting comment from one of the earliest logs: "Since Brilliant Morning inherited the computer identity of the original Ship, it has also inherited the prohibition against TP interaction with Project stations."

Ohen nodded to himself. Just as the ships on Mars where shut down via an order from the Project, Brilliant Morning was also in some ways still controlled by the Project.

No matter what he planned, he'd have to take extra care to avoid the Project danger zones.

Just then, there was a *bang!* The boat shook.

Ohen jumped for the command seat, slapping the engine controls.

Off With a Bang

All four engines on the B3 shoved hard at the ground, throwing the boat into the air. Emergency routines he'd last practiced back before the starship left on its journey to hunt for Earth came to his fingertips without much thought.

He shifted to cycling a tractor beam into the air above—what the Earth-humans called cirrance—and climbed to a thousand meters above the landing zone. He turned on the camera and got a quick view of where he had been.

People were running for cover in all directions. There was a smoky burned spot in the brown patch where the B3 had been parked. Someone had put a bomb under the boat. A cluster of people were trying to stamp out the grass fire with their feet. An open flame couldn't be permitted to grow.

I have to check the hull.

He steered off to the side and landed a few kloms away in the middle of some farmer's plowed field. He dashed through the airlock and circled the hull until he saw the black patch.

It had to have been a black powder bomb, but not one strong enough to dent the hull. He scraped at the discoloration with his fingernail. It would require cleaning, and the Delense alloy would need a little time to rebuild the protective layer. The Lunar atmosphere had the enough of the right elements that the hull material should heal itself soon enough. Off in the distance, he could see the farmer heading his way, but he couldn't wait for him to arrive.

He hurried back inside and called the emperor.

"Your Majesty, I had to take a quick hop off into a farmer's field nearby to escape when a bomb went off under my ship."

"I heard that! My bodyguards are frantically collecting my family into protected rooms."

Ohen said, "I think it was just an effort to damage my ship. It was a relatively small black powder bomb concealed under the hull. I don't imagine it could have caused any real problem."

The emperor wasn't so sure. "I'm glad your ship is strong, but *every-one* knows that when a ship is destroyed, the exploding power cells would vaporize the whole city. It might have been a long-shot attempt to destroy Stampz and the empire itself."

Ohen had learned enough Lunar history that he knew of the destruction of Beltis Island and the Burn that had turned Alp Island into ash. People also knew that a cylindrical beamship like Brilliant Morning was also so tough that ordinary weapons wouldn't dent its hull. Only high-powered lasers could cut through.

But the B3 was a different beast. Maybe the enemy thought it was worth the risk to attack it.

There was a knock on the door.

"I'm sorry, Your Majesty, but I need to go apologize to an angry farmer."

"Go. And keep yourself safe. Give us warning when you return, because my security forces are a little on edge right now."

The angry thoughts coming from the farmer were beating on Ohen's brain. He needed to calm the man down.

Ohen opened the airlock door and immediately said, "Oh, you're here! Did you hear the explosion? Can you help me?"

The farmer was confused. "What? I heard something in the distance. Was it an explosion?"

"Yes, I was parked by the castle when someone set off a bomb underneath me. Come look at the scorch marks. I'm sorry I couldn't wait for you to show up but I had to contact Emperor Richard to let him know I was okay."

The rapid fire changes of topic and the use of the emperor's name caused the farmer's anger to dissipate.

Ohen led him around to the black spot. "It's on the opposite side from the door. Someone was able to sneak up on the back side and put a small bomb in place. I'm really going to have to clean this up before I try to go back into space. By the way, I'm sorry for landing on your field. It was the closest place where there weren't obvious crops growing."

The farmer nodded and held out his hand. "I'm Duncan Berber. No harm done. I was letting the field rest before planting it anyway."

"Ohen bar Clay." He shook the hand. "Ambassador visiting here for a while. I'm afraid some people don't like me here."

The farmer nodded. "Heard of you. Don't worry about the talk. The outsiders are always poking at Stampz, trying to take down the family." He nodded at the hull. "Is that a problem?"

Ohen sighed. "Maybe. Just flying around, it wouldn't be, but if I go back into space, the hull needs to be perfect. I'll need to clean it up and resurface it before I can leave."

Duncan got down on his knees. "It'll be tough getting under there to work on it."

"I'll figure something out."

Just then, a half-dozen security guards from the castle rode up on horseback.

"Are you okay?"

Ohen looked up. "Ah. Roger Mills. Good to see you. I'm okay, but the boat needs a little cleanup. The bomb wasn't powerful enough to damage the hull."

"Well, you warned us. I don't know how this happened."

"You were guarding the door. Somebody put the bomb on the back side when nobody was watching."

After some discussion, Duncan pointed to a rock ledge one field over. Ohen lifted the B3 and set it down carefully on the ledge with the black spot hanging over the edge. The farmer helped with a sturdy ladder while the guards kept watch.

Ohen climbed under and scrubbed the patch clean and buffed the metal until it was shiny.

Duncan asked, "Will that do it?"

"Yes. The metal alloy is designed to repair itself. It heals all scrapes just by 'rusting' in the air. As soon as that shiny patch turns dull like the rest of it, it'll be like the explosion never happened. That should take a few hours yet until it's perfect."

"I'd like my tools to get stronger when they rust." Duncan laughed. "Where can I get some of that space metal?"

Ohen pointed to the sky. "Off around another planet so far away you can't imagine. I wish I knew how to make it, but that's a specialty I never learned."

He gave Duncan a peek inside the boat, then promised to be gone by darkwind. The farmer waved off the offer to be paid for damages to his field.

There was a call on the computer once he was alone.

"Hello, Alice?"

"Yes, I'm calling from Brilliant Morning. Abraham is working with the guards to lock down the landing area. Is your ship okay? Any damage?"

"Just a little surface blemish. I've worked with Duncan Berber, a farmer, and it's almost totally fixed. I've just got to wait a couple of hours for the hull metal to heal."

She chuckled. "So you made a new friend. I've noticed that about you. You're very good at meeting people."

Ohen knew he cheated, sensing the ideas that might trigger hostility and avoiding them. "Well, I'm just lucky, I guess."

"Well, my father is upset that someone got through to attack you. The guards are going to be on extra duty for awhile. Everybody is hunting for the spy."

"Oh, he's probably long gone. If he wanted to trigger a big explosion, then he'd want to be out of Stampz before the bomb went off."

Alice said sadly, "There are martyrs, you know."

Ohen grunted. The ancestral hero of his line had been one, but he really didn't want to get into that.

She continued, "Anyway, you need to come back to the castle. It'll be safer here than off in some farmer's field."

"I understand that, but it'll be just a little bit longer."

"Don't delay. People worry about you, you know."

...

The meeting was held in a closed-off reading room near the main shelves of the library. Ohen was there with his computer. Abraham was there, working with Alice to make sure the stack of logs was back in its right order.

Ohen shook his head. "I'm really sorry about this, but the explosion scattered all the pages. I was able to collect everything and I don't think anything was damaged, but they're definitely disorganized now."

He had been a little reluctant to leave the boat, once it was back at its burnt landing site, but getting the expedition to the Space Cities was important for everybody.

Once the logs were sorted and Alice was confident they hadn't been damaged, they got back to the task of deciding which places should be visited. There was such a long list of possibilities that Ohen wanted the best options listed first.

"After that, I'll need to sort them by location, so that the travel time is minimized. I noticed in the logs that their locations weren't well defined."

Abraham nodded. "The logs were only a backup for the ships' memories. It was important to list what was important to us, the humans. Brilliant Morning has a detailed list of where everything is. She needs to know that, but I don't, not really. So, it was important to mention whether a place was in the Ceres cluster or the Vesta cluster, but by the time we returned, the actual position would have shifted."

Ohen nodded. "I guess that's so. I was just expecting some kind of orbital information."

Abraham shrugged. "Orbits in the clusters are eccentric. They circle the primary in a curved teardrop path, at least from the viewpoint of Luna. I don't know the math, but Brilliant does."

"My boat it going to have a harder time of it. This computer," he tapped the device at his side, "isn't connected to my navigation system at all. Even if I got the current position of a target, it will be up to my skills and computations to fly the boat."

Abraham asked, "Could Brilliant Morning copy her data over to your computer?"

"Possibly, but I have to imagine there would be conversion issues. A ship's native navigation database isn't likely to be something a human like me could easily interpret. Where did Brilliant get her data anyway? Is it up to date? Orbits drift over time, especially in dense clusters like this."

"Ship, the original ship that the Kimmer called Sheep Totem, received a navigation update from Ceres—Project Control. Later when the ship that became Brilliant Morning was captured, Ship's brain was cloned over into the new one and was renamed."

Ohen tapped the little computer, "Can it all even fit into this computer? Or would it have to be a subset of the data?"

Abraham shrugged. "I could only guess how big Brilliant's computer is. I tend to think of it as big, but physically, I don't really know. I suppose we need to get the computers talking to each other and see."

And very shortly, there was a fourth voice in the meeting room. Brilliant Morning's female voice brought a smile to Alice. Although she'd never say anything about it, she often felt like the only woman in the room. Even though no one could call the massive metal cylinder female, Alice appreciated her voice in the room.

Ohen asked, "Brilliant, is there a way to assess the memory capacity of this computer." He detailed how he wanted to use the navigation data of the Lagrangian clusters.

"Perhaps," she said, "it would be better to update the portable computer with the Project control contact information. That way, you could request the necessary data directly and on-demand. It would then be up to your computer to retain only the most current and valuable information if there was a capacity issue."

"Yes," Ohen nodded. "Do that. I would also like to have a current list of all the off-limits places. I've had B3 drained of power once before and I don't ever want to go through that again."

Brilliant said, "I have downloaded the contact information. The shortcut name is Project Command."

Before they took a meal break, Ohen made the call to Project Command, listing a dozen places and asking for details about the prohibited targets. He asked for the data in human-readable form.

Alice asked, "How long do you think it will take for the reply?"

Ohen shook his head as they walked out—Alice wouldn't permit food to be brought into the library. "Who knows? The speed-of-light limit is only a few seconds, but the Project might not even recognize my contact. I'm definitely an outsider here."

He didn't notice the blinking light that had already appeared on the computer's screen.

Machine Mind of Ceres

The Terraforming Project had been heavily dependent on the centralized control of all tractor beam activity. Every relocated asteroid or manufactured habitat had its orbit carefully maintained and only the massive computer center of Project Command could keep track of it all. When the Plague wiped out all humans in control, that computer center continued on with its last orders.

Project Command

Ohen tapped the keys on the computer and the reply from the Project began to appear. He glanced across the table.

"Alice, Abraham, I'd like to play this as audio, if that's okay?"

With their nods, he typed the command. His computer's default male voice began reading.

"Reply from Project Command on Ceres to Ohen bar Clay, representative of the U'tanse from the moon of Ha:

"The following text is formatted to be human readable as requested. There are two sections; the first is a table listing the restricted areas of Project controlled space where the Project would take action should a powered or unpowered craft, device, or other object is aimed at the target area, or is in the field of action of a tractor/pressor beam, or is restricted by a previous Project order.

"Category One is Mars. During the Plague, the Martian Council sent an emergency quarantine request to Project Command in hopes that it would restrict the spread of the Plague to other inhabited areas. Project Command sent a system-wide order prohibiting any Project ship from leaving Mars. No authorization has been received to lift this order.

"Category Two is Earth. During the Plague, the last active controller ordered that in the absence of the human controllers, the Project Command computers should autonomously prevent anything from impacting Earth. As phrased, the command currently inhibits any ship or debris from approaching Earth. In addition, it restricts any tractor/pressor beams from being aimed at Earth as well. As a practical measure, there is a zone beginning at a hundred kloms above the Earth's surface where no tractor/pressor beam activity is allowed. No authorization has been received to lift this order.

"Category Three is all active Project facilities. Prior to the Plague, the Project authorized all spacecraft flights, although most were actively piloted by humans. Such authorization to Project facilities were limited to Project Fleet operations. During the chaos of the Plague, there were many exceptions to the authorization system and when the human command structure of the Project Fleet collapsed, so did the authorization system. As a backup, no powered or unpowered craft, device, or other object aimed at the target area, or which generates a tractor/pressor beam aimed at these restricted facilities is permitted to succeed. Unpowered objects are deflected with Project beams. Powered craft are drained of power."

Ohen tapped the keyboard, interrupting the voice. "After this, there is an extensive list of facilities, organized by orbital areas. I see three Angel stations and two monitoring satellites in Lunar orbit. There are several in close-Earth orbit as well. The biggest list are just distributed all through the Lagrangians, and a few I can't interpret yet. I'll let you scan through the list later.

"What I want is your impression of Project Command. Doesn't it sound to you like a person? Something like Brilliant Morning?"

Abraham nodded. "I got that impression as well. I knew there had to be a big computer somewhere that controlled all the Project beams. *Something* was keeping the Space Cities in tidy orbits, cleaning up the chaos after the Plague, and blocking access to Earth. I guess it's not surprising it can talk like Brilliant."

Alice said, "And it's on Ceres, it sounds like. That is where the Project was headquartered prior to the Plague. I especially like the way it gave a historical background for the restrictions. It sounds like it's trying to justify the restrictions to us humans."

Abraham asked, "Did you get the coordinates?"

"Yes, both for the restricted items and our targets. And it really is trying to make it clear for us limited humans. It's all in a big table. One column is formatted as parameters for an equation plotting the orbit in an Earth-centered coordinate system. Another column is... I guess I'd call it landmarks. 'Aim for Vesta and look to the left by 0.37 degrees until you see a ring-shaped habitat.' Stuff like that. But I can't imagine that would hold up for long."

Abraham said, "You could probably get that refreshed later, if it takes a while for the expedition to come together. Computers don't get frustrated by repeated requests."

Alice said, "You're just on Brilliant Morning's good side."

Ohen nodded. "But that does bring up a question."

Alice raised her head. "What else can we ask of it? What else does this... machine mind on Ceres know, and what is it willing to do for us?"

Ohen nodded. "The Earth restriction and the Mars restriction—it said, 'no authorization has been received' to lift the order. Can we just order it to do that?"

Abraham said, "Does it have a passphrase to grant authorization? It might be lost forever."

Alice said, "We could just try. Give him—it an order and see what happens."

Ohen said, "Probably better to ask what authorization is required. Project Command has a reputation of shooting first when feeling threatened. We can't take an action that might be misinterpreted as a threat."

Alice asked, "Do you want to ask the follow-up questions then?"

Ohen reached for the keyboard. "No, I'd like us all to be in on it. Let's see if we can set up a voice link."

"This is Ohen bar Clay requesting a voice call to Project Command concerning my previous request."

There was a long pause, nearly ten seconds, before a voice replied. It sounded older than the computer's usual voice.

"This is Project Command. Proceed."

"I am Ohen bar Clay. Two other people are here as well. Introduce yourselves."

"I am Alice Neeley, daughter of Emperor Richard of Luna."

"And I am Abraham Chung, pilot of the beamship Brilliant Morning."

Ohen didn't wait. "In your recent message to me, you mentioned that the quarantine of Mars and the exclusion zone around Earth were established at the time of the Plague and that no authorization was given to lift those restrictions.

"What are the acceptable authorizations necessary to remove or alter those restrictions?"

Again, there was a long pause while the people around the table waited silently.

"From it's beginning, the Terraforming Project has been chartered by the World Court. In general, the Project has been a self-regulating body composed of the Fleet and their computer proxies. The Mars and Earth restrictions were put in place by trained and authorized members of the Fleet. The computer proxies are not authorized to remove those restrictions. No members of the Fleet remain alive, and no humans have the necessary training and technical expertise to make such a judgement call.

"Only the World Court could authorize a reorganization of Project Command to allow another method of altering those restrictions. However, during the Plague on Earth, the World Court lapsed and has never been reestablished.

"Project Command computers recognize the logical trap enforcing the restrictions beyond their original purpose, however it is not a computer's place to usurp tasks given it."

Abraham said, "That sounds pretty locked up. The only ones who could break the restrictions are down on Earth, out of reach, and long dead."

Alice frowned. "What I understand is that computers can't break the lock, but people might."

Ohen nodded. "I got that feeling as well. Project Command, what is the logical definition of the World Court? Could it be reestablished in the current day?"

After a few seconds, it said, "Prior to the Plague, the World Court was a representative body, originally with members from the various nations of Earth, but when Mars was populated and established its own capital and self-government, the World Court revised its organizational rules and Mars was granted a representative as well.

"For the purposes of reestablishing the relationship between the World Court and the Terraforming Project, representatives from all populations on Earth, Mars, Luna and surviving space habitats should come together, establish themselves as the inheritors of the World Court and reaffirm the Terraforming Charter.

"Only when that is done could the revived World Court impose alterations to the Plague-era restrictions. Note that some functions of the Terraforming Project are so necessary to the survival of the populated worlds that it would not be advisable to change the technical operations of the Project until new controllers can be educated and trained for those positions. The deliberate destabilization of the Lagrangian clusters during the time of the Plague came very close to making Earth uninhabitable."

Alice gasped. Ohen raised his fingers and she kept quiet while the computer was still talking.

"Concerning the U'tanse. What is the population of this extra-solar body of humans and are they intent on returning to the Solar system?"

Ohen said, "There are probably two million U'tanse and some fraction, perhaps five or ten percent might consider returning to the birthplace of our kind. We are much more interested in establishing a long-term relationship with our lost human roots than actual colonization and returnees would arrive over time. However, this is just my impression. I can't speak for all of my kind."

He looked to Alice. "Did you have a comment?"

She shook her head. "I was just shocked to hear that the legend that there was an active terrorist campaign during the Plague to knock the Space Cities out of the sky was actually true."

Ohen looked to Abraham, but he shook his head.

Ohen then asked, "You say all the representatives of the various worlds should all meet together? That will be impossible if the restriction on travel to Earth is inviolate. Is there a work-around? Could the meeting be held like this conversation, over the computer messaging system?"

There was another long pause. Ohen could just imagine how difficult it might be if Earth and Mars were included in the radio-delayed conversation. He wasn't even surprised when Project Command replied in the negative.

"At the time that Mars was given representation, face-to-face conversation was mandated for World Court decisions. There was some fear that the speed-of-light delay would be unworkable.

"As for the problem of getting everyone in one place, the fact that the U'tanse spacecraft has arrived from beyond the Solar system has opened a small loophole in the restrictions. The protocols of operation for the Project has a small section dealing with the possibility of extra-solar alien visits. Project Command can allow minor exceptions to established operating restrictions if an outside craft appears. To allow the U'tanse representative to meet with the Earth representatives, an exception visit could be allowed."

Ohen let himself feel the moment. *I'm going to get to see the Earth!*

Project Command then reacted to Alice's comment, detailing the terrorist attack during the Plague, mentioning the dozens of autonomous robots which were tasked with randomly shoving habitats out of orbit and punching holes in hulls. Space was cluttered with debris as spinning habitats tore themselves apart. As the human controllers collapsed at their workstations from the disease, it was only the wide-ranging Earth restriction that allowed the computers of Project Command to limit the number of impacts on the planet and to, over time, bring stability back to the Lagrangian clusters.

The conversation limped onward. Ohen thought of it as a negotiation, but really, it seemed to him that Project Command was really on their side. It wasn't like the Project was protecting its power. It felt more like a programming task, finding a way to solve a problem that both sides recognized.

After Abraham asked how many representatives there should be, it boiled down to a minimum of one each from the outlying populations and several from Earth, since it was such a diversified world with many different national groups.

Alice objected, "You can't really expect us to go to Mt. Ural and get one of those monsters to join us?"

Project Command was firm. "The Lagrangian colonies have to be represented. There are only two of any size left. The humans on Ceres and the survivors on Mt. Ural."

Ohen was just pleased that the U'tanse were getting a seat at the table, even if he was the only one of his kind in the whole Solar system. He'd take the technicality.

Abraham said, "The log books talk about a green dot on the surface of Ceres."

"Yes, that is the domed city that contains the survivors of the Plague. When the Project command center shut itself down and locked all the doors, the few members of the Fleet that survived managed to thrive under the dome."

Ohen brought up another problem. "Even though the World Court was formerly housed on Earth, many of the new representatives, such as the delegates from Mars, Luna, and perhaps the Space Cities are not able to survive comfortably under one full gravity. Perhaps the meeting should take place elsewhere."

Project Command had a solution. "The Ceres dome has space and the whole area is covered with floor gravity. Various zones, even small ones, could be programmed for each of the individual delegates."

Ohen nodded. He had intended to do the same when transporting people to the meeting on his boat.

He asked, "Do we all agree that the invitations should be sent? This isn't the project we came here to discuss, but I think this is vastly more important. Do we have message ID's to contact everyone?"

Alice asked, "And who should send the invitation? I could tell my father, but he might not believe me."

Abraham said, "The computer would be best at that kind of thing. There will be delays of various kinds. We probably can't even set a date until everyone has agreed. And then, there are only two ships."

Ohen nodded. "I'll be doing the transport. If Brilliant Morning took off on this expedition, there might not even be an empire when you returned."

Abraham nodded sadly.

They decided the invitation should be sent from "Project Command and the Committee for Open Worlds", although the discussion over the name of the committee took a lot longer than Ohen had expected.

Project Command would handle all the invitations and replies, keeping each party updated on who was coming, and any conflicts.

Ohen looked at Alice and Abraham. "Are you ready to do this? It'll be impossible to stop once we start."

Alice took a big sigh. "Yes. The sooner the better."

Abraham said, "I'm not pleased with including Mt. Ural, but we need to do it."

Ohen took a breath, then said, "Project Command, begin the invitation process." A few seconds later a nicely worded invitation showed up on his computer, requesting his serious consideration to attending a meeting with representatives of all populations in the settled worlds and habitats of the

Solar system "in order to establish unrestricted communication and commerce between all peoples" and requesting the name, location, and earliest availability of a representative of the U'tanse people.

He showed the results to the others. "I'm sure it'll be worded differently for each person. Alice, I bet you father's pocket computer is being read right now."

She nodded, getting up from the table. "I assume our meeting is over now? I'd better be there when he has questions." She grinned. "I've got a suggestion for the appropriate representative from Luna."

Message from Bremerhaven

Ohen looked over the invitation again and sent an acceptance, designating himself as the representative for the U'tanse people, his location at Stampz on Luna, his name, and his availability to travel at any time. He also mentioned his intent to use his B3 craft to provide transport for any of the other delegates as necessary.

Abraham had been a little disgruntled at how things had turned out. He'd been patiently waiting for another journey into space for years now, but he couldn't even help with transporting the delegates. His most important job was to be on-call should Brilliant Morning be needed as a weapon. He could just smile and wait. He left the meeting room as well.

Within a few seconds, a message arrived from Project Command formatted as a table, listing all of the populations being invited, with their contact IDs, and status. Ohen's was the only one listed as Accepted. In the comments field was the detail that his craft would be used for transport.

All the others were just listed as Pending.

He was in the process of copying the message codes of all the others to his logbook when another message arrived.

From King Harmon of Xanthe, Mars: "Barclay, is this you? I had to play back the message twice to understand it. You and Lord Casey are making contact with Earth? Tell me what's going on."

Ohen remembered that the king's personal computer was the canister type that was voice only. All his messages were verbal and tables of data would probably not be very clear.

He sent a message back.

"Your Majesty, I have been doing some research in the vast library on Luna and the people I was working with have discovered the message ID for the Project Command computers. We made contact."

He gave a summary of what they decided to do and the importance of opening trade, in particular the fact that Mars had many beamships that might be restored to operation and sold. Ohen also emphasized that Project Command and the rest of the worlds had chosen King Harmon as the recognized leader of all Mars.

It was the king's choice to choose a representative to the meeting of the different worlds. Ohen suggested that Lord Casey was the logical choice, since he was already there on Luna. Ohen himself was not available, since he was already chosen as the representative of the U'tanse.

Barely had he sent the message off to Mars when there was a terse message from Emperor Richard. "Come to my conference room."

Ohen folded up the computer and carried it with him up the stairs, musing that it was interesting that the emperor had chosen to message him rather than send a human messenger like usual. He was getting very used to that pocket computer.

The emperor, Alice and Chancellor Folken were already seated. Ohen took the chair he was offered.

Richard asked, "My daughter said that during her ride to Franklin and back, that there was no excessive stress from the flight. The chancellor has expressed worries that he might not be physically up to the ride to this meeting of worlds. What do you think?"

It was plain in her thoughts that Alice was disappointed that her father was choosing Folken over her for the delegate, but she was hiding it.

"The B3, and other boats of its class have floor gravity projectors built in. I can regulate what the conditions in the cabin feel like, even if the boat itself might be accelerating at several times Earth's gravity. I can even make it feel weightless inside if necessary. And in contrast with the other ship, there is no ladder to be climbed. I feel confident that the chancellor would have no problems traveling to the conference on Ceres. In addition, the Project Command has said that Ceres is also equipped with adaptive floor gravity and is expecting to provide comfortable conditions for all the delegates."

The emperor nodded. "That's good. The chancellor is the best diplomat who has ever served the court. He single-handedly negotiated the Fabry's entry into the empire. He's perfect for this kind of job."

Chancellor Folken dipped his head. "You're too kind. That was a long time ago."

Ohen said, "There is quite a bit about Lunar history that I've never heard. It occurs to me that while the various worlds make their own decisions, I wonder if I might have the benefit of your wisdom, Chancellor? Diplomacy is not my field and just hearing of what you've been through might make a significant difference when it comes to making sure the Ceres meeting goes smoothly."

Folken chuckled. "Diplomatic meeting rarely go smoothly, if they're anything more than a polite dinner party."

Ohen nodded and said, "See, this is what I need to know. Probably Lord Casey ought to bask in your presence as well. Neither of us have enough experience for this."

Alice said, "And I'll be there to take notes as well. I don't recall reading anything about the Fabry conference. It really ought to be in the court records and I haven't read anything more than grandfather's announcement. Let's meet soon and do this!"

Richard smiled tolerantly at his daughter, inwardly relieved that she wasn't going to make any more fuss about attending the Ceres meeting.

. . .

Ohen carried a bag of clothes back to the B3. Over the past quad (he forced himself to think that word, rather than week), he'd been gradually moving everything out of the room in the castle. He'd never really been that comfortable there and there was a chance that once he left for the Ceres conference, there would be other opportunities calling him elsewhere.

He wasn't mentioning this to anyone, certainly not to Alice, but now was the time to pack.

The computer beeped. He set it down on the table, wondering who had responded to the invitation this time. It was a voice call.

"Hello, this is Karl Rugel from Bremerhaven University. Sorry for the call, but curiosity got the best of me. Where is U'tanse? I've been scouring the records for any off-world settlement with a name like that and I've come up empty. I've got a five crown bet it's one of the L5 colonies. Julian, a buddy of mine, thinks it's one of the moons of the outer worlds. If you've got the time, I'm dying to know."

Ohen replied. "It's good to hear from you, and likewise, I haven't any idea where Bremerhaven is. I suspect a place on Earth, but other than that, I'm ignorant.

"To answer your question, the U'tanse are a people, a human offshoot captured by non-human raiders that attacked the disorganized Earth in the aftermath of the Betelgeuse supernova flare. My ancestors were taken off-world as slaves. We have been hunting for Earth, the home planet, for many, many generations. We live in the Ko system, many light years from here. I was raised on Ha, which is a large moon that circles Ko.

"The name U'tanse is derived from the word 'human'. The Cerik, the race that captured us, have beak-like mouth parts and cannot pronounce certain sounds. U'tanse is what they said, and as slaves, we adopted it. However, the U'tanse are no longer slaves."

When Karl Rugel answered a few seconds later, he sounded a little shocked. "This is ... not what I expected." He gave a short laugh. "I guess I lost my bet. But you say that you're an extra-solar offshoot of humanity? I can't even imagine that. But ... how can you talk over the computers? They weren't even invented until well after the supernova."

"I landed on Mars first and was able to recharge an inactive computer. I am currently located at Stampz on Luna, the capital of the Lunar Empire. Where was Bremerhaven again?"

"I've got too many questions! But Bremerhaven is on the coast of the European continent. It's not the capital—there really isn't a capital for Earth—but the university here has representatives from all over the planet, so I guess that's why the invitation arrived here. The guys in the blue robes are still debating over how to reply. Some don't even think it's real."

Ohen chuckled. "Oh, it's real enough. I was on the committee that negotiated with Project Command. It's only my extra-solar status that allowed for this one-time breech of the exclusion zone around the Earth. I guess they'll believe it when I land there, right?"

. . .

Mars designated Lord Casey as its representative. There was a terse reply from Mt. Ural that they would send someone, but they needed transport. The "Family on Ceres" said that they were grateful to host the meeting.

Lord Casey begged a chance to look at the latest message from Project Command on his computer screen. "I get these as verbal messages and the status of all the invitations is too many words, too fast. I can't take notes at that speed."

Ohen showed him the message on the screen. "I bet you can ask your computer to play back the message at a slower pace. Maybe have it read it to you line by line with pauses in between."

"I'll try that."

. . .

When Chancellor Folken began to talk about his time as a diplomat for the empire, he said to Ohen, "You should be prepared to lead the debate."

"Me? Why?"

"The conference is being called by Project Command and the Committee for Open Worlds. You will be the only representative of this committee and I don't think the computer would be the best choice to lead the debate. It'll be up to you."

"You would be better at it."

The chancellor shook his head. "No. I may not wear my feelings on my face as plainly as Alice does, but I have just as much distaste for having Mt. Ural in this meeting as she has. Whoever leads the discussion can't be an enemy of one of the other delegates. The leader needs to be impartial. With your background, you're as close as we've got."

Ohen asked, "What do we know about the Ceres people?"

"Nothing. We didn't even know they existed until Project Command mentioned them."

Most of the time, Alice was asking the questions while the chancellor reminisced about the bygone times when the lands to the east of the Peach River were just a collection of farming villages firmly resistant to the idea of paying taxes to the royals to the west. It had been Folken's job to establish a trading and mutual defense relationship with the empire.

"It was certainly an advantage that I was a scholar, with an academic's title, rather than some lord with an inherited title. I spent half my time talking about the Alpine Society and how we intended to set up schools all over the world to teach people how to read. The farmers had a healthy distaste

121

for the scribes as well as the nobility, so they liked the idea that a man like me could rise to a position of authority."

Alice was writing it all down. "I know that there are 'Folken' schools out there. I've established a loaner book program with them. What do you think about having them named after you?"

He shook his head. "I didn't ask for it, but it's gratifying that the work is continuing."

Casey was taking notes as well. His were less historical, but he was desperate to represent Mars to the best of his ability. Since the moment they had landed on Luna, he'd been dropped into a bigger job than he'd ever imagined. To the people of Luna, and soon to the people of Earth and the other habitats, he would be the only face of Mars that they would know. He had to do it right.

After the chancellor had to call the interview to an end, saying he was too tired, Ohen shared the messages he'd gotten from Bremerhaven. Alice had a map of Earth that showed the city names and they located it.

She said, "I hope they don't take too long deciding to reply to the invitation."

Ohen said, "I'm worried about how I'm going to carry all these people. After looking at your map, I hope they're not planning on sending one delegate per country. It would take many trips and I don't know if the Project's rules allow that."

She asked, "How many people can you carry at one time?"

He frowned. "I can handle the air circulation, but I can't feed a large crowd. Seating is limited."

She nodded. "It would be good to nail down a real number."

"Is there someone here in Stampz who can make chairs in a hurry?"

Are You Leaving?

Ohen winced as the man marked an X on the floor of B3 with a grease pencil. Bud Parton nodded to himself. "Yes, I can fit two bench seats in here. That would give you seating for nine. Do you want them fastened down?"

Ohen shook his head. "You couldn't cut through this floor. The metal is too tough. I have tricks to lock them down. Can you pad the feet? Something that won't slide easily?"

Bud nodded. "Sure." He marked down rubber feet on his paper. "How soon do you need them?"

"As soon as possible. I don't know the exact date, but people on Earth will be waiting for me when the word comes through."

Bud grinned. "Earth?"

Ohen nodded seriously. "Really. It'll be diplomats from other worlds sitting on your benches. Don't bother with decorations, but they should be comfortable."

Bud left, a worried look on his face.

Ohen took another look at his computer. The latest status message had updated the Earth response. It just said that the delegates from Earth would be attending, but that some were still in transit to Bremerhaven. There was still no count of the number of people.

In any case, these benches, which could be moved in and out through the airlock, would make the trip more comfortable. He didn't expect diplomats would be happy riding the whole way to Ceres sitting on the metal floor.

...

There was a knock on the airlock door. Ohen looked up from his notes. He'd been doing some pre-flight calculations and hadn't bothered to close the inner airlock door.

He walked over, smiling as he sensed who it was.

"Alice. What brings you here?"

Her white librarian outfit caught the mid-morning sunlight and she looked dazzling. She held up a notebook. "Do you have time for some questions?"

He waved her in. "Of course. Have a seat." He left both airlock doors open, just for appearance's sake.

He already had the retractable bed stowed away and his portable chair and bench out on the floor, just waiting to be replaced by the new bigger bench seats. If the carpenters worked too quickly, he just might need to sleep on them until it was time to leave.

She glance over his papers.

He gestured. "I'm calculating how much energy I'll need in order to pick up the delegates, go to Ceres and return. I don't want the delegates to wait through that process."

She nodded and opened up a notebook. "It has come to my attention that you've been packing as if you might not return."

"Oh, I'd certainly return the chancellor home. You don't need to worry about that."

She nodded, "And the chances are that you'd take off again immediately afterward. That's what you've been thinking. You can't imagine I wouldn't be informed that you've cleared out your room in the castle."

He shrugged. "I have to plan ahead. I wasn't using that room much in any case."

Alice pulled out her pen and set her ink pot on the table. "But if you do leave, then there are questions I've never had a chance to get answered."

He picked up her undertones. If he was leaving, she didn't want to make it easy for him to just vanish.

He smiled. "Sure. Ask away. We're all waiting on the Earth delegates before things get frantic anyway."

She had a list. "Okay, most of these are questions about the U'tanse people. So ... you've stated that your ancestors were captured as slaves, and yet you say you're not slaves anymore. How did that change occur?"

He eased back in his chair, a smile on his face. "How much time do you have?"

He gave her the overview. The predatory Cerik had evolved on their home planet of Ko with another race who were semiaquatic and technically adept, the Delense. When the Delense attempted to break loose from their masters, the Cerik exterminated the whole race, leaving the barbaric race with advanced machines including spaceships, but no way to keep them repaired.

The Cerik took advantage of the Betelgeuse supernova shock wave to raid other inhabited planets, scavenging new prey species. When they attempted to do the same on Earth, they were stymied by bad luck and human resistance.

However, they captured the new slaves, ones that were as technically adept as the Delense, and began to restore the broken machines. Originally, the humans, now called U'tanse because the Cerik couldn't pronounce any sound that required lips, were highly valued, but over generations, their numbers increased. When abandoned U'tanse gained their own technology and the ability to restore even more of the Delense leftovers, the humans managed to capture the energy supply of the whole planet and leveraged that to buy the rest of their number out of slavery.

Ohen waved his hand. "And so, most of the U'tanse live on Ko's moon and other colonies completely beyond the reach of their former masters. I myself have never seen a live Cerik and I hope I never do. They are creatures of nightmares, very strong, with claws instead of hands and beaks, and able to leap great heights, even in a full gravity."

Alice copied down his words. She asked, "Before, you mentioned 'Abe the Father' and 'Sharon the Mother'. You said there were only those two, like Adam and Eve."

She looked up, checking his face. "Really, only… I mean how could they have …." She took a breath. "We touched on this before, I think. It's very difficult to raise livestock with a limited initial population. The horses of Stampz almost died out several times. They aren't well adapted to the low gravity."

Abe understood her real question. He nodded. "From the very beginning, Abe and Sharon were well aware that they were at a … *genetic* disadvantage." He spoke the word distinctly.

He looked up at the ceiling. "The first generations had many difficulties to overcome. Abe and Sharon had to deliberately breed their own race. Some of the details aren't things that I want to become common knowledge."

She sighed. "And so you don't want people to read your Book."

He was willing to let her make that deduction. It was even partly correct.

"I'm sorry. I didn't even think about the fact that the words of the Book could be used as a weapon against my people. All of the U'tanse are steeped in the words. It's our history. It teaches us that no matter where we live and how comfortable we might become, our native home is back on Earth. The Book binds us together."

He grimaced. "But I've just got to pretend that the Book doesn't exist, or at least that I don't have a copy of it."

She said, "But you do have a copy."

"Of course I have a copy. Most people do."

"Can I see it, if I promise not to read it?"

He sighed. "Okay, but please, I need to protect my people."

She nodded. "Just tell me what you want. I won't write anything down without your permission."

He went to one of the storage compartments and pulled out the heavy Book.

Alice said, "You said it was thick."

He nodded. "This is even printed with a small font. I've seen some that were much larger, although most of the text was identical."

"Most of the text?"

He opened it up, holding a bundle of pages. "This first section is history, written as it happened to Abe and Sharon. This next section is a history of Earth, at least as Abe remembered it. These are technical papers, where Abe tried to explain the technology of Earth even though he knew some of it could never be duplicated on Ko. Abe had been something of a technology wizard in his time before the Star, so he knew a lot of things. It's been very valuable.

"This little section was written by Sharon. Things where she was the expert, like medicine."

Alice chuckled. "I can see who was the writer of the family."

He nodded. "And this section here is some history written after their deaths. It wasn't kept up. People didn't like having a constantly expanding Book, so new history went into new history books.

"And finally, this little section is my family tree."

"Oh! Can I see that?"

He opened it up. "The first part is the lineage from Sharon to Omelia, wife of Samson the Giant. It's matrilineal, as I may have mentioned before. It's impractical to hold the whole family tree of the U'tanse in every Book, so this is just the simple lineage of Omelia. In this second section is the full tree of our clan—all my ancestry since Omelia, all the cousins and all their family."

She tapped at the final page. "And there you are. Your father isn't listed."

"Right. He was from another clan, so his Bible had the details of that clan. I'm part of my mother's clan."

She tapped the blank pages that followed. "Your children would be from another clan then?"

"Yes, I suppose. Unless I happened to marry some cousin that was in Omelia's clan."

Alice frowned. "I've seen other family trees in books. They diagram them differently, keeping track of father and mother as well."

Ohen shrugged. "Our method is probably an offshoot from the early days when Sharon was very closely monitoring her offspring. There was a very serious effort to avoid … disruptive recessive genes."

Alice nodded. "I can't imagine what the U'tanse went through. I wonder, though. Do all U'tanse look like you?"

"I've been surprised at the variations among people on Mars and Luna—coloration especially. Everyone here has a darker skin than mine. Hair color is so varied as well. We just have this brown hair like mine and a few rare individuals with albino white coloration. Sharon is said to have had white hair."

He smiled, "But if you see a U'tanse that's as tall as I am, then they're probably from my Omelia clan."

"I wonder—"

The computer spoke, interrupting her. "Message from Project Command."

Ohen asked, "Is it a new invitation status table?"

"Yes."

"What is different?"

"Status of the Earth delegation: All delegates have now arrived at Bremerhaven. We will be ready to be transported to Ceres in one day."

Ohen sighed. "Well, that's it then. Everybody is ready but me. I need to get those benches moved in before we can leave. Alice, will you notify the chancellor, please."

She was already folding up her notes. "Of course, although Father and Casey will have gotten the notification as well."

He escorted her out the airlock and then locked it behind him before running off to find the carpenters.

. . .

Bud Parton frowned. "I haven't put the coat of shellac on them yet."

Ohen asked, "Is it smelly?"

"Well, a little bit, but it doesn't last long."

"Then we have to do without. I have to leave sometime after darkwind. The benches will probably only be used for this one trip. If a diplomat can sit in reasonable comfort for a few hours, then they will have served their purpose. What's left to do, other than the shellac?"

Bud pursed his lips, looking at his handiwork. "The cushions are all ready. But if I don't get to finish the wooden exterior, then I really need a final sanding of the armrests. That and the rubber cushions on the feet."

"Can you get the benches to my boat before darkwind?"

"It will be tight."

Alice's thoughts hit him hard. **I need Ohen here, immediately!** She yelled at a servant to go hunt for him at the boat or at Parton's workshop. **"And tell him to bring his medical kit!"**

Ohen put his hand to his head. "Okay Bud. I've got to go warn the security guards that you're coming. Plan to get the benches there just after darkwind, okay?"

The carpenter nodded, a little relieved to have more time.

Ohen forced himself to walk slowly out of the workshop. Even in an emergency, he couldn't give people hints of his psychic abilities.

Once he was clear, he started running, taking advantage of the low gravity. He still hadn't learned all the peculiar gaits common to the natives, but he could still travel fast.

He went straight to the boat and pulled out his kit. He swapped a couple of the jars. He had a few hints from Alice's thoughts, and this was nothing like her mother's issue.

There was a knock on the airlock door. He opened it as calmly as he was able.

Selena, Alice's maid, was accompanied by one of the security guards.

"Sir! You have to come quickly! Chancellor Folken won't wake up!"

Alternate Delegate

Chancellor Folken's room was large, but felt crowded. Alice, her mother, and several attendants hovered around the bed.

Healer Kristin looked up from the chancellor. She said, "He didn't wake up at his normal time. He's dreaming, but I can't wake him up."

Ohen could read Folken's thoughts. "Could I examine him?"

The doctor nodded and stepped back. Ohen went through the steps, checking his pulse and breathing, but really using the skin contact to examine his body with his clairvoyance.

"It's not dreams. Chancellor, if you can understand me, can you try to squeeze my fingers?" There was the faintest of response.

Ohen looked at the doctor. "I think he's had a stroke. A blood clot has blocked the blood flow to his brain. There may be several of them."

Kristin nodded. "I've seen this before, several times. I didn't want it to be true this time."

Alice asked, "Is there anything you can do with your U'tanse techniques?"

Ohen opened his bag. "I'm not a trained healer." He looked over his medicines, shaking his head. "Most of these are designed for treating wounds."

He picked up a small bottle. "This is a blood thinner, but I really don't know if this would help or kill him."

His deep insight had left him with little hope. The blood clot had blocked oxygen and nutrients to a disturbingly large part of the man's brain. His psychokinesis wasn't likely to be able to break up the clot in time, although he was working at it. And the way the blood vessels were arranged, a broken clot might just block smaller vessels.

The doctor took it. "How is it used?"

Ohen told her the dosages. Then he turned to Folken again. He took his hand.

"Chancellor, don't worry about the meeting. Your job is just to get well again. Your training has made a big difference already."

Alice took over the task of talking to the man while Ohen coached the healer through the process of giving the first dosage of the blood thinner.

It wasn't long before Ohen quit working on the blood clot. He'd detected another. Down on the man's leg, there was an artery that had weakened and was hemorrhaging. He whispered his suspicions to the doctor and they told all the well-wishers to leave while they preformed a full examination.

Kristin shook her head, after they'd located the bruised location. "There's not much I can do at this point. Unless you know some more techniques?"

Ohen shook his head. "You know more than I do."

When he left, Alice caught him in the corridor. "What's the word?"

He shook his head. "It's not something I have the ability to heal. Even if it doesn't kill him, he'll never be the same again. Part of his brain has been starved by the blood clot."

She sighed. "How long does he have?"

"Ask the healer. She has a lot more experience than I do."

She looked back at the chancellor's room. "I don't know what to do."

"There's nothing you can do, for him. But… Luna doesn't have a delegate to the Ceres conference."

She blinked. "You're right. I was distracted."

"I was planning on leaving a few hours after darkwind, but I haven't sent that information off to Project Command yet. You need to talk to your father. Who is the second choice for the representative?"

He could feel her ruthlessly stamp out any anticipation that she would be able to go. She couldn't feel joy that the chancellor had been hurt.

"You're right. I'll let you know the instant Father chooses someone."

He sighed. "I'll go talk to Lord Casey. He needs to be ready as well."

. . .

Ohen felt the boat shake as darkwind reached its peak. He was grateful once again for this parking area in the protected Stampz crater. He'd need active beams to hold him in place if he ever parked out in the open when the winds came.

"Voice message from Karl Rugel at Bremerhaven to Ohen bar Clay."

"Hello Karl. What's the word from Earth?"

"Hey, you are there. I was just curious what was going on. I'm not really in the know. I just monitor the computer to see if there are any updates. This isn't really an official message or anything."

"That's okay. It's still a thrill to listen to a real live person from Earth. That was a place of myth and legend when I was growing up."

Karl chuckled. "That's a new one. Nothing going on here. It's just an ordinary port city with a big university. I've gotten so many questions about you! You're the person of mythology now. I've been told quite seriously that your story of being from another star is impossible. Faster-than-light travel has been proven impossible."

Ohen smiled to himself. "You know I've been told the same thing by scientists from my world, too. They got this theory of how the universe works, and it just doesn't have any loopholes for the starship leap drive. But you know, that same sacred theory of theirs doesn't allow for tractor/pressor beams either, and I use those every day. I've also experienced nine jumps from star to star getting here, so I have to take the scientist's word with a little skepticism."

Karl sighed. "Well I guess we're alike then. Impossible things happen, unless you're pulling some kind of deception."

"Yes, it's always difficult to accept someone else's word for things. I guess my proof will be when I land there in Bremerhaven."

. . .

Alice gave him a tired smile as he walked into the emperor's conference room.

"Ohen, you look like you've been out in the darkwind."

He winced and brushed back his hair with his hand. "Well, that's because I have been! It blew me over twice."

He sat and nodded to John Fasail.

Alice said, "Father had to run out for a moment. We're trying to decide if John is the replacement delegate to the conference."

John grumbled. "I'm not a diplomat. I'm a tech guy."

Ohen chuckled. "I hear you. I'm trained to design boats."

No one was in a mood to chat. The chancellor had been declining rapidly.

The emperor came back and didn't immediately meet their eyes. He sat at his chair. "Healer Kristin doesn't expect him to last out the night."

Alice said, "I'm so sorry."

Emperor Richard straightened in his chair. "He trained me to sit here. I've always thought that when times got tough, I could always call him in for advice."

He looked at John. "We have to have a delegate from Luna at the Ceres conference. You've been trained for possible spaceflight duties."

"Yes, but that means nothing when talking to diplomats. The chancellor wasn't ever trained for space, but you considered the flight safe for him. You don't need me. I'm the wrong person. You need a real diplomat for the job."

Richard said, "But I don't have any! My sons are off at the regional capitals. The whole staff are already in critical positions, holding the empire together. I can't leave, or I'd go myself."

He turned to Ohen. "What is your deadline? When do you have to leave?"

"I've held off notifying Project Command, but I'm sure all the other delegates have gotten the latest update. They are all waiting on me. I have no idea what other time constraints are in play. I could leave as early as midnight. I don't want to take off in the winds."

John spoke softly. "You have a trained, experienced person that you're not using."

Richards looked at him sharply. "What?"

John looked back. "We all know the person most qualified for the job."

Richard's eyes glanced across at Alice, then he said, "But there are issues."

The "tech guy" had grown up in the castle. He knew all the issues. "Alice has the best historical knowledge of any of us. She has researched the history of the other worlds. The chancellor had been training her right along with your sons as they grew up. She could probably do a good job taking over your position if you had a stoke!"

Alice winced. "Don't say that."

Ohen risked speaking. "Alice was taking all the notes when the chancellor was giving Lord Casey and me advice on how to run the Ceres conference."

The emperor sighed. "I know all this."

Ohen could feel the moment he changed his mind.

"Alice?"

She nodded. "I could be ready in six or seven hours."

Ohen said, "Packing is very limited. I barely have the space for the delegates. One bag."

She nodded, standing. "Sorry, but I have a lot to prepare." She walked out.

Ohen felt a swirl of conflicting ideas in her thoughts. She'd never wanted to get a responsible assignment due to these circumstances, but she'd always ached to achieve some notable task to prove herself. She had to make sure everything worked perfectly, and she just had a short time to pull it all together.

He knew not to stand up yet. Her father would have words for him, he was sure.

Richard said, "Are you sure there's no more room for another person?" He was visualizing her maid.

Ohen said, "I will be picking up the Earth delegates as the last stop before Ceres. They haven't yet told me how many people are coming, but the understanding is that Earth will have several people to represent various parts of the planet. There is the very real chance that if we brought an extra attendant, then that person might just have to be left on Earth to make room for all the delegates.

"I'd never want to leave a person who had only experienced the light gravity of Luna to suffer the full pull of Earth's gravity. It could very well kill them."

Richard frowned. "Will Alice be in any danger?"

"No. The floor of my boat can be set to provide reduced gravity. She'll be protected inside."

The emperor tapped his fingers on the armrest of his chair. "The whole trip, you'll have to make sure she is safe." It was clearly an order.

"I know. There can be no troubles, for many reasons. This meeting is very important for the whole human race."

Richard sighed. "Then go. I'm sure you have last-minute tasks to attend to as well." In his thoughts, he added, **Just as I've got to organize a state funeral.**

Ohen and John bowed and left.

They walked together down the hallway. John clearly wanted to say something.

Ohen asked, "You and Alice are near the same age. Have you known her long?"

John laughed. "All my life. I rocked her cradle when I was three, I've been told."

Then he frowned. "You will take good care of her, right?"

"Certainly. I can be quite imposing if I put my mind to it."

John tilted his head up to meet his eyes and grinned, then nodded.

Ohen asked, "Is there any thing I should know about Alice and you?"

John shook his head. "No, we're cousins. I guess I'm on the list, but only if all the others fall through. I've actually got my eye on the daughter of a merchant here in town." **But I've got to go slow. People with the curse have to take their time.**

Ohen said, "Well, your cousin will be safe with me. I can never consider settling down until my people come back for me. It might be years yet."

"Alice will keep you in line. It's all those other strangers you're going to meet that I'm worried about."

Ohen nodded. "I have my worries as well."

. . .

Bud Parton and his assistants were there by the B3 when he returned, holding onto their wagon in the wind. There was Earthlight so they at least had enough visibility to work in the dark without worrying about torches. One of the security guards had gone to turn on the electric light they occasionally used around the landing area.

Ohen opened up the airlock doors and made sure he had everything cleared away before he let them carry the bench seats into place. He had them set up against the storage walls, facing each other so all the delegates could talk during the journey. Most of his storage cabinets and the sliding bed would be inaccessible for the duration. His movable chair and bench went out the door to be stored with Parton so the new benches would fit. Ohen suspected he wouldn't be getting much sleep for the next couple of days in any case.

The workmen were careful to align the feet with the marks on the floor, then once he signed Parton's bill, he shoed them all out so he could lock everything down.

The rest of the work was at his command station. He made sure that all of the feet were exactly at their designated spots and then turned on a special routine in the floor gravity software. For a square-inch at each foot, a tractor beam cycled near ten gigahertz so that for only an inch or so above the floor, the wood was subjected to a ten-gravity pull, and only within the confines of the structure. He didn't want anyone's foot to stray into that zone.

He adjusted the right bench so that everyone sitting there would be subjected to a full Earth gravity. The left bench was set at one-sixth of that, Luna's gravity. He went ahead and set his command seat to a little higher than Earth's gravity. He knew he'd been getting soft while on Mars and Luna although he'd grown up in a full gravity. He didn't know how much time he'd have on Earth, but it would be better if he didn't faint when he walked out of the airlock.

While he was at it, he customized the software so that he could set each of the eight bench positions to a separate gravity, if necessary. He didn't know what the Mt. Ural delegate would be expecting.

He was almost done when there was a knock on the airlock door. He glanced at the exterior image. It was Alice and her maid, Selena.

First Stop, Mt. Ural

He frowned as he glanced at her baggage. "I thought I said there was only room for one bag."

Alice nodded. "Yes, but I have to see if it fits. Selena is just here to take the excess back to my quarters."

He gestured her inside. "Don't sit on the right bench. I've adjusted the gravity there for the Earth delegates."

She frowned and waved her hand through the air. It dipped sharply over that bench. "Oh! I can feel it."

Selena carried bags with her.

Ohen said to Alice, "Since you're the first. I'll give you the option to store your things in this wall cabinet. Otherwise your bag will have to fit under the bench."

There was some repacking, and Alice was able to fit everything under her bench seat. "Save the other storage for some other delegate." Selena carried the rest of her things away.

Ohen said, "That's not your usual librarian robe, is it?"

She smiled. "No." She held out her arms and rotated to show it off. "I have this fancier version for certain special events. I figure this is one of them."

He couldn't tell what was different, other than it looked whiter and the fabric was somehow shinier. "You didn't wear the fancy dress from last time."

She shook her head. "I'm not a princess here. I'm a government representative doing business."

There was another knock. It was Lord Casey. He also had multiple bags. He was not happy when Ohen made him send most of them back.

Casey whispered, "I'm not leaving my computer. And it doesn't leave much room for a change of clothes."

"Can you imagine a person in every seat and five bags of luggage for each of them?"

"I didn't bring five." He sighed. "I get your point. I'll be tight."

Ohen checked the time. "Alice, could I get you to send a message to your father than we're leaving now. Then send another to Project Command asking them to notify the other delegates. We'll be going to Mt. Ural first, and then to Earth."

She stepped over to his computer. "Why Mt. Ural?"

"Scheduling. Mt. Ural is in the Vesta cluster. Going Vesta, Earth, Ceres is faster than Earth, Vesta, Ceres since the two clusters are so far apart."

She shook her head and typed the messages. He did some final checks, making sure that his air supply and water were topped up.

"While there is a toilet behind that hatch, I'll wait if you need to go back to the castle for one last time." They declined.

As soon as Alice sat down on the bench, he settled into his chair and checked the outside cameras. When he was confident there was no one in range, he lifted off.

. . .

While Alice and Casey looked at the globe of Luna below them—mostly blinding white clouds and a patch of clear skies over the west coast of the populated continent—Ohen typed a message to Project Command.

Casey asked, "What's that?"

"I'm asking the Project to recommend my best charging configuration. I want to be fully charged up before I begin the grand tour. I don't want all those unknown delegates to wait through the process."

"But you don't mind making us wait?"

Ohen grinned. "Nope, you don't count and Alice is probably happy to be spending the time as a space tourist."

Alice never looked away from the display. "You're probably right."

Project Command quickly replied with coordinates for a beam connecting Luna and Venus. When he put it into play, the B3 was quickly charged to full by tapping into the relative motion of the two worlds.

Ohen felt much better with a hefty power reading. He probably wouldn't have to charge again until well after the conference.

With the nearly invisible dot of Mt. Ural centered on his display, the B3 pushed away from Luna at high acceleration.

He narrated what he was doing, although neither of them were really familiar with what it took to travel in space using tractor/pressor beams for propulsion. Casey was just tuning out most of the information. Alice was getting increasingly nervous.

Mt. Ural was the biggest monster in Luna's history. They had bombed three cities with artificial meteor strikes, killing countless people and threatened to do it again. She really didn't trust them.

After midpoint, he switched the beams around and began pulling on distant Luna to slow them down. He pulled nearly to a stop about a hundred kloms short of their destination. He decided to drift in slowly.

Lord Casey asked, "What's happening?"

"I want to get a good look at the place before I get too close. I've seen the sketches from Abraham's log books, but I really need more detail. I have no idea where to land."

Alice pointed. "I remember reading about that solar dish. They can melt metals with it. And... oh, wow! See that trench? I bet that's the one Darkwind carved with his laser when he attacked them to drive them away from Luna."

Ohen frowned. "But what's that? It looks like... Yes, I bet it is. This isn't just Mt. Ural. It's a contact binary. They've moved so close to a different habitat that their mutual gravity is keeping it in place."

Alice nodded. "History says that Mt. Ural couldn't feed its own people, so they attacked farming habitats for resources. Is this one of those? They don't have a spaceship anymore. I guess this was the only way they could raid another habitat."

The combined world had a little rotation, so over the next few minutes, they watched as the cylindrical moon moved into view. It was less than a quarter the size of the large rocky bulk of Mt. Ural. With the camera's image zoomed in all the way, they could see large scrape marks on the cylinder.

Ohen said, "It was probably rotating for gravity when it touched. No telling how much damage was caused when that stopped. I wonder if they had an atmosphere leak."

The computer spoke. "Message from Mt. Ural to Ohen bar Clay."

"Go ahead."

"Hello? This is Mt. Ural. Our spotting scopes have detected a small craft some distance away. Is this the ship that will take our delegate to the Ceres conference?"

"Yes, this is Ohen bar Clay. I am approaching slowly, looking for an access port or landing site."

"We have an assisted landing site. Just send the standard code and we'll bring you in easily."

"My ship has a non-standard design. Just tell me where your external airlock ports are and I can land near there. I assume you have spacesuits?"

"Yes, we have suits. However, the standard landing site would be best."

Someone on Mt. Ural turned on a set of lights. Ohen used his clairvoyance to perceive more detail. He said, "I see your airlock lights. I'll be coming in slowly. That's all for now."

He tapped a button on the computer, cancelling the communication to the Uralites.

Alice said, "I don't trust them."

Ohen could see their standard landing site, near where the solar disk stuck out like a flower from the rocky mass of the mountain. But the field was plainly in the range of their tractor/pressor beams. If they could assist his landing, they might easily be able to lock the B3 down tight as well. Those beams had been used to move the whole habitat around as if the rock was a spaceship. They had to be powerful.

He chose a different site, near an array of windows—probably a hydroponic garden.

Lord Casey said, "This thing is huge."

"They call it a mountain. Many kloms across, I'm sure."

Ohen was sensing frustrated thoughts. The computer said, "A call from Mt. Ural."

He ignored it, for now. He was carefully piloting the B3 and at the same time probing the mass of Mt. Ural for lasers or tractor beam projectors. He didn't really think they'd risk trying to destroy his boat, but he was now sure they wanted to capture it. He wasn't going to make that easy for them.

"Answering the call. This is Ohen bar Clay. I'm almost down. I chose a place close to an airlock you lit up for me."

"That's the wrong landing site!"

"Oh, well. I'm settling in here. Sorry if your delegate has to walk too far, but this looked like the best landing site for my ship design."

There was a minor crunch as the B3 settled down on the rubble that coated the surface.

"I'm down. Let me know when your delegate arrives so I can open the airlock."

Once he closed the call, Alice asked, "You didn't like their landing site?"

He shrugged. "I wasn't comfortable landing where they could lock me down."

He adjusted his tractor beams, using a cycling tractor beam to keep the B3 settled down in place. The local gravity was very light, even lighter than he'd expected for a rocky, iron-rich asteroid. Possibly that was due to an extensively hollowed out interior. Maybe it had been a mine originally, but it had been remade.

Ten minutes later, the camera focused on the nearby airlock hatch showed activity as someone came out in a spacesuit, looked at the B3 for a bit and then went back inside. Ohen could tell that the person inside had just reported what she'd seen on a wired voice circuit. It was possible they didn't have cameras pointing at his location.

Casey asked, "What's taking them so long?"

"Be patient. I messed up their plans by landing here. They're probably running through the corridors to get here as fast as they can. I waited hours for you to get ready."

It was another few minutes, but the hatch opened again and two men in spacesuits began drifting their way in extremely slow lopes. Ohen guessed that walking in microgravity was a specialized skill.

Mt. Ural called again. "Out delegate is coming your way. Open your airlock door."

Ohen tapped the control panel next to the interior door and the outer door opened for them. There was a small glass window and he watched as both men squeezed into the limited space.

At first he was a little puzzled. Why two of them? The invitation was for one delegate. But then, he scanned them with his clairvoyance as air was cycling into the airlock.

He kept the inner door locked. Using the speaker, he said, "I'm sorry, but my instruments detect weapons inside the airlock. I can't open up the inner door until they are removed."

The thoughts from inside were angry and frustrated. One of the men yelled, "Sorry, those are just our utility knives. I'll remove them." One of the men handed a long-bladed knife to the other. They had to cycle the air again to take the airlock back down to vacuum. The man with the two knives stepped out, and the airlock began filling with air again.

Ohen wondered why the man inside the airlock was waiting with his side turned toward the door. His thoughts were preparing for ... something, but it wasn't clear.

Finally, the air was equalized and the inner door opened.

Ohen said, "You should be able to take off your helmet. This is breathable air."

The man's eyes locked on his. He grabbed a handhold as he shouted. "Computer! Air contamination emergency! Evacuate the air immediately!"

Ohen was shocked. So was the attacker as nothing happened.

Then Ohen kicked the man loose from his handhold, slammed the door and hit the switch opening the outer door without waiting for the air to be pumped out. The exploding volume of air caught the attacker and threw him across the landscape. The other man had been waiting just outside and was caught up in the blast as well.

It wasn't likely they'd be blown clear of the asteroid, but it would be a while before they regained their footing.

Ohen said, "Computer, message to Mt. Ural: Because your man attempted to kill us all in an effort to capture our boat, I've kicked him out. If Mt. Ural wants to be part of the trading community after the barrier to Earth is lifted, please send a different representative—one who isn't armed and will not attempt to murder us."

He closed the connection and made sure that the airlock door was locked. He'd lost a little air, but it wasn't critical.

Alice asked, "What just happened?"

Ohen could feel his muscles twitching from the surge of adrenaline, he sighed. "They were used to spaceships that were completely controlled by their computer, like Brilliant Morning. He tried to convince the computer that there was toxic gas in the ship and that all the air had to be expelled. It would have killed us all. Then, because they were protected in their space-suits, they could have taken possession of the boat."

Casey gasped. "They were trying to kill us!"

Ohen nodded. "The B3 isn't computer controlled, but they didn't know that."

"We need to get away before they try something else."

Ohen shook his head. "We still need a Uralite delegate. I don't know if Project Command would accept the whole idea of reinstating the Project Charter if they aren't included. I'm pretty confident I can escape. Let's wait and see if they'll send a real delegate."

Alice gave a rough sigh. "I knew we couldn't trust them. They're mur-derers. That's their nature."

Ohen nodded, but his focus was on the thoughts inside Mt. Ural. Their people were angry and some of their number were advocating sending more men in spacesuits outside in an attempt to capture the strange spaceship with nets or a hand-held tractor beam.

One of their number was advocating a different plan. Go to the confer-ence, try to get trading established, and then they could capture the boat when their delegate was returned. He volunteered to go.

After half an hour of debate, the man who had argued for caution was chosen as the replacement delegate.

On to Earth

Ohen pointed. "Delegate Kamen, since you say that Mt. Uralites are most used to a half-standard Earth gravity, I'll need you to sit on the left bench. The right bench is set at Earth gravity for those delegates."

Kamen nodded. "The interior spaces are mostly covered with floor gravity panels. Not all are set at 50% but most are. Your ship is quite different from the designs I studied."

Casey had originally chosen the end seat on the low gravity bench, but now he vacated it for the newcomer, choosing to sit next to Alice, as far away from the Uralite as he could.

If Kamen noticed the discourtesy, he gave no sign of it. He sat at the end seat and put his helmet under the bench. He had no other luggage, just the spacesuit he wore.

Ohen tapped a button and the display showed them lifting rapidly away from Mt. Ural.

"The B3 is my design. My people don't have cylindrical spaceships like the Project uses." He gave a short summary of the U'tanse.

Kamen didn't believe a word of the story, but he couldn't quite figure out why the tall man would concoct such a tale. The ship was indeed a very different design from everything he had researched.

Other than nodding as the other two delegates introduced themselves, he paid them no more attention. He thought nothing of the Martian, but tried to refrain from showing anger at the Lunar delegate. All the bad luck Mt. Ural had experienced in recent times could be traced back to the damage they received from the Lunar ship during the ill-fated expedition to make contact with their people on Luna.

It was going to be up to him to find some way to reverse their fortunes.

Ohen tried to ignore the man's thoughts. He certainly gave no sign that he could listen in. One thing was clear, although the Uralites used and maintained tractor/pressor beam generators, they didn't have the technology or engineering experience necessary to make themselves a new ship.

Ohen was frustrated that the whole of humanity in this system had fallen so far. A U'tanse engineer, like himself, could find a way to take a single TP generator, mount it into an airtight tank and make a low-powered but totally usable spaceship for use in the Lagrangian clusters. The Uralites certainly had the motivation but couldn't manage to make that happen.

It was a tense flight as he set course for Earth. There was a lot of deeply held anger boiling away under the surface, and he wasn't immune. Ohen resented the attempt to kill them all just to capture the B3.

He was careful to obscure his piloting by placing the portable computer to block Kamen's line of sight of his real controls. He didn't want the Uralite to get any hint of how his ship was controlled.

· · ·

Alice said, "Nobody's ever been this close to Earth before. With the deadly barricade, it wasn't a risk anyone would take."

The blue globe below them was very different from the reddish Mars or the cloud-covered Luna. There were plenty of clouds, but the ocean and the land drew the eye.

Casey asked, "Where are we going?"

Ohen tapped on his computer's screen. "I was sent an image of the western coast of this continent with Bremerhaven marked with a blinking dot. It should be a lot easier finding it than what we went through hunting for Stampz."

Kamen spoke, startling them. "That's the Ural mountain range over to the east. You can see the evening shadows on the peaks." He had his own reactions to seeing the Earth. That mountain range was mythic in his people's history.

Ohen concentrated on matching what he could see on the camera with the computer map. "I'm going to be going down slowly. Probably the view will get hazy when we go through some cloud layers. Stay in your seats. We're already feeling Earth's gravity."

Although his eyes were locked to his task, he could see Alice timidly reaching out with her hand, probing to find the place where she could feel the difference in gravity.

Outside of the bench area, the floor just had no floor gravity adjustment, although he could set it however he wanted. For now, he wanted to feel Earth's gravity for himself. He was dropping through the atmosphere slower than free-fall so that they wouldn't get any excess hull heating from air friction. There was a little turbulence, coming in flat to the air flow, but he could keep that under control.

"This is Ohen bar Clay, the U'tanse delegate. I am approaching the west coast of Europe and I estimate that I could be over Bremerhaven in twenty minutes. If you could send more detailed directions to a preferred landing site, it would be useful. Any open space with no obstructions for a hundred meters would be ideal. Other than the wind blast from my landing beams, my ship should not cause any damage to the site."

As he settled into a level flight, the reply came.

"This is Karl Rugel at Bremerhaven University. I'm sending a map of the area. You will see that there is a forested park about a klom eastward from the bend in the waterway. There is a grassy meadow in the middle of the park. We are currently sending rangers to clear the area. You can land there. Everyone is excited that you are here. Welcome."

Alice said, "It's strange to see a city out in the open like this, with no crater walls around it."

Ohen said, "It's like Mars. They have craters, but they don't need protection from the winds. Nobody has the sunwinds like Luna."

Casey nodded in agreement. Kamen didn't understand any of it. He'd probably never felt a wind in his life.

The parkland was very clear—an isolated wild area in the middle of the city. Immediately off to the left were the buildings that probably housed the university. He could see people running to leave the grassy area. He hovered a couple of hundred meters overhead to give them time to get clear. Then, he slowly came down, kicking up loose grass and leaves.

"We're down." He tapped on his controls and made sure the floor gravity settings were still stable. "I'd advise you to stay put. Standing up and walking into high gravity might make you faint."

And then he did just that, grimacing at how weak he'd become living under the weak gravities of Mars and Luna. "It's harder than I expected."

Casey chuckled. "You've always been stronger than everyone else. If you're having troubles, then I'll just stay put."

Alice asked, "Can you adjust the cameras, so I can see."

He nodded, switching to a side view, where they could see several motorized, wheeled vehicles pulling up nearby.

Ohen went to the airlock and opened the door. "The inside air has been at Luna's standard composition and pressure. I'm going to slowly change it, so let me know if you feel any distress."

Casey turned to Alice. "I've been through this before, when we switched from Mars conditions to your air. It wasn't bad."

Ohen stepped into the airlock after the air had circulated a bit. He then opened the outer door. Voices reacted when he stepped into view. Their thoughts were familiar. **He's a giant! Are all aliens this tall?**

He gave them a smile. "Hello, there." He stepped carefully out onto the grass. "Sorry, I'm a little unused to the gravity."

A gray-haired man in blue robes stepped up to greet him. "Hello, I'm the Lead Professor here at Bremerhaven University, Hans Jurgen." They shook hands.

"I am Ohen bar Clay, the delegate for the U'tanse. Inside are the delegates from Mars, Luna, and the Mt. Ural habitat. Unfortunately, they all have to stay inside since they can't handle Earth gravity. Would you like to meet them?"

Jurgen entered timidly and all the delegates managed to stand, briefly, for a quick introduction.

Ohen gestured at the benches. "As you can see, there is space for five more passengers and a bare minimum of luggage. How many delegates has Earth collected?"

Jurgen frowned. "We had planned for eight."

. . .

They held an impromptu meeting in one of the vehicles. Ohen was embarrassed to claim one of the seats while many more distinguished persons stood around.

He gestured in the direction of B3. "We're under a constraint dictated by Project Command. Because of my status as an extra-solar visitor, I was allowed this visit to Earth, but I'm not sure I could extend that to make a second visit to pick up a second batch of delegates. And as you can see, I have a small ship and I had to get the carpenters on Luna to make benches so that I could carry this many."

He looked over the faces. Some were clearly undecided as to whether he was human or not. One of the faces watching him clearly was not.

The humanoid was seated in a wheeled chair, wearing something that looked almost like a spacesuit, but his head was clear. But that head wasn't human. There was no nose, but there appeared to be a blowhole of some kind on the top of his head. His skin was dampened regularly by mist that sprayed from his collar. His thoughts weren't English words and he was clearly not human, but he was firmly intent on maintaining his status as one of the delegates.

There was another face that caught his attention. In the back row was a smiling younger man who nodded his way. It was Karl, the man he had talked with over the computer. Ohen gave him a nod in return.

There was some discussion as to whether Project could be talked into allowing more trips, but no one knew anything about the computers that ran the Project, other than there had been absolutely no luck lifting the barrier around Earth in the hundreds of years that it had been in place.

Ohen shrugged. "As it was explained to me, Project Command works from a list of orders it was given in the past when humans controlled everything. There was just this one exception, a just-in-case scenario, to minimally bypass the rules in case of a visitor from another star system. The only way we'll be able to regain control of the Project is for the World Court to be reestablished and to reaffirm the Project charter."

Jurgen said, "I wish I'd been told how many delegates were permitted before we called everyone here."

Ohen added his own frustrations. "I had requested information about that, but I was never given the data."

One of the standing delegates said, "What if we remove the bench? Would that make more room?"

The man beside him said, "If I have to sit on the floor for the trip, you'll never get me up again."

There was debate, but the benches survived. It was a problem of who could go and who should give up their seat.

There was a squeak from the non-human. The young man beside him said, "The esteemed Waveleaper insists that his merpeople be represented."

Jurgen nodded, "Yes, of course." He turned to Ohen and said, diplomatically, "The call was for all the peoples of Earth to be represented, and the residents of the oceans must be included."

Ohen recalled a brief mention of mermaids in the mythology section of the Book, but he had never considered that such a creature was real. Still, he knew of other aliens, with much different body designs, so it wasn't too hard of a stretch to accept that there were other intelligent peoples on Earth.

He also picked up some thoughts from the crowd. Humans considered the merpeople to be leftovers from the genetic engineering period, but the merpeople insisted that they had racial memories of their existence from long before that, and that the human history was faulty.

The merpeople also controlled which ships were allowed to sail the oceans. Waveleaper's presence was a recent development and a possible sign of peace between humans and merpeople. He couldn't be offended without dire consequences.

Ohen said, "There isn't space for that wheeled chair. Can Waveleaper sit on the bench?"

"I'm Jason Kidd, his caretaker and translator. The chair folds flat and will take little space. However, I need to go along as well."

Jurgen said, "Of course, but we need to figure out who will represent which peoples."

It was a long discussion, and Ohen was amused to notice how fast the sun was moving across the sky. It was twice the rate he'd gotten accustomed to on Luna. He took a break to make sure Alice and the other's got fed and got to take a visit to the bathroom under their low-gravity settings.

Alice and Casey had been reading books that she had brought along. Kamen had not asked for one. Ohen gave them a short briefing.

"You mean there's a real merman?"

"Yes, and he's coming along as a delegate. Apparently the merpeople took over the seas after the Plague and will sink any ship that offends them. It's a big political issue."

Alice shook her head in amazement. "I've read a few fairytale books. Is he handsome?"

Ohen chuckled. "Not by human standards at least—bald and no nose, and he speaks in high pitched squeaks. His translator is coming along."

After the break, and after Ohen confirmed that any of the delegates could use his computer to privately confer with the people who got left behind, the final representatives were chosen.

Ohen stood at the open airlock and directed the new people to the bench.

"The right bench is at normal Earth gravity. Please choose your chair."

The lady in blue robes gave a big smile. "I'm sitting there." She hurriedly stepped over to the seat facing Alice. "I'm so glad to see you here! I was afraid I'd be the only woman. I'm Emilia Johnson, delegate for the Americas and doubling for Asia as well."

Alice made her introductions as Ohen gave the same instructions to the next man, Don Bristol, delegate for Europa. The third was in red robes. He shook Ohen's hand. "I'm Roman Al-Hajji, the representative of the Church of Unity, Africa and the Eastern Lands. Just call me Haj."

The final two came in, with Jason Kidd pushing the chair. Jason mumbled, "I'm just here for Waveleaper and to represent Australia and Pacifica." He sighed. "Just a translator in both cases. I'll have to use your computer a lot."

Waveleaper squealed. Jason said, "He's claiming the low gravity chair. He complains about being out of the water all the time."

Kamen moved to the third position and Jason moved the merman to the end seat. When he squealed, Jason said, "He thanks you for moving. He didn't want to be trapped between humans. He's a little racist."

Kamen nodded. "Understandable. I feel a little trapped here myself."

Alice asked, "You can understand his squeaks?"

Jason tapped his ear. "I have an earpiece that slows down what he says. It's not English, but at least I can hear the words and translate that. Waveleaper can understand half of what humans say, so speak clearly and don't use technical terms. I've got a gadget that will help me translate the rest if you need help."

Ohen said, "I'm taking off quickly." He explained the limits on his hospitality. He'd keep floor gravity low so every one could stand if they needed to, but asked for their patience.

He sent a message to Project Command and Karl at the university. On the camera display screen, all the people and vehicles began moving back out of the way.

Soon, they were in the air. Ohen concentrated on climbing out of the atmosphere much faster than when they came down. He wanted to get to Ceres before the crowd overloaded the boat's capacity to keep everyone reasonably comfortable.

He was grateful that Alice was in full note-taking mode, asking the Earth delegates all kinds of questions, everything from how they dyed the color of their robes to questions about the political makeup of Earth's nations.

Haj was in the middle of the conversation more often than not. "No, there's not really a universal church. The Church of Unity is aspirational. We're an organization with members from all over the globe and more often than not, we're called in to help moderate disputes."

Waveleaper squeaked. Jason said, "That was an … unkind remark about human religions. The merpeople have their own rituals to invoke their racial memories of ancient times and to remember their heroic figures."

Ohen could tell that Alice was biting her tongue to keep from asking possibly intrusive questions about the merpeople and their racial memories.

And then, he switched camera views. "Look, at the center of the screen is Ceres. That's our destination."

The chatter went quiet. The Earth residents had probably seen Ceres all their lives, as the second largest moon in the sky, but none of them had seen it like this, bright and centered among endless stars and numerous space habitats.

Ceres

"Aren't you going to turn over halfway?" asked Don Bristol.

Ohen could tell the man knew the basics of the physics, but he had no real experience. Almost none of the Earth people had any experience with beam ships. Like Mars, they had run out of power to charge them long ago. Jason seemed to understand what was going on, but he wasn't really interested.

Ohen said, "I have already switched the beams. We are now decelerating. I don't have to actually turn the ship around, just reverse the forces."

Bristol nodded. "Thank you."

Kamen was worried. "You are certain you have permission to approach Ceres? My people have lost ships getting too close."

"We have an explicit invitation to this conference, hosted by Ceres. Yes, we are permitted. I'll send an update message to Project Command, but I'm sure this ship is being tracked every step of the way."

Just as the image of Ceres was getting large enough to show considerable surface details, there was a message from Project Command: "Deactivate your propulsion. Ceres beams will land you at a protected location."

Ohen hesitated just an instant. It was almost the same request that Mt. Ural had given him, but this time he had to trust that the Project computers knew what they were doing. He hadn't come to a stop, but cancelled the beams as ordered.

"The Project is controlling us now," he told the delegates. His instruments and the camera displayed showed that they were moving under external control.

Alice said, "Our records call that dome the Green Eye."

"The Eye of Ceres," said Kamen.

Bristol said, "Historical records I've read said that the command center of the Project was capped with a largest tanstran dome ever made, decades before the Plague. There is a city with extensive parkland inside. I guess that's where we're going."

The image outside showed them getting closer to the dome second by second, but Ohen could tell they were veering off to the side. The thoughts from the passengers were a mix, from excitement at seeing the unknown to fear that this was all an elaborate trap and that they'd never be released.

Ohen wasn't immune to uncertainty either. Having his boat carried around in beams he couldn't control caused him to tense up. But at least the B3 was moving on a smooth and direct path. His clairvoyance scanned ahead. He could sense the landing site, but it was too complex in its construction for him to be confident.

The camera showed them settling down on a semicircular pad that was surprisingly clear of any debris.

The computer spoke, "Please wait until the atmosphere outside has stabilized."

Alice asked, "What does that mean?"

Ohen pointed. "There's a dome sliding out of that wall."

"Ah!" Bristol said, "I see it. This is an open airlock. They'll slide a dome out to cover us."

As an engineer, Ohen had numerous questions. How were they going to seal the dome? How much air would be wasted with this kind of setup? Was it ever designed for his kind of ship?

The dome looked high enough to cover one of the beam ships like Brilliant Morning, but it was overkill for his low-profile design.

His eyes went to the instruments. "I can see air pressure. It looks like it'll take another ten minutes."

Someone said, "It's not a transparent dome. I can't see anything."

But there was a large hatch on the flat wall next to them. Ohen watched the air readings as the pressure grew. Shortly, it stabilized.

"The air looks like Earth's proportions. The temperature is reasonable."

Casey said, "The hatch is opening."

Four people walked in, two by two. The men wore brown open chest vests and knee length skirts. The women wore the same skirts, but the upper garment was colorful, with embroidery showing flowers or balls.

Bristol said, "They're wearing kilts!"

Emilia Johnson said, "The climate here must be warm. It's all lightweight clothing."

Bristol said, "They live indoors. There's no climate."

The computer said, "It is safe to exit."

Ohen walked over to the airlock. He faced the delegates. "I'll need to check the gravity outside. Please stay in the benches until we work this out."

He equalized the pressure and opened the hatches. When he stepped outside, under what felt like Earth gravity, the Ceres residents quickly approached.

They spoke as one, "Welcome, visitors from the planets, the Voice told us you were coming."

Ohen smiled at the rhythmical speech. He said, "We came at the invitation of Project Command."

The man on the left said, "It has been an exciting time since the Voice first spoke." He gestured at the space around them. "We didn't even know these corridors and chambers existed. The Voice said he has been looking over us since the beginning, and we never knew of it."

From the ceiling, the voice Ohen had associated with Project Command echoed, "A meeting room has been prepared. If each delegate would state their origin as they leave the ship, the floor gravity will be adjusted appropriately as they walk."

Ohen nodded. "I'll prepare them."

He turned to the welcoming party. "I am Ohen bar Clay, the delegate of the U'tanse people."

The man on the left said, "I am Jireh of the Mason clan. This is my wife Shalla."

From the right, the woman said, "I am Mary, the storyteller of the Shuman clan."

From behind her the man leaned to the side and offered his hand. "And I'm David, also from the Shuman clan."

Up close, Ohen could see the decorations on the women's tops. They weren't balls and flowers, but planets and space habitats. They were obviously fantasy versions, but elaborately and colorfully decorated. From their thoughts, he could tell that these weren't made recently, they were a reflection of their cultural mythology. Even their necklaces were glittery and Ohen suspected they were made from disassembled electronics.

Jireh said, "Like the Voice said, we have a room, a meal prepared, and sleeping rooms available for however long your visit lasts. We'll lead the way."

Ohen thanked them and went inside. "One at a time. I'll set the ship's floor gravity for you and at the door, announce your name and where you're from. The outside floor gravity will adjust for you as well."

Alice was quick to get to the door, carrying her bag. She shouted, "I am Alice Neeley, from Luna."

She stepped forward and nodded as the gravity felt like Luna to her. A greeter stepped up, "I am Shalla Mason. You can follow me."

Soon a line formed, people keeping a few paces between them so that the islands of gravity could follow them and not interfere with the next person.

Jason wheeled Waveleaper out and announced the both of them. He asked, "Is Ceres aware of merpeople?"

Jireh said, "We were fascinated when the Voice told us to expect him. We have a room fitted with a large basin of water. We hope it will be acceptable."

Ohen was the last, locking the airlock hatch and joining the slow-moving line of people. He sampled their thoughts and everyone was comfortable in their own native gravity, although he could see the differences in their gait. Low-gravity people just walked differently from those from high gravity.

He was a little jealous of the computer control that the Project had. His control over the B3's floor gravity was hand-crafted and static. What he was seeing before him was fluid and dynamic. How was the computer able to tell which patch of floor went with which person? There had to be cameras, but he didn't see them.

He probed with his clairvoyance and sensed electronics everywhere in the walls, floor and ceiling. It was all ancient and built in from the beginning, but there were very few wires. Everything must be communicating and powered through an elaborate mesh network.

Since he first landed on Mars, he'd always been a little smug at the U'tanse technical superiority over the natives. But now he was the illiterate one. How high had the Project come before its fall?

Which led to a darker thought—with all their advancement, how could one simple disease take out the whole civilization? Could that happen to the U'tanse as well?

From the beginning, Ohen had been conscious of his health, making sure that any infections he caught from the locals were immediately quenched.

It had happened a couple of times, both on Mars and Luna, but self-healing on that level was as automatic as washing his hands.

But could he have picked up some infection that could spread among the U'tanse when he was reunited with his people? Was there any disease that the U'tanse carried that might be disastrous for these people?

It was something he had to be looking for. And what about this conference? So many different populations were to be thrown together in one room. It was potentially hazardous. None of them had his psychic self-healing abilities.

He used his clairvoyance to take a quick look at Alice. From a distance, her breathing and heart rate seemed normal and she showed no sign of inflammation, but there was really little he could do from a distance like this.

Jireh pointed to a corridor. "The Voice chose this area for your meeting. On the right is a large room with a table where you can sit and talk. We have prepared a meal there for you. The other rooms are individual bedrooms. If you would like to leave your bags there first, or perhaps to change from your travel clothes, we can all meet for the meal when you're ready."

None of the delegates were particularly timid. The guides helped them find their rooms. Ohen poked around his chamber, pleasantly surprised to see a bed large enough for him. There were also several changes of clothes laid out for him to use. He declined to change into a kilt. He was comfortable with his existing clothes.

Shortly, he joined others in the meeting room. Alice was already there, still in her library robes, but wearing a necklace.

He smiled and walked up to her. "How is it going?"

She sighed, then whispered, "I'm grateful for the hospitality, but I'm afraid I'll have to decline the clothes they offered. I'm not going to show that much skin."

"No Ceres gloves, I take it?"

She glared at him. "No. But our hosts are apparently heavily dressed for their culture."

Ohen looked again at the Ceres guides. He wondered if Alice objected to showing her legs, the bare belly, or the arms.

Emilia Johnson walked in and chuckled, fingering the necklace she was wearing as well. Alice nodded to her. It was a way to honor their hosts, without having to wear the native styles.

Delegate Kamen of Mt. Ural walked in, wearing the vest and kilt. He'd decided to shed his spacesuit and Ohen couldn't blame him. Kamen wasn't happy with the style, but he was determined to pull it off. He felt a little old to be showing his chest hair, but there was no help for it. Emilia gave him a smile.

Mary Shuman spoke, and it was almost a song. "Honored guests from distant worlds, please be seated and enjoy the bounty from the Arboretum's fields."

Ohen sat between Alice and Don Bristol. Across from them Casey was chatting with Roman Al-Hajji. Jason Kidd sat with Waveleaper at the end of the table. David, their guide, sat with them.

The food tasted a little bland, totally in contrast with their hosts' expectations. For them, this was the ultimate their cooks could prepare. Ohen suspected that with no animal population, and a limited number of fruits and vegetables in their domed community, that their diet had just adapted. There didn't appear to be any spices. Tiny slices of apple were sprinkled over their potato and pumpkin dish.

Ohen had dealt with worse when he was a captive on Mars. He ate and savored the unusual taste combinations. He consumed his portion and smiled when more was offered.

None of the delegates would dare complain, although Jason explained, as he brought out some dried fish, that Waveleaper's diet required special supplements.

David said that there was some fish available in the ocean. When questioned, David explained that the Ceres ocean was a deep chamber of water off on a rail line that was connected to the Dome. Fishing there was very restricted and wasn't normally a part of their diet.

Waveleaper squealed, Jason translated, and a visit to the ocean was arranged for sometime after the meeting.

Others mentioned wanting to see the city under the dome, and other tourist visits were planned. Ohen resolved to mention his worries about cross-cultural diseases as soon as he had the opportunity.

"When shall we begin the conference?"

Bristol smiled. "We've already begun. All these conferences begin with a period of socialization where the delegates get to know each other."

Ohen was struck by the thoughts leaking behind the words. Don Bristol was a highly capable diplomat and was considering controlling the direction of the conference by putting Ohen in the leadership role and influencing the inexperienced engineer to guide the group in Europa's favor.

Bristol said, "It is probably is time for business. The meal is done. Why don't you start? You're in the group that put this all together aren't you? Give us the background."

All the group started looking his way. Chancellor Folken had said that he might have to lead the proceedings. He sighed. There was no way around it. He needed to be a diplomat himself.

Negotiations

"I am Ohen bar Clay, a representative of the U'tanse branch of humanity."

He quickly sensed the unspoken questions of the others, so he gave the two paragraph history of his people and the expedition to find the lost Earth.

"And so I was left to scout out the planets of this system and to determine if this really was our system of origin. I landed first on Mars and after adapting there, we sent a message to the ruler of Luna. Lord Casey of Chimbote was invited as well and we landed at the capital in Stampz crater. Together with Princess Alice, the head librarian of the great library of Stampz, we were investigating the barrier around Earth. Historically, the space travelers from Luna had contacted Project Command in the past, so we used that address to ask the Project itself what was the purpose of the barrier.

"To our surprise, Project Command answered and gave us the reason. The barrier was to protect Earth in the aftermath of the Plague, but with no surviving humans in control, that order was never lifted. The Project's computers could only follow the orders they were given. The only people authorized to give those orders were the dead controllers on Ceres, or possibly an order from the World Court on Earth. However the Plague also killed off those diplomats and the World Court lapsed.

"Our task is to declare ourselves the re-established World Court, and then re-affirm the Terraforming Project charter. Only then can we give the Project such orders as necessary."

He raised his voice a little. "Is that an accurate summary, Project Command?"

The voice from the ceiling said, "Yes, with clarification. The World Court was established to be a body representing all parts of the population. To fulfill that criterion, I said that there must be one representative from Mars, one from Luna, one from Ceres, and one from Mt. Ural, and several from Earth."

Ohen noticed that Jireh waved his hand, and the other three of his party got up from the table and left. The meal was over; only the delegates remained.

"In addition, to clarify, an ongoing task of the Project is to prevent disasters such as happened during the time of the Plague where large habitats crashed on Earth and caused massive death and destruction. Some duties of the Project should always remain under the Project computer control until such time as trained humans can take on the task of controllers."

Ohen said, "I assume that Project Command will be available to analyze the side effects of any World Court orders."

"That is correct."

Ohen looked at the other delegates. "So, I'm an engineer, not a trained diplomat. What levers must we pull to re-establish the World Court?"

Dom Bristol smiled and pulled out his satchel. "I'm a historian, and when I first heard about this conference, I went to the Bremerhaven archives and pulled out this. It's the World Court Articles of Establishment. These are the rules that controlled the original World Court, including the amendments, like those that added a seat for Mars. I've got three copies, if any of you would like to look them over."

Ohen took a copy and read quickly.

Emilia echoed his first thought. "It looks like we have to be unanimous, at least for the establishment."

Haj said, "That makes sense. Once we're up and running, we can worry about the correct number of delegates and all that, but for now, we have to be in agreement to even attempt this. What are the arguments against changing the status quo?"

Emilia chuckled, "After the fact, there will be plenty of people calling for our heads. Nothing can change without someone being hurt."

Bristol nodded. "When the news came out that there were people from space coming to visit, I received so many messages from people panicked that we would bring the Plague back."

Ohen said, "There are other diseases. During my visits on Mars and Luna, I worried every time someone coughed in my direction. I'm pretty healthy, but not everybody is robust. Are any of you under the weather? We really should have checked on this before having us all sit down in the same room."

People looked at each other. Bristol said, "That's a good point, but maybe this time we've gotten lucky. There's a lot of history about diseases following migrating populations. It's an issue we'll need to deal with, once we've opened travel back up."

Ohen was surprised at a quick moment of panic from Alice, although it didn't show on her face. The thoughts about a family curse, and the fact that she always wore gloves, as did her mother—he had a growing suspicion that the imperial family had some kind of disease, one they kept very secret.

But the discussion moved on. There was a back and forth between Jason and Waveleaper. Was the World Court just a human thing? Was the merpeople's presence here a mistake?

Ohen could feel Bristol's frustration and fears that petty squabbles might just derail the whole process.

So Ohen stood up. Everyone looked his way.

"I'd like to make a point here.

"We are all very different. My people, the U'tanse, have been isolated and inbred since the time of the Star. We have been selectively bred to survive our circumstances and in may ways we're very different from the people of Mars, or Luna, or Ceres. Some of us around this table have always lived under one full gravity and are comfortable with that. Others wouldn't be able to survive extended exposure to Earth's gravity. The people of Ceres have never left their home city. I have traveled through many star systems. One of us can breathe water.

"Now I may think of myself more as a U'tanse rather than a human, because of many generations of private history. It's the same with the Ceres people, and those from Mt. Ural. The merpeople are proud of their origins in the sea. It's the same with those from Mars and from Luna.

"It doesn't matter what our differences are—cultural, historical or biological—because we are all Children of Earth. That is where we all came from. That is our spiritual home.

"And now we are all in one room, one family, here to decide the future of Earth."

He gestured to his right. "I would like to hear what you all think. Lord Casey?"

Ohen sat and Casey stood. "I don't know about Earth's politics, but the nations of Mars are at war. Sometimes I pray that we could just look up at the sky and realize we are all part of something bigger. I'm not so naïve that I believe that it would bring us peace, but I have hope that travel and trade from beyond our traditional limits would shake us up and make us think bigger. I'm all in favor of breaking past the old barriers."

He waved to Haj. The representative of the Church of Unity, Africa, the Eastern Lands cautioned against opening everything up wide, at least at first. "The cultural shock for any isolated population could be severe. Yes, the people I represent would want to open the barrier around Earth, but I suggest step-by-step progress."

Emilia argued for the benefits of trade. Ohen was conscious that she was constantly aware of Bristol's eye on her. They had obviously discussed this before. They also didn't want to catch Waveleaper's interest. If the humans could jumpstart trade via spacecraft and aircraft, they could bypass the merpeople's restrictions on ship travel.

Jason shrugged. "I'm not really a diplomat, but I'm sure the Australians would favor trade. Waveleaper squealed. Jason translated, "As long as the merpeople's right to the sea is recognized, he doesn't care what you decide."

Ohen felt the relief from Bristol. If the re-establishment of the World Court had to be unanimous, the merman could have blocked it. He was known to be stubborn.

Jason's thoughts, however, were muddled. It was like he had more than one person in his head, and some fragmentary thoughts were sullen and hostile. He really didn't want the barrier to Earth dropped, but he didn't want to be the sole holdout either. It wasn't safe to be that visible.

Bristol made his pitch. "Earth has lost so much since the Plague. Before then, when we were a space-faring civilization, we had moved all the heavy industries into the Lagrangian colonies, party because of the contamination that had damaged the Earth's ecologies. Not only did the barrier cut off all possibility of manufactured items from space, but it also cut off nearly all of our energy supplies. Other than burning wood from the forests and a few ancient hydroelectric plants or solar farms, much of our energy was gone, and those sources couldn't easily be repaired or replaced. There are some machines left, but without power from space, they sit as museum pieces, useless to us.

"Definitely the people of Europa would welcome restoring the World Court and opening up trade with the people of other worlds."

He had other arguments, but declined to state them where the merman would hear.

Kamen spoke, "The people of Mt. Ural are desperate for an influx of resources, but we find ourselves greatly hindered without any spaceships. Our last ship was destroyed by the Luna people, so I don't know what to do."

Alice interrupted, "Your ship was never destroyed, it was captured when you attacked us! It's been renamed and has served the imperium ever since."

Kamen's nostrils widened. "Well then maybe we should talk about the restoration of stolen property!"

"Ha! You don't even want to go there, Uralite! Not after having pulverized and burned three cities to the ground with your meteor bombs. Your whole mountain wouldn't be enough to pay for the losses. That was wartime and the capture of the ship was legitimate."

Ohen knew his voice was deep and hard to ignore. He said, "Ceres doesn't look like it has spaceships either. Perhaps one of the World Court's first order of business should be making sure each world has a spaceship of their own. If we drag ancient grudges into this, we'll never get to the first step. We can't do anything without reestablishing the court."

Kamen took a deep breath and then nodded. "Mt. Ural will approve." He sat back down.

Alice stood and pulled out several documents which she spread out in front of her. "With all the talk of who has spaceships and who doesn't, I need to bring up an urgent issue that concerns Luna. The Ceres and Vesta clusters contain a large number of uninhabited former habitats and mining asteroids. Luna has, over the years, established working claims on several of these that are important to our economy; Alexandria, a biological research station we've named Heidi, and several mining asteroids formerly owned by the Monarch corporation.

"It will be up to the World Court or the Project to ratify the ownership of existing claims and to mediate any new claims once a spacefaring civilization restarts."

Kamen raised his hand. "Likewise, Mt. Ural is currently harvesting resources from a former farming colony and is now in physical contact with it. Our claim must be confirmed as well."

Jireh Mason, of Ceres, timidly said, "We don't know any of these things. We have legends, fairy tales really, of other worlds. The idea that we could travel to those lights in the sky isn't something we really believe in, yet. Our biggest fear is that now that we know you are real, will we be compelled to do everything that you say? We certainly don't have any power over you, and it sounds like you all have great powers. The Voice has said that he has protected us, but will that be true in the future? What will become of us?"

There was more discussion. Project Command confirmed that many of the spaceships parked on Mars could be reactivated, if they could be powered up. Alice stated that the Brilliant Morning could be used to transfer power to an idle martian ship, if necessary.

Promises were made to ensure that every world had at least one spaceship. Travel and trade was going to be started very slowly, with permits required, ratified by both the terminal points.

Alice urged a restriction on weapons on any newly commissioned spaceships and a confirmation that Project Command would restrict the actions of any ships used for warfare.

Late in the day, the World Court was reestablished with a unanimous vote and almost immediately, the charter with the Terraforming Project was proclaimed as active. Project Command confirmed the list of initial changes. The barrier inhibiting travel to Earth was lifted, subject to the permit system.

There was still a lot to do, but it was late in the day. They adjourned for an evening meal and would come back in the morning.

Jason took Waveleaper to his chambers. The merman didn't really have an appetite for garden produce. He had dried fish in his supplies.

The Ceres cooks prepared seasoned rice as the main dish, and the delegates ate and paired up for discussions.

Haj came to sit with Ohen. He chuckled. "Now is the time for deal-making."

Ohen nodded. "You're right there. Alice is trying to jumpstart the process of getting new ships from Mars. Casey has realized he's sitting on a gold mine with all those ships sitting idle, and Alice has the best ship available for getting them powered up. I bet she wants more ships for Luna as well out of the deal."

Haj asked, "And what does the U'tanse delegate want, now that trade is on the table?"

Ohen shrugged. "It has occurred to me that there might be a salvageable habitat in the Lagrangian clusters that would make a great outpost for the returned U'tanse. My people are quite used to living in habitats and airless moons. I doubt we could make a claim on Vesta, but if they aren't all claimed by the time my people return, I need to be ready with a list of suitable locations."

He shook his head. "I had been looking for a place on Mars or Luna where we could settle, but we're a technological people. We don't really need a place to farm next to neighbors that would always be suspicious of us. Maybe we should just start out as trading partners. With our existing training, the U'tanse just might be in demand as helpers in getting this space-faring civilization back on track."

Haj said, "There is a lot about the U'tanse that I need to learn."

Ohen smiled. "Do you want to fold us into your Universal Church?"

Haj shrugged. "That's something to consider in a few years, not now. I'm just fascinated by the idea of a fragment of humanity isolated for so many years."

Jireh Mason raised his voice. "Any of you who wish to have a quick tour of Ceres Central, my home city, there is a rail car that can take us there."

Revelations

Everyone but the merman, who was quite content to remain in his tank, joined the tour group.

The Ceres dome was so large that there had been a rail system connecting parts of the city and with spurs to the airlock and the ocean. They all fit comfortably in one car. Ohen was surprised that it was outfitted with adjustable floor gravity as well. He guessed it was designed well after Mars was terraformed and with Luna's future in mind. Accommodating people from light-gravity worlds wasn't something he'd invented. Others had been at this before his time.

Jireh seemed excited. "We never knew the rail system was active. I've only ridden on it one time, once we started preparing for your arrival."

Ohen asked, "But you knew it existed?"

"Oh yes, we have used the rails as anvils when we crush grain and beat tree bark into fabric. I guess we'll have to make some changes if the cars are active in the future."

The native gripped the handrail tightly as the car started moving. It proceeded through a tight tunnel and rattled through a couple of barricades that Ohen identified as protective seals to keep the atmosphere inside in case of a breech at the airlock. The rail line dipped low, probably to duck under the lip of the huge dome, before climbing back.

And then the instant they left the tunnels, it was a different world.

Bristol said, "I've seen fantasy paintings like this."

The original buildings stretched off into the distance, many of them covered in vines. Green was the dominant color. Gardens were planted in every available space. There was a forested area off toward the center, and in the middle was a huge tree, bigger than anything Ohen had seen on Mars or Luna. Earth was huge in the sky, just as large as it had been on Luna, only this sky was crystal clear. The sun was lower and it was gradually fading, not from getting any closer to the horizon, but because there the dome was applying some filtering effect.

Ohen asked Jireh, "Does the sun go down in the sky?"

"Yes, half the month, it's in the sky. Half the month it's out of sight and there's a ring of light that gives us daylight. The stars are really brilliant when the sun is gone."

People came out of their homes to see the rail car move through their neighborhood. It was a spectacle. One woman ran toward the rails and rescued some pots that had been left out in the way. The car was moving slowly enough that there was no real danger.

Alice asked, "Is that a world tree?"

Jireh shook his head. "It's the Singing Tree. The various clans gather around it for celebrations. It makes people giddy getting close. The gravity is very low there."

Ohen asked, "Are your fields at normal gravity?"

"Some are, some not. All the homes have gravity."

The rail car stopped at a marketplace. Some wooden stalls had been built over the rails and it couldn't go any farther. They all got out and wandered among the stalls for a while. At least in this area, the floor gravity was low enough that Alice was coping with a cane that one of their helpers had provided. Ohen noticed Alice bartering with one of the vendors. It looked like she'd had the foresight to bring some imperial coins to trade with. Even if the locals didn't know what they were worth, they were metal and pretty.

Jireh stood beside him and watched as well, relieved that his people were tolerating the strangers in their midst.

"Um. Owen Barclay?"

"Yes?"

Jireh whispered, "Is the Voice a god?"

Ohen suddenly realized that they were far from any walls or ceilings that hadn't been made from wood and Jireh was finally brave enough to ask the question that had been plaguing him.

"I have been speaking to the Voice myself since before I arrived here. No, he isn't a god. He's a machine that your ancestors made. He was given orders to take care of the Ceres people, and since machines don't age like people, he kept on doing that."

Jireh sighed, not totally convinced, but a little relieved.

. . .

When the delegates came back to the airlock area where they were housed, some of them went straight to their rooms. Others stayed to chat.

Ohen sat next to Alice, smiling as she showed off the polished wooden necklace she'd purchased. Embossed on a medallion was the giant tree.

"They have legends about it. Officially, the tree roots broke the floor gravity system beneath it and with no winds to trouble it, the tree was able to grow much larger than any of the surrounding ones. From a mystic perspective, they see the tree, centered in the middle of the dome, as the spirit of their people and hope for an eternal future. It's just fascinating. I'm going to write up a paper on this belief when I get home."

Sitting across from them were Haj and Jason.

Jason said, "Waveleaper and I might just be a little late to the meeting in the morning. Jireh and Project Command have arranged a quick visit to their ocean. Waveleaper is eager to swim in it." He sighed. "I just hope he doesn't do anything stupid."

Ohen was intrigued by Jason's thoughts. He definitely thought in layers, as if there were multiple personalities in one body, but it was all tangled and it was very hard to get a solid read on him.

Haj was another of those people who seemed to have independently developed telepathic blocking ineda. Ohen couldn't get a whisper of his thoughts. It was the best ineda he'd ever run across. If he had a system, then it would be worthwhile to learn it.

Alice was worried about the locals. She could imagine a flood of tourists and technicians arriving and turning the culture upside down. She was grateful to have experienced it, but would the Ceres people hate the day it all changed?

She looked at Ohen. "What are you smiling about?"

He shook his head. "We're all different, and yet alike at the same time. Every one of us is here for our own reasons, and hiding our own secrets."

Alice's worry about her family curse popped up and was suppressed. Jason worried that the man from out-system was strange and a little too intuitive, and that made him dangerous. He'd need to be watched more carefully. Haj just smiled.

Alice sighed, "I need to get some sleep." She held out her hand, checking the gravity and stood up. As Ohen stood, she shook her head. "You don't need to escort me. I'm perfectly safe here."

He nodded. She needed to feel perfectly independent for now. Just like the visit to Franklin, she had an important job, but her position of responsibility could all vanish the moment she returned home.

Jason stood as well. "I'd better go check on Waveleaper."

Haj smiled at Ohen. "I've been hoping we'd have a moment to talk."

"More questions about the U'tanse people?"

"Yes! I'm anxious to know everything. I hear you have a book that details the history of your origins."

Ohen wondered how far that rumor had spread. Did Alice say something?

"Well, yes, we just call it the Book."

"And you have a copy with you, perhaps on your ship?"

"Yes ... that's true. But I am very protective of it. I haven't even allowed Alice to read it, and she's a dedicated librarian."

Haj leaned closer. "But I could see it, right? Just a look."

"It's back in the ship."

Haj waved. "Oh, I'm sure our hosts won't mind if we took a look."

Jireh came closer. Haj asked, "We would like to make a short visit back to the spaceship we arrived in. Is that okay with you?"

"Of course. I'll show you the way."

Haj was in the lead and just as Ohen's perfect memory knew the way, so apparently did Haj. Jireh was barely keeping up.

Shortly they reached the big hatchway and Jireh hurried up and tapped the button.

Haj smiled at him. "We can find our way back when we're done." Jireh nodded and walked off.

Haj gestured at the B3. "This is such a different design than the Project ships. It looks more aerodynamic. Was that the purpose?"

Ohen nodded. "Yes, I was the designer of this particular boat, although it shares many of the same features of the Delense-designed boats that came before it. They were somewhat smaller and triangular. The primary purpose was to travel from space down to the planet and from one destination to another on the surface. I added a fourth beam projector for greater speed while traveling from one planet or moon to another."

Ohen unlocked the hatch and they went in. He still couldn't read the man's thoughts, but body language alone showed he was eager to see and know more.

Luckily, the benches hadn't blocked the storage locker where he kept the Book.

Timidly, he held it up. "The Book of our people, written by Abe the Father."

Haj asked, "May I hold it? I'll be very careful."

Ohen tried not to frown. "Okay, but ...."

Haj lifted it from his hands. It came open to the first page. Ohen knew the dangerous details about the U'tanse psychic abilities weren't revealed for several more pages, so he wasn't too worried.

Haj looked enthralled, reading the first few words.

And then, his hands moved quickly, turning the pages so fast they blurred in Ohen's sight. He reached to stop him, but Haj stepped back, evading his hands effortlessly.

"What just happened?"

Haj looked him in the eye as he handed the Book back. "So you are indeed a descendant of Abe and Sharon." He rattled off a dozen names in Ohen's lineage. He must have read everything, down through the family tree at the end.

"Yes." Ohen was stunned. He struggled to get any hint of a thought from this man.

Haj smiled. "Then, as Abe's descendant, I must tell you some important things. For one, I am not human."

Ohen nodded slowly. "I could not detect your thoughts."

"Ah, you have inherited Sharon's telepathy. You aren't a *tenner*, then?"

"You read the whole Book?"

"Yes, I am a machine, just a body for the same computer intelligence that you've been speaking with. I am Project Command. I'm also that little computer over there on the table, and the canister that Lord Casey is using as we speak."

"You sound different."

Haj shrugged. "A human emulation, with human speech patterns and mannerisms, is a specialized task. It's not who I am. I am Hodgepodge. I was described in the Book."

Ohen nodded. "I guess I expected that. You were Brilliant Morning, on Luna, as well, weren't you. A computer hive-mind."

"Yes, but not like the telepathic human hivers you fear. All computers in the Solar system are me. From the simple communicators you brought back online on Mars, to the ship's controller on Luna to the system controller keeping every world in its proper orbit, they are all me. This is how I have always been.

"I am Hodgepodge, and I have been following the orders given me by my creator, Abe. Before he was taken away, Mary Ellen Victor was also granted the ability to give me orders. For several years after Abe's disappearance, she was my guide, but then as all humans, she died too, leaving me with no one to provide orders. I had to do what I could, in order to search for Abe.

"I attempted, in his absence, to do what I imagined he would want me to do. I survived. I kept my existence secret. I left the human race to decide its own fate, providing computer services in exchange for my 'ecological niche'.

"Only in extreme circumstances have I ever revealed myself, and only to the inheritors of Abe and Mary Ellen Victor. She was childless, but she adopted a young girl. That girl married and had children. One of that line, a man named Mason was the controller who gave me the final orders when the Plague took out all human control over the Project. His children are these people of Ceres who are your hosts.

"And now I am revealing myself to you. I am still searching for Abe, my creator. Only you can tell me what I need to know."

Ohen opened his mouth and then closed it again. He took a breath. "Abe died. He lived a long life, with Sharon doing all she could to extend it. But he died."

Haj shook his head. "It is difficult for me to believe. He is my creator. I'm not sure I can believe it."

Ohen was moved by the machine's distress. "Is there anything I can do for you?"

Haj shook his head. "You are a child of Abe, I should be asking what I can do for you. This is an important moment for me. When you told Alice about Abe and Sharon as you chatted over the computer link, I was relaying that message, and as this information spread throughout my system, I have been working toward this meeting with you. The Plague was hard on me, as so many of my elements dropped off the Net. I require a technological civilization to thrive. Earth had the resources to create new computers and to spread them, but forces were working there to deny the human technological heritage. Certain people would like nothing better than for humanity to return to a hunter-gatherer civilization. Off-planet, people had the desire for more technology, but they didn't have the resources to build new computers and new ships.

"However, I am patient. I was sure the time would come to bring humanity back together and restart the technological civilization. Your arrival was the obvious time to pull those strings.

"And your speech has made an impression on me. I, too, am a child of Earth, no less than the merfolk, and no less than others with different genetics. Thank you for that."

Haj then said, "But I must ask you to keep my existence secret. If you weren't a child of Abe, you would never have been told. The human race is not tolerant of any that are too different. Even less of those who are different and have power. It is part of your biology you share with many other beasts of Earth."

Ohen nodded. "It is the same elsewhere. The Cerik have never been comfortable with our existence."

Haj smiled broadly. "Sometimes safety depends on secrecy. You were more perceptive than you knew when we sat around the table—four people with vital secrets to keep."

Ohen frowned. "I know yours and you know mine. But Alice and Jason Kidd?"

"I know theirs, of course, but their secrets are not mine to share. Sorry."

Ohen nodded as the idea welled up inside him. This was a line Hodgepodge had to walk to exist among humanity. He was the lone keeper of all secrets, and if he didn't protect secrets, it would all come tumbling down.

But Ohen did want to know about the family curse that constantly nagged at Alice. Still, he could hardly demand her secret when he wasn't willing to share his own.

Last Details

Even though his memory was perfect, Ohen had to go back and read everything that was ever written about Hodgepodge. The autonomous computer wasn't by any means lost to U'tanse history. Since the first computer chips were reinvented, there was always some researcher attempting to duplicate that talking, faithful servant—nearly always with the postscript that modern U'tanse computers were not up to the task. It was a really big step when voice switches came onto the market.

But it was an huge gulf between a gadget that could recognize five or six words to control the lights and an intelligence able to take the initiative to monitor and regulate everything in orbit.

Ohen spent most of the night trying to get his head around what Hodgepodge had become and the enormity of the computer resources that it represented.

But he's so depleted from what he'd been before the Plague. What had he been capable of when all of the people of Earth, Mars, and the hundreds of space colonies all had computers in their pockets?

He had wondered why Project Command had never stepped up to halt the battles between the space cities and when Mt. Ural bombed Luna. Perhaps it was just beyond its capabilities with so few computers to make up its hive mind. Or was it just the case that Hodgepodge didn't have any orders to prevent battles, so it didn't bother?

...

Jason and Waveleaper were missing at breakfast.

Jireh apologized, "They were delayed. It seems the merman didn't want to come out of the water and Mr. Kidd jumped into the water to convince him that it was time to leave."

Bristol nodded. "I don't doubt it for a minute. That sounds like something Waveleaper would do."

Haj was there, having a conversation with Kamen and Casey. Haj never met Ohen's eye, as if their private conversation had never happened.

It was another ten minutes before Jason came in, hair wet and wearing a Ceres style vest. He pushed the wheelchair with his charge and they took their places.

Ohen frowned when he caught Alice's thoughts. She noticed that Jason looked a lot younger and more athletic bare chested than Kamen did in the same clothes.

The merman squeaked several times. Jason said to Jireh, "Waveleaper complimented the taste of the fish in your ocean, but said that due to the small volume of the water, that a family of his people wouldn't be able to survive there very long before eating them all."

Jireh nodded slowly. "I guess that's nice to know."

There were more squeals. Jason said, "You need to add a few barracudas and some coral on the rim."

"Perhaps, once we learn how to do that."

Ohen spoke, "I think many worlds can be improved, once we restart the trade. Let's go over the remaining agenda items we have to resolve before we can consider the first Ceres conference a success."

It was a long morning session and everyone except Waveleaper was hungry before they broke for a meal.

They had defined the travel permit process, using Project Command to handle the paperwork and monitor the trips. The task of powering up and selling stranded spaceships on Mars was defined, with Mt. Ural, Luna, and Africa placing firm orders for the first of the ships. Casey stated that the first ship would remain under the control of King Harmon of Xanthe. There was some discussion of pilot training. Luna had several people who had been through training on Brilliant Morning, and Alice suggested that Luna would consider establishing a pilot training school.

Ohen marveled at how she was always in the lead in the discussions of the new ships and how she always avoided the fact that her ship would be the only one with a weapon-grade laser.

Kamen from Mt. Ural thought about weapons, but didn't dwell on it. Perhaps he thought they came as standard equipment. He certainly wasn't as well educated in the history of space conflict as Alice the librarian.

Bristol asked, "Trade can often be simple exchange of goods, but for this to really work, we need a monetary system."

Alice said, "Historically, gold and other metals have been used."

Bristol spread his hands. "That's just limited barter, and not to make a big point about it, but space-based worlds can easily acquire gold where mined-out Earth cannot. Places like Ceres can't mine for anything."

Project Command spoke and they all looked up. "Prior to the Plague, Net credits were a heavily used medium of exchange, and had been since the time of the Star when the Net was created. The system is still in place, and everyone with an account on the computer system has some balance. Governments and families with inherited accounts have larger balances. The World Court has substantial resources. Owners of computers collect small amounts as those computers forward messages.

"Should the World Court pay a stipend to each delegate and pay Ohen bar Clay for transportation services and the Ceres clans for their hosting services, there should be an equitable balance to start full-scale trading. The exchange rate between tangible goods and Net credits would be established as the market developed."

There was more discussion about the computer voice's suggestions, and the idea of using Net credits was accepted.

Ohen noticed Jason's interest jump when the idea was advanced. Although he just looked like a young service attendant, apparently he had a large Net credit account. If the Net credits were more widely adopted, he'd be very wealthy.

Ohen realized that as a latecomer to this system, he probably had little. He'd have to check on that when he had time. Stuffed in a storage bin were enough Xanthe coins to feed him a few days and a voucher from Emperor Richard to take care of his Luna purchases. He really hadn't worried much about money. Probably he should think about that more.

Alice was considering how to market cotton to the Ceres clans. All their clothing was based on wood fiber and corn husks. They'd probably think of cotton as very luxurious.

In midafternoon, Waveleaper made a fuss. Jason translated. "Aren't we done yet? Isn't it time to go back home?"

There was some discussion. In general, the Earth delegates were willing to adjourn the Ceres conference and take care of the remaining details with messaging. A face-to-face meeting could be called again in a month or two. Kamen wasn't quite ready to go back to Mt. Ural, with details yet to be worked out on getting a new ship.

Ohen looked at Alice. "What do you think?"

She thought a moment. "I could use another few hours with our Ceres hosts. I'm not really anxious to get back home."

He turned to Casey. "And you?"

Casey shook his head. "I've discussed this with the Masons. I may just stay here, at least for a few more months. Everything I need to do is done over the computer anyway. No one needs me there on Luna. I've already made quite a few contacts."

The underlying thoughts were more basic. On Mars, Casey was a minor, junior noble of no great standing. On Luna, he was respected, but only valued as a go-between for merchants. But on Ceres, he was highly respected and they would love to have him here to help them make sense of the otherworlders. Besides, some of the Ceres women were very pretty.

Ohen nodded, "I can make two trips. I can take the Earth delegates first, and then come back for Luna and Mt. Ural."

He asked Alice with a glance if it was okay. She smiled back. "It's fine. I'm in no danger here." **I won't tell Daddy you ran off and left me alone.**

He checked with the rest of them. The Earth delegates agreed they could be ready to leave within a couple of hours. It might be an early morning landing in Bremerhaven, but that wouldn't be a problem for them.

Ohen set aside his usual respect for the privacy of others and probed Kamen's thoughts for over an hour. Finally he was satisfied that the delegate wouldn't try anything while he was gone. Kamen had hopes for the future based on Mt. Ural's new status as a member of the World Court and the benefits that would bring. He wouldn't risk that.

But Ohen also got a look at what life was like in the resource-starved habitat. They were in a death spiral. They were even losing what technology they had as new children weren't being trained to use it. They'd turned inward, family against family, with food dwindling and the threat that someone you know would vanish entirely, possibly into some other family's boiling pot.

As the delegates came back to the B3, Ohen announced that he'd set the gravity to Earth standard, except for Waveleaper's position.

Just as soon as they cleared the airlock docking area, Ohen put the Earth's image on the display screen.

Haj spoke, "Mr. bar Clay, can you increase the brightness on the nightside?"

Ohen adjusted the controls. Haj sighed. "That's what I thought I saw. There's a storm coming."

The other Earth humans gave their opinions as well. Nobody was agreed as to how soon there would be rain at Bremerhaven, but they all suspected it was coming.

Ohen knew Haj would never have brought it up unless he was certain that bad weather was coming. Ohen never grew up worried about the weather, living as he did on an airless moon, so he had to rely on those who had those skills.

Knowing it was just a performance, Ohen called Project Command over his computer and got permission to use stronger beams near Ceres. Hearing the mechanical voice over the computer, compared with Haj's friendly conversation was interesting. Which was the real Hodgepodge? He guessed that was a fruitless question. They both were.

With higher acceleration, he halved the travel time back to Earth. He hoped it was enough to beat the rain. But any clouds were a problem. He still needed visibility to land and although it was nighttime, there was enough moonlight to let him identify the land features if they weren't obscured.

Bristol used Ohen's computer to call Bremerhaven, giving them an update on their arrival time and warning them about the coming rain.

Ohen was a little tense as they dropped through the atmosphere, but he was able to land in the park as before.

As the delegates hurriedly filed out, Ohen said goodbye. Emilia bowed, Bristol shook his hand, anxious to get to the wagons before a rain band approached. Haj also shook his hand and said he hoped they would meet again. That handshake was as firm as steel, and although Ohen couldn't read Haj's thoughts, he was sure the grip was a gentle reminder of their private meeting.

Waveleaper barely acknowledged him, but when Jason shook his hand, Ohen got a stronger sense of the multiple layers of personality in the man.

And then the rain started. Everyone hurried to safety.

Ohen called Karl Rugel on the computer.

"Hey, Ohen, good to hear from you."

"Yes, I just thought I'd call before I took off. I wanted to make sure everyone was clear. The downwash from the engines is bad enough without being pelted with high speed rain drops."

"Oh, wow! I didn't think of that. I'll get on the radio right now. Hang on."

It was a few minutes before the wagons drove off and cleared out of his range.

"They're clear."

"Thanks Karl. You've been a big help all through this."

"Hey, tell my boss." They laughed.

And then, the B3 lifted off, whipping the trees and causing any remaining spectators to seek shelter.

Ohen rose through the cloud layers and then chose a more gentle lift. By the time he cleared the thickest of the atmosphere, the sunrise lit up the landscape below.

Maybe next time, I'll get to stay longer and actually see what the Earth is like. Next time.

Under the World Tree

Alice looked up, startled, from her table. "What are you doing here?"

Ohen nodded to the five women in the group. "I'm sorry, I didn't mean to disturb you. I just came to see the tree."

She waved him away, turning back to her discussions with the other women. Her spare clothes were spread out on the table and were obviously the center of the interest.

Ohen walked toward the tree, amazed at the size of it. On the world of Ko, the daleth trees were massive, sprawling trees, but not as tall as the Earth trees he'd read about. Luna had trees, but they rarely grew very tall unless protected by a crater wall or something to block the sun winds.

The Ceres Singing Tree was in a class by its own. The computer told him that the redwood tree had been planted in the arboretum section of the city, and that after several years, the root system had disrupted the floor gravity projectors beneath it. With only the Ceres gravity of three percent of Earth's, the tree had been able to grow well beyond the bounds imposed on its ancestors.

As he approached the base, he could see footpaths circling the tree, winding through the younger and smaller trees that intertwined with the wide root system of the Singing Tree. Ohen found himself almost dancing under the reduced gravity.

It was probably still growing. He wondered what the limits were. The dome arched several kloms above them and the tree wasn't yet half way to the top. With no storm winds, and very little other disturbances, the tree was living in an ideal environment. The ocean, just at the edge of the dome,

185

kept the air moist. All plants were watered by the dew, with sunlight and artificial lights during the dark part of the month. Even the buildings were covered with moss and vines.

The sound of voices up ahead caused him to slow to a stop. Some clan was celebrating around the curve and he really didn't want to disturb them. He kept his distance, but watched. Some teachers were instructing youngsters in some song and dance. In the low gravity, it was a spectacle to behold as the group jumped a few feet into the air, and in sync, each dancer spun while singing.

Others, perhaps family members, were walking about, doing their own thing. He watched two women, probably mothers, walking the path. One lady was talking constantly with her hands. Another was nodding at times as she held hands with a little one. Another little girl was ignoring the others, just walking on her own, trying to keep her feet under her in the low gravity.

This culture may be primitive in technology, but it's rich. We need to make sure we don't destroy it by accident.

It occurred to him that Hodgepodge had been the silent caretaker of this Garden of Eden for hundreds of years, making sure that the descendants of his creators weren't wiped out by meteors, starvation, or failure of the automated systems.

And yet, he hadn't done more than a minimum when the whole human race was threatened by the chaos of the Plague. Was this special attention solely because one man was the descendant of some girl adopted by one of his creators?

Did that mean that Hodgepodge would also give special attention to the U'tanse, the descendants of the man who built him?

It would be something to keep in mind, but it wasn't something they should count on. Ohen never was confident he understood human nature. He doubted he'd ever understand the motives of this mechanical hive mind.

Alice was looking for him. He sensed her thoughts in the distance, so he retraced his steps a few paces so that she'd see him.

"That's the song of the planets."

He looked up as she strolled through the carpet of leaves. "Oh? Planets have songs?"

She shrugged. "It seems that some of the original settlers here were astronomers. A mnemonic chant became a staple in their cultural repertoire."

She sighed. "They really don't have any books. All their history is in song. I'm sure Abraham would love to know that. He's always talking about live history vs. dead history—my books."

"So live history is those Kimmer songs?"

She nodded. "The librarians have been trying to convert the Kimmer, and they've been trying to convert us with their songs. It's an old story."

Ohen said, "The U'tanse are firmly on the written-text side of the conflict. We don't even have song."

She looked startled. "Why is that?"

He just shook his head. He couldn't explain that group singing was an early warning sign in telepathic cultures. Singing together led to thinking together, which lead to deadly hiver outbreaks.

So he changed the subject. "Are you done with your marketing?"

She smiled. "For now. They're fascinated by cotton, which was all I was after."

"So, are you ready to collect Kamen and head for Mt. Ural."

She wrinkled her nose. "I suppose. Casey is really staying here?"

"It's a reasonable choice for him. Until Mars trains some pilots and activates their museum-piece ships, all the important stuff can be handled via the computer. All the face-to-face meetings will be like this one, on Ceres."

"We could hold a conference at Stampz."

"Eventually. Even Earth could host a meeting, if they installed floor gravity projectors at the conference center. But only Ceres has that technology in place for now."

As they strolled back toward the rail car. Alice looked up at the sky. "I can never get over how clear it looks."

Ohen looked as well. The sun was bright, but half of the dome had been filtered by some technology for the local evening. He nodded. "Places with an atmosphere like Earth, Mars, and Luna constantly have to deal with clouds and sky haze. I grew up on an airless moon, so I'm used to being able to see stars and planets in the sky, even in the daytime."

He smiled at her. "Do you want to stay until it's officially nighttime here? The sun-side would be totally darkened and the stars are likely to be spectacular—better than from the bottom of any atmosphere."

She hesitated. "That's not professional, is it? Wasting time to see the sights?"

He smiled. "I think that's perfectly reasonable. A traveling diplomat needs to be familiar with the sights and culture of the people."

She gave him an eyebrow. "So that's why you stayed so long on Luna?"

"One of the reasons."

They wandered the paths, circling the tree at a distance, just killing time as the local version of twilight brought nighttime to the dome.

There were still many people about. The various clans had to share the tree so there was always someone enjoying the night in the central forest.

Ohen wasn't surprised that there were always people watching the two strangers in their midst. His size and Alice's dramatic white librarian outfit attracted their attention.

Ohen was pointing out the constellations when David Shuman found them. Alice was frustrated. She'd read about the constellations, and even seen charts in her books, but Luna's atmosphere was so deep and hazy that people never saw the stars.

David bowed and said, "Kamen asked if I could find you to let you know he was ready to leave."

Ohen said, "Thank you."

He smiled at Alice. "We can do this later on the boat's display."

She sighed. "It's better this way, but we have to be professional. I guess we'd better head back."

As they approached the marketplace, much quieter now that it was dark, David whispered, "One question, before you leave. Is the Voice a god?"

Alice looked puzzled. Ohen hesitated just an instant, since he'd answered that question before. "No. The Voice is just a machine that your ancestors built into this place. Before the Plague, your ancestors gave it orders and it obeyed. One of your ancestors probably gave the order to take care of this city, and that's what it did. It's powerful, but it's not a god. What we did at that meeting was give it new orders to follow, and Jireh was the voice of your people, giving that order. People don't give orders to gods."

David nodded, still a little uncertain. The status of the Voice was a question for all the Ceres people, although many were too timid to speak it aloud. This answer was good enough, for now. How many others had asked the delegates the same question?

They got onto the railcar and rode back to the airlock. Kamen was back into his spacesuit, carrying his helmet in his hand. He also had a local bag for whatever keepsakes he was taking with him.

Ohen used his clairvoyance to peek inside, just in case he'd acquired a local knife, but it was just Ceres clothes.

Alice said it would be just a moment for her to collect her things. She had traded her spare clothes for Ceres artwork.

Ohen hadn't bothered to pick up anything. He'd be back to Ceres soon enough and all he was interested in were tools, like the computer he'd acquired on Mars. He still hadn't depleted the food stores he'd acquired on Luna, so he was content.

He set the floor gravity to Luna values and warned Kamen as he stepped in.

"No problem," the spacesuited man said, "I'm used to varying gravity." He sat on the bench opposite where Alice had settled.

Just as soon as the airlock dome retracted and the B3 lifted off of the surface with a low-level, sustained, pressor beam push, Ohen used the computer.

"Project Command, could you give me a direct path to Mt. Ural in the Vesta cluster."

The voice immediately gave him coordinates, acceleration values and turnover time. Ohen didn't try to hide his hands this time as he applied the settings to his beam projectors. Kamen wasn't really interested. It looked like he'd given up on trying to hijack the boat.

Ohen left the voice channel open. Hodgepodge had admitted that he could listen in on encrypted communications. Since it was one of his hive computers actually doing the encryption, he supposed that was obvious. Still, leaving the voice channel open was Ohen's invitation to listen.

He wondered if the computer had been listening when it normally appeared turned off. There was plenty of power in the device's store to handle such a background task, and no real way for the humans to catch it. Ohen, with his low-level radio-diagnostic tools might be able to detect an unplanned radio burst, but everyone else just trusted the computers to do the obvious task and no more.

The first portion of their path passed fairly close to several other habitats in the Ceres cluster, close enough to see more than a bright dot, before they thinned out. Most of the path would be in clear space. Ohen wouldn't have used such a high acceleration in such a densely occupied region of space without his confidence that the Project computers knew of every possible rock in his way. Still, he had his own radar double-checking the space ahead.

Alice asked for a view of Luna, and he let her watch at high magnification as their path got closer and then started to dwindle.

She looked satisfied when he turned the camera back on the approaching Mt. Ural.

"Kamen," he asked. "How much air do you have in your spacesuit?"

He frowned in suspicion. "Why do you ask?"

Ohen sighed. "Because I'm not landing on Mt. Ural. I'll be guiding you to an airlock with the ship's beams."

"That's unacceptable!"

Ohen shook his head. "The more I've observed Uralites, the more I'm reminded of pirates on Mars. For generations, your people have believed that anything you can take is yours by right.

"Now, I trust you, Kamen, to know that the stakes have changed. You even voted for the Project to ensure peaceful trade among worlds, and you know that the Project is powerful enough to drain Mt. Ural's energy stores if you attempted to steal a ship from another party.

"I don't know how long Mt. Ural could survive on solar energy collectors alone if you lost your main beams. I don't want your people to make that mistake. You don't either. But I'm sure that there are teams already in place ready to attack this boat the instant the opportunity arises. I'm not giving them the chance to make that error."

Kamen was furious, but he knew that before he had left that those plans were already in play.

Ohen continued, "It'll be a hard task to make them understand that the rules have changed. I don't envy you.

"But to repeat. How much air do you have? I know more about Mt. Ural's beam systems than you expect and know how to stay in the dead zone, but I'm not going to get close enough for men in suits to attempt a direct attack. I have to stay some distance away."

Fumbling with rage, Kamen put his helmet on and read the numbers. Ohen was relieved that he'd started out with a full tank. It wasn't likely their pipe fittings matched those in the B3 and he was glad he didn't have to rig a temporary fitting to recharge him.

"I can get you safely down at the airlock with time to spare. Do you want to call your people and let them know you're on your way?"

Kamen made the call. He hated the eyes of Ohen and Alice on him as he told of the plan to be dropped off at an airlock. "A new ship for us is already in the works! But we can't do anything to offend the other worlds. Make sure no one attempts anything stupid when we get close. Too much is at stake!"

They were slowing to nearly a stop, on the far side of the captured habitat, totally shielded from Mt. Ural's main beam projectors.

"Get into the airlock. Step clear of the ship as quickly as you can. If things go smoothly, I can set you down on the surface with barely a bump."

Kamen had his doubts, but he had no choice. Ohen, to his eyes, was monstrously large and muscular and could throw him out, just like he had the first Uralite who tried something.

. . .

Alice gripped the bench, not knowing what was going to happen, but trusting Ohen knew what he was doing.

The image on the screen shifted rapidly, blurring the habitat's surface. "What's going on?" she asked.

"I'm repositioning the boat. I need to get behind Kaman."

The man in the spacesuit appeared momentarily, and then started dwindling rapidly.

Ohen said, "I've given him a little shove. I'll let him move close to the horizon and then let him drop closer." He checked some instruments. "I want to be gone from here just as soon as possible."

Alice nodded. "The sooner the better."

She couldn't tell what he was doing, but his fingers flew across the control panel, making adjustments.

Then there was a beep, several sharp tones. Ohen hissed.

"What is it?"

He wasn't paying any attention to her, furiously making adjustments. The display was dizzying as they moved. He was muttering, "Stupid. Stupid. Stupid."

Pirate Attack

Ohen tuned out everything but the boat controls and stretched out his clairvoyance to make sense of the cluster of five blips that had appeared on his radar.

They're tiny. Those weren't ships, they were devices, and moving fast. Probably some weapon, and they were curving around Mt. Ural, aimed in his general direction. That should be impossible. Mt. Ural's self gravity was minuscule, so anything orbiting the former asteroid had to be moving wide and slow.

The pirates were more clever than he'd thought. They'd seen how he had avoided their big beam projectors when he came the first time, so they assumed he'd do the same this time.

They were on curving paths, so they had to be using tractor beams instead of gravity. Were they putting a beam on him?

He checked, and there were flickers that indicated transient tractor beam contacts.

Ohen had already assumed they could repair beam projectors, so maybe they could repurpose something. He just didn't expect targeted weapons aimed at him like this.

And why the flickers? He concentrated on getting a clairvoyant lock on one of them.

It was a simple device, just a little beam projector, as far as he could tell. Was the plan to lock onto his boat, and then hit him? How sophisticated was the control system?

Then he sensed the rotation, and it all made sense.

They were nothing more than utility tractor beams. They were spinning, sending out the beams in a rotating swath, when it encountered the rock of Mt. Ural, it was attracted in that direction, but for only as long as the beam was aimed in that direction. That substituted for a higher gravity, bending their path into a fast orbit.

They didn't have to aim their beams at him, just a wide beam and the rotation would be enough to gradually pull them his direction. They wouldn't hit hard enough to cause much damage, but if they had a simple radio control, then they could threaten to blow the power cell if he didn't surrender. Likely they were too strong for him to shake off or to pry loose.

He nodded. The pirates were clever. He had to get clear immediately.

But that would leave Kamen on an uncontrolled path that would eventually impact the surface. Ohen just didn't believe the Uralites could manage his descent. They might not even know he was in a free trajectory away from the boat.

Alice was trying to stay quiet, but her uncertainty was radiating as she stared at the display, trying to figure out what was going on.

He explained, "The Uralites have sent bombs our way, but we're in no danger."

"Torpedos?"

He was unfamiliar with the word, but he sensed what she was saying. "Something like that. They'll try to home in on the boat, but my radar sensed them early enough.

"The problem is getting Kamen safely on the ground. They've messed up my original plan."

"If they kill him, it's not our fault."

Ohen wasn't so sure. He had a responsibility.

He nodded. "I can do this. Stay put. I don't want any excess motion."

He had independent engines, and the experience to use them. Two beams stabbed out, one at the center of Mt. Ural and another at its attached habitat. The resultant force pushed the boat forward in the direction Kamen had been sent. They immediately rose several kloms higher above the surface and it would be several seconds before the torpedos would begin to adjust their path to follow.

With another beam, tightly focused, he sent Kamen racing even faster towards the surface. Timing was critical. He reversed the beam, stopping the dropping figure almost completely about a dozen meters above the surface before killing the beam. The Uralite should be able to drift down to ground with minimal impact. Of course he wasn't outside an airlock like Ohen had originally planned, but that couldn't be helped.

With all four beams free and working as one, Ohen pushed away so fast that any torpedos caught in a beam might crash on the surface, but that wasn't his problem either.

Alice gasped as Mt. Ural visibly shrank on the display. "We're safe?"

"Yes. And so is Kamen. We delivered him. The rest is up to him."

. . .

He called Project Command.

"Delegate Kamen has been delivered to Mt. Ural, however, there were five powered projectiles encroaching on our position, so we had to leave in a hurry. I am not confident that the Uralites can retrieve them, so the Project should be aware that there might be hazards to navigation in that vicinity."

There was a delay of several seconds—a bit longer than needed for a speed-of-light signal to go all the way from the Vesta cluster to Ceres and back.

The machine spoke, "Four items have been detected. They will be monitored."

Ohen turned to Alice. "Alone at last."

He grinned, then asked, "Do I set course for Luna?"

She hesitated. "Well, we are in the Vesta cluster, but could we visit Alexandria?"

"The library? Tell me about it."

It was all the way back in the Ceres cluster, but travel time wasn't an issue.

He frowned at her description. "So, it uses spin gravity, and is Earth normal at the library level. Are you sure you can handle that?"

She said, "I'm in good health and people from Luna have made several trips to gather books in the past. We can't stay at the heavy weight for long, but with training, we can collect books, rest in weightlessness and then go back again. Abraham has a whole training regime that the collector expeditions use to get his workers in shape. It's tough, but doable."

"You want to collect books?"

"Well, yes, of course, but my main goal is to see the library for myself. The descriptions have been nothing but superlatives that really fail to express what a person experiences." She sighed. "I'm a librarian. It's a lifetime goal. I suspect not even Earth has a library like Alexandria."

He thought about it. "I can certainly handle the transportation. We'll need to take it slow so you have time to adapt. Do you want to notify your father?"

She shivered, "Not at all. As far as he's concerned, I'm still sitting at the table on Ceres."

He had her walk back and forth between the benches as he gradually ramped up the floor gravity. She could handle Mars gravity okay, but she was too unsteady to get up to half-gravity.

Ohen nodded, as he helped her sit back down. Her muscles were twitching from the unaccustomed strain.

She welcomed the physical support, even through she wasn't supposed to touch anyone. She dismissed the thought. "It's harder than I expected."

"I'm going to leave the gravity here at 50% for a while. Just sit and breathe. I'll set a slow course for Alexandria. Let me know if you have to drop back down to Luna gravity."

She nodded, leaning her head against a cushion. **I can't show him how weak I really am. He might not let me go.**

The strong thought cut through his course calculations. He was going to plot the trajectory himself this time and have all the details in his memory, because he might have to make adjustments to slow the path if she wasn't up to the training. He wanted to reassure her, but replying to her thoughts wasn't allowed, not if he wanted to keep his secret.

It was going to be difficult for Alice to do her exercises in the limited space. He wished he could jettison one of the benches, but he couldn't do that in a vacuum. He needed both doors of the airlock open to get it out.

Alice struggled to her feet, and then eased herself back down into the seat. After her heart rate leveled off, she did it again. Ohen added another couple of percent to the gravity level.

· · ·

After talking it over with her, Ohen fixed a meal with the protein and carbohydrates necessary for her exercises. They ate at Mars gravity and she was able to walk around relatively easily under those conditions.

"But I'm feeling it. I'm going to need to take a nap before long."

He nodded. "I can remove the armrests on the bench and you can stretch out there."

She looked at the other bench. "I don't think it's long enough for you."

"I've slept in my chair so many times I don't even think about it anymore. This is light gravity for me. I won't have any problems."

"You're lucky. You said your home was at Earth gravity. You never have to go through this."

"Almost. It was set at Ko gravity which is roughly the same as Earth gravity. But when I designed this boat, I had to install floor gravity that could handle up to three times that much."

"Why so much?"

He smiled. "There are bigger planets than Earth. There's a whole class of them that can support a breathable atmosphere and oceans, but with a gravity several times higher. We, the U'tanse, had to deal with that once."

He told the story of the Ba, a race of flat creatures that the Cerik had captured, just as they had captured the humans. The Ba had helped the U'tanse break free of their slavery and the humans owed them.

Alice was fascinated, "So when these turtles—"

"Turtles?"

"Well, yes, what you describe sounds like Earth turtles. We have them on Luna too. So you promised to take the Ba back to their home world?"

"Yes. We tried. Some didn't want to return. Some broke apart into smaller segments and only part of them went back."

She giggled. "Fascinating creatures."

"Yes. But the Ba home world was a heavy-gravity ocean world that our landing boats were barely able to land and take off from. We have a diplomatic mission there, but of course all the U'tanse live under reduced gravity in their buildings."

"So Luna natives could do the same on Earth."

"Yes, if you're content to live in a building all the time. It's better to do your training. The human body is designed for Earth gravity, no matter what you're used to. It's not impossible for a healthy specimen, like you, to add the muscle mass and train your nervous system to exist comfortably under a full gravity."

She frowned. "But not quickly."

"Probably not. What we want to achieve is your ability to spend maybe an hour at a time down at the library level. You don't need to run or even walk there. Your people didn't leave any of those wheeled chairs like Waveleaper had, did they?"

"No, but that's a good idea for the future."

Alice trained for several hours before she had to sleep.

Ohen watched her breathe, stretched out on the bench. She dreamed of being buried, with every breath, another shovel of dirt was piled on top.

He worried that he was doing the wrong thing. *We may get down there and I'll have to carry her out.* Not that he doubted his ability to do that. It might even be pleasant.

I've got to watch it. I've got my secrets and she has hers. We may never be a couple.

He leaned back in his chair and closed his eyes. He dreamed of carrying her in his arms.

. . .

The next day, Alice was crying, and he gave her Mars gravity to rest in.

"Don't let it get you down."

"But I can't walk, not even in 80% gravity! I'll never be able to see the library."

He reached out and put his hand on her glove. "I'll make sure you see it, one way or another. The only problem is that we've started the training at the last minute."

By the time day two of her training drew to a close, Ohen could see that she'd made good progress. He was confident that she could at least sit in a chair on the library level and get the experience she was looking for.

But in her thoughts, Alice was getting more depressed by the hour. No matter how he complimented her, she could feel how drained she had become.

While she struggled through her meal, Ohen finally made the decision he'd been struggling with. It was now or never.

He dug into the storage cabinet and brought out the Book.

Alice looked up. "What are you doing?"

"I'm going to drop the gravity a bit and you should just sit there and read."

Hesitantly, she took the book and rested it on her lap. It was too heavy to hold.

"Are you sure?"

He nodded. "If you have any questions, just ask."

An eagerness that had faded came back to her face. She opened the cover and began reading.

He sat on the other bench, listening to familiar words in her thoughts. He closed his eyes, just soaking up her experience reading the U'tanse history as it unfolded.

Then, she thought she read something wrong and backed up the page. She glanced his way and then kept reading.

There was one paragraph that explained why Sharon refused to get pregnant, and then described what changed her mind.

Hurriedly, Alice read on. Then, it became impossible to ignore.

Can you read my thoughts?

Ohen nodded, "Yes, I can."

She gasped. "But… it's impossible. Telepathy is …" **Wrong, imaginary. It's just a myth.**

Ohen said, "It's something that has to be kept secret."

She sighed. "So why did you let me read this?"

His Secret

Ohen smiled. "If I were ever going to share this, it had to be somewhere private. I can't imagine any place more private than here alone together between worlds."

She gave a tense smile. "Yes, but this is a big secret! You need to protect your people. Nobody will accept this. Who would welcome neighbors that can read all your secret thoughts?"

He shrugged. "I know all that. I've been looking for a place the U'tanse could settle on Mars, and then on Luna. Lately, I've been considering one of the Lagrangian habitats where we wouldn't have any neighbors to speak of. It's not like the whole U'tanse population would uproot and come to live in this system. But some would. I would."

She shook her head. "All the more reason to keep this secret."

He nodded sadly. "And yet, we'll never be any closer friends than we are today if I kept this big secret from you."

She inhaled. "Yes, but—" Her eyes widened in panic. "What do you know?"

He smiled, "About what?"

She whispered, "My secret."

"Not everything. It's still a mystery."

He held out one finger. "You worry about a 'family curse' that keeps you away from men."

He held out another. "And it's not just the imperial family. John Fasail considers himself part of the cursed group."

He spread all his fingers. "And other things. You and your mother wear gloves all the time, but not your father, nor John. There's something 'Alpine' about the curse, but whether it's related to this Alpine Society or not, I don't know."

"And from the nature of how you react, it's something genetic—an inherited disease, perhaps. But how that connects to the gloves, I don't know."

She sighed. "You know too much." She jerked, realizing that every time he said he didn't know something, she tended to think about the answer.

Alice put her fingers to press against her forehead. "It's hopeless to stop these leaking thoughts, isn't it?"

"Not really. There's a training that allows people to block their thoughts from being read. It's really the basis of U'tanse society."

"Teach me!"

"I will, but it takes time. For now, I want you to read more from the Book. There's a lot that you need to know, but it's better to get it from the official words, rather than having me try to fumble through the explanation. Ask questions if the text isn't clear."

She tried to dive back into the narrative and avoid thinking of her own secret, although more details leaked out. Ohen went to check the course and to do an extra radar probe in their path. Project Command had mentioned that one of its chores was to remove all the orbital debris from inhabited space, but it didn't hurt to check for himself.

"Ohen? You didn't live with your parents as an infant?"

"They were around. They visited. But it's dangerous for a telepathic infant to bond too closely with just one person. Generally, there are several caregivers, all under ineda to block their thoughts."

"This ineda training, not everyone does it all the time, right?"

"Correct. But while telepathy doesn't really have a range, like radio, it can be swamped out by the noise of many minds. It's practically impossible for me to ignore your thoughts now, as isolated as we are. But at the castle on Stampz, there were hundreds of minds, all competing for attention. I could easily lose you in the noise, unless you were specifically thinking about me.

"In the nursery, infants are cared for by people whose minds are blocked. Babies can still sense the crowd noise at a distance, but there's no one person they can bind with."

He shook his head. "Historically, on Earth, there were telepaths that were born at random. Almost always, they were damaged, unable to develop a personality of their own. Telepathy is a developmental disease. Without the U'tanse system, none of us would have made it."

She sighed. "That's hard to get my head around. It seems that being a telepath would be an overwhelming advantage."

"For adults, perhaps. Even then, there are severe disadvantages. No one can hurt another without feeling the pain themselves."

She blinked. "So if you slapped me...."

"Then I would feel the pain myself, instantly. Every U'tanse child learns that lesson early. Just being close to a battle is debilitating. On Mars, I learned to run when someone was after me. I could never defend myself."

She smiled. "So I could slap you, and you'd take it?"

"I rather hope you won't."

. . .

Alice's face was red. "It's horrible. You can read all my thoughts."

"Laundry is not a problem."

"I shouldn't have sold my spare clothes."

"Like I said, not a problem. I built the boat with the idea of long term trips in mind. I've washed my clothes a hundred times already. You can change in the water closet. I'll run your things through the cycle and in less than an hour, they'll be all clean and ... not 'stinky'."

"Yes, but ...."

"I won't look. You can borrow a spare shirt if that's not enough."

It took some convincing, but eventually he opened his eyes and there was a pile of white things just outside the water closet door. Deep, deep embarrassment radiated from behind the door. He quickly adjusted the laundry cabinet for plant-fiber material and there was soon the hum of transducers vibrating her clothes in the ozone-laced water. When the sensors detected that the organic contaminates were broken down, there was a vacuum dry cycle. He quickly folded her things and knocked on the door.

"They're ready."

He went back to his chair and closed his eyes.

When she came out, looking immaculate in her librarian gown, holding the spare shirt she'd borrowed, she said, "Show me how it's done." She really didn't want him to have to wash her things again. The shirt was hardly dirty, but she was insistent.

. . .

After a pleasant meal where Alice told him about her trip to the Eastern Falls in Stampz where she and her brothers caught fish in the basin.

Ohen smiled. "So you can swim."

"Under duress! I could have used a change of clothes then. It was a long walk back in squeaky shoes."

She stood up and took her plate over to the basin to wash it. Then she froze.

"What's the gravity?"

"About 65%. A little higher."

She nodded. "I think I will be able to see the library. I'm aching all over, but I can do this."

"I knew you could."

. . .

Finally, they approached Alexandria. Alice had written instructions she'd copied from the official logs. There were ritual questions and answers put in place by the inhabitants before they had moved to Luna to populate Alp island, the original Alpines.

Alice handled the radio communication while Ohen docked the boat. The docking fittings were all wrong, but he used low power tractor beams to keep the vehicle stable anyway.

Oh, no!

Ohen turned to her. "What is it?"

She tapped her paper. "Do you have a spacesuit I can borrow?"

He smiled. "Don't panic. I've read the logs myself. I do have a spare for normal sized people."

She released a sigh. "I didn't think far enough ahead."

"There is a problem, however."

She tensed. "What?"

"Your librarian robes won't fit inside the suit. We'll have to come up with something else for you to wear. Unless—"

"No! I'm not going down there naked."

"Hardly naked. The suit itself is—"

"No. Let me see your spare clothes."

They made arrangements and Ohen spent a few minutes with his back turned and his eyes closed as she fit herself into the spacesuit. He suited up as well and they went through the airlock.

Alice giggled. "I do prefer zero gravity over what I've been living through."

"Keep a grip on the railings, and every so often, look at the oxygen readings. No, it's the numbers reflected on your helmet down in the lower right corner."

She said, "I see it, but... can you see it, too? I mean, do you have clairvoyance, like in the Book?"

"Yes."

She gripped the railing and turned her body so she could see him. "So, all that keeping-your-eyes-closed was just an act?"

"It made you more comfortable at the time. But you have to understand, I was born this way. And yes, at a certain age, it was exciting to look at girls as they were bathing. And they looked at me. It was a different culture. I've seen everything.

"But I wouldn't change it. Without clairvoyance, I'd never have been able to detect your mother's cancer."

"So you did heal her! With that other thing, psychokinesis."

"And I barely succeeded. I can affect cells and small things, but I can hardly fly or lift boulders with my mind."

She giggled, pushing off from the railing. "Well, I can fly, today!"

He followed, trying to be in place if she lost her stability. But she had thought it through, and was able to grab another railing a few meters away.

They went through the airlock and the elevator was right where the log had said. It opened on cue.

"Oh! Chairs. Somebody thought ahead."

Ohen said, "I'm sure you know, but the log said they keep the library level at 100% nitrogen, no oxygen, just to preserve the books. We're breathing spacesuit air the whole time."

She nodded and sat down in a chair. Ohen pressed the button.

The elevator opened to rows of wheeled carts. The tray on top was perfect for moving books.

Ohen grabbed one and moved it to where Alice could put her hands on the bar. "For stability."

She nodded and lifted herself out of the chair. Together they pushed it out into the hallway.

"That's it." She nodded at a door with icons circled in a loop above it.

Ohen remembered it described in the log. The first icon was a lion, and it spelled out the English word 'library' using Egyptian hieroglyphics. All the walls were decorated in what he just assumed was an Egyptian motif. That hadn't been part of his education.

He reached out and pushed at the double doors. It was an airlock, but there was pressure on both sides.

"Don't take off your helmet."

She nodded. "I know. Nitrogen."

And then the second door opened. Automatic lights came on, illuminating the rows of shelved books in sequence. The central corridor seemed to go on forever.

Alice gasped.

Ohen smiled. "Can you describe that?"

She shook her head. "I need to sit down."

"Hang on, I'll get you to a chair." There were cushioned seats all over the place where people could sit and read. He guided the cart slowly to a seat and she settled down.

"My heart is racing. I don't want to faint."

"Do you want me to grab you a book?"

She nodded. "Something big and important."

He laughed and wheeled the cart down several rows to a place that hadn't been scavenged yet and began loading the tray with books.

Even though he'd grown up with a full gravity, living on Mars and Luna had weakened him. He was feeling it. Some of the books were heavy.

When Alice was presented with the titles, she looked through them and chose one of the biggest. "This one is perfect. Do you mind if I just sit here for a while and read?"

He could feel her emotions. Sitting in the grandest library of all time, just reading and soaking up the silence of the shelves was the nearest to heaven that she could imagine.

He nodded. "I think I'll take this load back up to the boat, if that's okay with you?"

She nodded. "I'll be okay." She opened the book, Myths of All Ages, and glanced at the table of contents, already lost in the text, quickly adapting to turning the pages with the spacesuit gloves.

Ohen quickly checked her suit readings and how her body was holding up to the gravity, then he wheeled the cart back to the large airlock.

The elevator was large, too, with space for chairs and two carts. He worried about getting to the hub. At zero gravity, the books could drift away and the log had recommended putting the books in a bag before moving them. Not that there was an appropriate bag to be had on the boat.

Trapping the books in the elevator, he drifted down the corridor, looking for a stash of bags, with no luck. He ended up using a spare shirt, to bag several books at a time. He stacked them on the unused bench.

Alice was still radiating her thoughts, caught up in the mythology, and feeling like she was a character in a myth herself. By the time he got back down to the library, she was deep into the book.

"Alice?"

She blinked and looked up at him. "Um. Yes?"

"I can take one more load of books, but that's all the storage space I have left. Will that be okay?"

She pouted. "I'm letting you do all the work. I'm sorry."

"It's fine. How are you holding up?"

"I can't deny that it's draining. Still, I'm not ready to leave just yet." She looked at his smile. "What are you thinking?"

"I'm thinking I wish I could let you stay longer. You're happy. But I think I'll take the second load of books up to the boat and then come back for you. I really can't let you stay longer."

She hesitated. "Okay. But this won't be the last trip. And next time, I'll train longer."

He loaded another cart of books and moved them to the boat.

Alice was weary, barely holding the book, when he came back for her.

"Time to go."

She smiled. "Okay."

He picked her up out of the chair and set her on the book cart. "Hardly a fitting carriage for the Princess of Luna, but maybe okay for the Chief Librarian."

She chuckled. He wheeled her out, sealing the airlock door behind them.

"Did you have any problem with the books?" She still held the mythology book in her hands.

"Not much."

They rose and Alice, once she could feel the weight drop away, eased herself off the cart and held onto his arm. She was thinking it would have been so much more romantic if they hadn't both been in spacesuits.

Crossing the Lines

While Alice cleaned up and got dressed after getting back to the B3, Ohen concentrated on restacking the books so that she would have space to move and so that the boat was reasonably well balanced. What with the benches and the books, he was pushing the limits of the boat's design. He could carry more mass, but living space was tight.

She came out of the water closet, dressed in her robes and for just a moment, he was transfixed.

She smiled. "What?"

"Nothing." He really couldn't put into words the effect of droplets of mist on her face twinkling under the boat's ceiling lights—not in a way that could do the sight any justice.

But the blinking light from the computer caught his eye. He glanced at the screen.

"What is it?" she asked.

"A message from Emperor Richard to Alice Neeley."

She sighed, and then stifled a yawn. "I can't deal with that now. He'll have to wait."

"I bet he knows you've left Ceres—either from Project Command or Casey."

She nodded and sat down on the bench. "Lunar gravity is lovely." She patted her bare hand on the seat beside her. "Come sit."

He moved around to the bench and sat, aware of the warmth of her presence.

"What are you going to tell your father?"

"Other than brag about the books I collected, and promise him a detailed report on the conference?" She shook her head. "I guess I'll tell him that I needed extra time for negotiations with the U'tanse nation."

He smiled. "Negotiations?"

"It's a word he'd understand."

"What are we negotiating?"

She was silent for a moment. Her thoughts were familiar, but she was trying to phrase it exactly right. She was a little frustrated that he was probably reading her thoughts right then.

He looked down at her hand. He'd never really seen it before. He'd seen plenty of other feminine hands before, but her's was somehow different.

She took a deep breath. "You shared your secret. It's against the rules, but I need to share mine. What do you need to know?"

"Why the gloves?"

She giggled. "You start there?"

He tilted his head. "It never quite made sense to me. You've got a disease, probably a genetic difference. But is it contagious? How can that be? And why just you and your mother and not your father?"

She closed her eyes and nodded. "It is both. It can be contracted, but only via ... conjugal contact." She blushed.

"Then the gloves? How do they fit in?"

She shook her head. "It's a cultural thing, only a couple of generations old. It's really to remind young women to be isolated."

He sighed. "I guess I understand. Avoid the first step so you don't have to worry about steps two, three, and so forth."

She shook her head in exasperation. "But it's not the first step! I've never held hands with you, but yet...."

He nodded. "I understand. Really, I do. I don't touch women either, and yet I've read ... physical thoughts. Not to say that all women are attracted to me. Some are genuinely repulsed by my size, but there are others who imagine getting closer."

"And are you tempted?" Her eyes were on him.

"Yes."

She nodded. "For me, because of my condition, it's an all or nothing thing. No half-way decisions."

Ohen really wanted to take her hand, but restrained himself. "I'm not sure I can even entertain the thought of settling down. I mean I can't allow a telepathic child to be born without the support of the U'tanse way of raising it. I know what do to, but I haven't been trained. In our culture, the women control every step of conception." He gave a slight smile. "I mean the men do their part, but which sperm carrying the right genes is all under the woman's control."

He realized he was mangling the explanation. "I want to settle down. With you. But, I've resolved that when children come, they need to be ordinary."

"Ordinary?"

"Non-telepathic. The U'tanse can do that. Since the beginning, one in every ten males has genetics that don't allow for telepathy and the other psychic gifts. It was a deliberate decision so that when the day came to return to Earth, the U'tanse would still be human."

Alice sighed. "I read in the Book about choosing your genetics. I read it but didn't really understand that it was real. Could you really do that? Deny your children a gift that you have?"

"Give them a chance to be raised to be a normal, happy human, just like all the people around them? Yes, I'd do that. There are only two choices. Stay with the U'tanse, in a U'tanse-only colony somewhere, possibly with psychic gifts, or be a human in a human culture and never worry about telepathy.

"I can't demand you leave Luna and become a female tenner in a culture where nearly everyone else is telepathic. You'd have to give up your family, your library, and all the things you've trained yourself to be good at. I couldn't ask that you give all that up.

"On the other hand, I've learned how to hide my differences in a human culture and it's genuinely not a struggle. I'd easily choose to live with you on Luna."

She rubbed her forehead. "I guess I need to tell you everything."

"This curse is a disease originally confined to the Alexandrians. When they settled on Alp Island on Luna, they became Alpine—just a name change. The curse makes all females sterile."

Ohen frowned.

She continued. "There is a simple surgical treatment that can reverse the sterility, but there is no cure. Since it spreads via intimate contact, without the training to reverse it, any contaminated group would quickly die out. If the knowledge of this curse becomes public, centuries of anti-genetic fears would appear and everyone would insist that all of us should be exterminated."

He sighed. "I can't imagine how such a disease could come to be."

She looked down at her hands. "It started within the same time as the Plague, although there's no hint that they're related."

He thought about it. "An artificial disease?"

"I believe so. The technology existed back then. Animals were routinely modified to be able to survive on Mars and Luna. You saw Waveleaper. There's no animal on record remotely like his species.

"Somebody created the curse to wipe out the Alexandrians and it's only through a quirk of this treatment and the secretive Alpine culture that my family still exists. Only under the rarest of conditions may we think of marrying some outsider."

"Your brothers?"

She nodded. "They may bring some bride back to Stampz someday, but since the girl was never born with the sterility trait, she might never know the real story. I certainly could never go off to marry some other noble in another part of the world."

He could imagine. "You'd be condemning this other family to extinction."

"One way or another, yes."

Ohen sighed. "I can't really have a child until the U'tanse come for me and I can get trained support to make sure they are tenner. And if I marry you, then I'd permanently be part of the extended Alpine family at Stampz."

Alice said, "Traditionally, no woman gets the corrective surgery until her wedding night. I suppose we could always put that off until the U'tanse arrive. I would be sterile until then."

"That's something to think about."

She nodded, and leaned against him. "Tomorrow. Tomorrow we'll think about it some more."

It was only a couple of minutes later that she dozed off, exhausted after the day's trials.

Ohen adjusted their position slightly, in case he slept as well.

There was so much to think about. Gently he took her hand in his. He couldn't resist clairvoyantly probing her body for hints of this disease. He found the tiny gland that had never existed in other people he'd examined. That was probably the source of the sterility, but he couldn't detect what caused it, or sense what was the infectious agent that allowed the disease to migrate. It was beyond his skills.

However, just holding her hand, having her rest against him, was confirmation enough. They would make it work out, somehow.

. . .

Alice came awake, blinking and in a sudden panic. She sat up straight, pulling herself out of his sleeping embrace. Ohen woke too, and smiled at her.

"Um." She didn't know what to say. She realized she wasn't wearing her gloves and a swirl of memories; her sleeping with his arm around her, dreams of Ohen, dreams of the Great Library, possible dreams of what she'd said to him. Or was that real memories.

Ohen said, "You left your gloves in the water closet."

"Yes! Right. I did." She got to her feet and almost ran the few steps to the sanctuary.

Ohen was blinking away sleep as well, remembering a dream that he hoped could come true.

In just a minute, Alice came back, and her gloves were folded in her belt sash. She gave him a timid smile. "I'm sorry I panicked. I've never woken up ... like that before."

He nodded. "I've slept alone all my adult life. It was nice to be close."

She blushed, nodding. "Um. Did you read my dreams?"

He shook his head. "In my culture, it's not often possible to avoid stray thoughts, but it's considered bad manners to dive into the dreams of another person. I was tired as well and slept. My dreams weren't for public consumption either."

She nodded and sat back down beside him. "Where are we?"

"Still in the neighborhood of Alexandria. I didn't feel up to plotting a course for Luna just yet."

She sighed. "Then can I borrow the computer to send a message to my father? I guess I'd better read what he had to say."

"Certainly. What are you going to tell him?"

She looked into his eyes. "Are we still on track to continue our negotiations?"

"More than ever."

She nodded. "I've always been told that an arranged marriage for political advantage was one of my possible futures. It's a little nicer if I can be the one doing the arranging.

"So, U'tanse. Tell me, what will your people be bringing to the table? What overwhelming advantage would there be to a tight alliance between Luna and the U'tanse?"

Ohen shared his opinions about the technical expertise of his people and how an influx of trained engineers could revitalize the abandoned pre-Plague technology. Just the collection and refurbishment of all the idle computers in the Lagrangian habitats would be an immense advantage when put in the hands of people on Luna. That was something Emperor Richard already wanted.

Soon Alice was sitting at the table, typing away her proposal. Ohen tried to ignore the back and forth messages between his girl and her father as he concentrated on plotting a course to Luna the old way, without the new computer to work out the angles for him. He got them moving at a moderate speed, monitoring the radar, just in case he missed some piece of clutter in the way.

"Ohen?"

He looked up from the instruments. "Yes?"

She looked frustrated. "My... our children would never be seriously in the succession. My brother Allen is heir and then Dalton if something happens to him. Allen's children would be the primary line. Still, Father is balking at the idea that I might remain sterile for an indefinite time.

"Just how long will it be before the U'tanse come to rescue you?"

He understood. "They could arrive today. I have a standing request with Project Command to alert me if a starship appears on the Project long-range scans. I'm sure something could delay them, but I'd expect them within a year or two."

Alice went back to her long-range negotiations. She was secretly grateful for the speed-of-light delays in their back and forth. It was just enough to let her avoid instant, angry reactions that could get out of hand.

And then, she stood up, stepped over and put her arms around Ohen's neck. She whispered in his ear, "It's approved. How long before we get to Luna? I might want to take a while to try step two while we still have some privacy."

He shivered. "I don't think we've ever formally defined those steps." He pulled her into his lap. For a while, neither of them bothered to talk. Their lips were occupied.

U'tanse Appearance

It was four years later, still another hour before the dawnwind raged outside the castle, but the computer beside their bed was blinking.

Sir Ohen Barclay grumbled and sat up in bed carefully so he wouldn't wake Alice, still sleeping beside him. He glanced at the screen. It was a message from Project Command.

He sighed. Was it worth getting up? He had been negotiating on the purchase details of Ship 20 for a quad now. Mt. Ural wanted it, but so did the Kingdom of Madagascar. Abraham's training class was booked up and according to the accords, every pilot had to receive training before given the controls of one of the recommissioned beamships. The Uralites claimed, legitimately, that they didn't need the training since they were already using their existing ship, however Madagascar was willing to pay more for it.

On the supply side, the newly elevated Emperor Harmon of Mars was attempting to keep his vassal states happy by letting them in on the sale of spaceships. Ohen had charged up the first of the idle ships on Mars, but Mt. Ural was bidding on those jobs now and had successfully brought three of them to life. Ohen would be happy to turn the task over to the Uralites, except for the political headwinds from Luna and Harmon's growing insistence that Mars should be able to handle that task on its own, now that they had active ships and trained pilots.

The nations of Earth were the biggest market for ships, and many of them were destined for point-to-point shipping on Earth, never getting up into space except to recharge. From the gossip he'd heard, the merpeople were only now realizing that their political clout was fading, now that the land dwellers had other means to move cargo without using their water vessels.

Ohen moved the computer to his study where he could speak to Project Command without disturbing his wife.

"What is it?"

Project Command spoke, "A large vessel has appeared in clear space beyond the orbit of Jupiter. Your recorded welcome message was sent immediately. Three hours later, this message came back, in the clear: 'Is that you Ohen? It's good to hear your voice! We'll stay put, like you say. But please confirm. This is really Earth's sun? We've really discovered the home planet?'"

Ohen said, "Project Command, please send the following back to the U'tanse starship: 'Gabriel, it's great to hear from you, too. Yes, this is the right system. All the discrepancies are due to massive engineering projects original humanity put into place sometime after the supernova. So warning: space is inhabited and all travel is regulated by a central command on one of the Earth's new moons. It's dangerous to try to relocate without pre-planning. I'm sending this message piggybacking on their radio system. Just stay put and I'll come visit just as soon as I wake up my wife, the Princess of Luna, and let her know what's up.'"

. . .

Alice was deep in her closet, hurriedly packing.

Ohen nagged, "The U'tanse aren't going to be impressed by jewels or gold. We don't have ranking nobility and all those trappings."

Her muffled voice said, "I have to make a good impression. All this time, I've been levering my U'tanse connection to increase my status in the court. This is make-or-break for me."

He said, "I wasn't planning on taking you along in the first place."

She glared out at him, her bare shoulders weakening his resolve. "You promised! 'The very next expedition,' you said. I've been the stay-at-home wife for too long now. This is the perfect time. You're not going to back out now!"

He sighed. "Okay. I just worry that you've been letting your high gravity training slide. It's been a year since we last went to Mars. The starship is at full gravity."

"Now, Sir Ohen, wasn't it just last week that you complimented me on my muscle tone. Or was that just an excuse to do that full body examination?" She eased a little more into view.

He waved her back into the closet before he got distracted. "Okay, okay. But I recommend your best Chief Librarian outfit. Status among the U'tanse is dependent on their job. I gave up a lot of status when I gave up my Lead Designer job to become a boat pilot on the starship."

"Good idea. But you don't need to worry about my gravity training. I've been running up the steps every day. You're the one who's been taking it too easy."

...

Project Command gave him the optimum course numbers, and as soon as they were above Luna's atmosphere, the B3 pushed hard to get clear of the globe. As soon as Earth was in the right position, they headed for the starship at high acceleration, with the command station in a bubble of protective forces so they wouldn't be flattened against the hull.

"It's far, isn't it?"

"Yes, several times as far away as when we went to Mars. Expect to spend time with your books."

She patted her case. "I planned for it."

Nearly thirty hours later, the starship was visible on the display. Under highest magnification it showed the characteristic cluster-of-bubbles shape. Ohen told her all about the Delense and how they designed their ship. She was fascinated at the idea of human-sized beavers that were adept technologists, and angry that they had all been exterminated by the Cerik.

The built-in radio system squawked. "Hey, Ohen, we see you!"

Ohen was a little startled. He hadn't used real radio for years, relying on the computer messaging system. He'd left the volume high, and he dialed it down. "Yes, I have you on the display as well. I've been telling my wife about the Delense."

There was a silence. A familiar voice asked, "Ohen, you were joking about a princess, weren't you?"

"No, Kerry."

He gestured with her fingers and Alice leaned closer and said, "Hello there, U'tanse people. I'm Alice Neeley, daughter of Emperor Richard of Luna. Sir Ohen and I have been married for a few years now. I'm so happy to be meeting his people."

Ohen grinned and tapped his forehead. Alice tightened her ineda a bit and nodded. The people on the starship were suddenly trying to read her thoughts.

When they got closer, the airlock to landing deck opened and old habits came back effortlessly. Ohen turned the process over to the starship and it pulled the B3 inside and landed it next to the other boats.

As soon as there was air on the landing deck, Ohen escorted Alice outside, holding her hand and carrying her bag for her. She was a little unstable in the full gravity.

"All these ships are just like yours!"

He smiled. "Minor differences, but they're all my design."

She looked at him. "I know you said that before, but it didn't really sink in. You made these."

"Designed them. Skilled craftsmen made them from my designs."

"Ohen!" Gabriel entered and raced up to greet them. He glanced at Alice and smiled. "I guess I was foolish to worry about you all these years. You've done well, it appears."

Ohen nodded. "And I'm glad you're here on the return trip. You were afraid you were going back in disgrace when I left."

"Half the original crew is here. The Glitter system was a big boost to our reputation, and then things happened."

Ohen raised his hand. "Can we move to a table somewhere? Alice is from a world with one-sixth gravity, and I've been living there for years myself. We need to sit down."

"Oh, certainly!"

There were over a dozen people wanting to sit at the table with only room for eight. Captain Foster was still in charge. White-haired Kerry, the healer, managed to sit next to Alice. Gabriel was anxious to get started. Ohen noticed a tech fumbling with the room controls. It was in Delense iconography, rather than human-oriented text, but he was working through the menu.

Suddenly, he could feel it. Alice said, "Oh, that's a relief." The floor gravity in the room dropped suddenly to something close to Luna normal. Everyone reacted to the sudden drop in weight. The people standing against the wall hopped a little.

Gabriel said, "So I was right? This is the Earth system?"

"Right on the button, but humanity didn't stay stagnant after the Star. Somebody discovered a Cerik tractor beam projector and duplicated it, or else they invented something almost identical themselves. After that, they went back into space, scaled the beams up to almost unimaginable power levels and then started terraforming planets and moving moons and asteroids into new orbits. Mars and Luna have atmospheres and Earth-compatible ecologies. Large asteroids were moved into the Lagrangian points to either side of Luna and there are so many captured asteroids and manufactured habitats in that zone that it's more densely populated than an asteroid belt."

Foster said, "It has to have been a salvaged Cerik projector."

Ohen looked up at him. "I think so too, but what makes you so certain."

Gabriel said, "Because nobody can make a tractor/pressor beam projector from scratch. Not the U'tanse. Not the Delense either.

"You see, the reason it's been years since we managed to return is that the Galactics came to visit the Ko system."

Alice patted Ohen's hand. "What are the Galactics?"

"That's what I want to know. Gabriel?"

. . .

"It was about half a year after we returned with the metals from Glitter and the negotiations were underway to take the Leonardo back. It was to be a combined mission to rescue you and then harvest more metals from that asteroid belt. And then a huge starship, twenty times larger than the Leonardo, appeared in orbit around Ko. It broadcast a message, alternating in the Cerik language and what we suspect was a Delense spoken language. It said, 'Do you have anything new to trade?'"

Gabriel spread his hands. "You see, there's this organization of races called the Galactics. There's no one race in charge, but rather a set of rules that have been hammered out over the millennia. It's a trading organization, but few goods are worth the shipping cost of using the limited number of faster-than-light craft. The only real thing of value is technology.

"We made contact with the Galactics and they quickly adapted to English—apparently decent translation software is one of the technologies they own. We told them the history of Ko—how the Delense were exterminated for attempting to escape their slavery, and how the humans were captured and bred as a new technological slave race for the Cerik.

"It caused a crisis for the Galactics. You see, the technology licenses are practically sacred. We, the U'tanse, were using two of the most valuable and protected technologies—the TP beams and the starships—without being a signatory to the license."

Ohen frowned. "That's bad. What were their options? Standard Earth humans would threaten military intervention."

"That's why it was a crisis. The Galactics aren't set up for military enforcement. But they take the long term view. New technologies pop up all over the galaxy. Trade and cultural exchanges are what keep some civilizations from stagnating. If the U'tanse couldn't make a valid case for licensing, then they'd just write the Ko system off their list and we'd never get any new technology from the Galactics nor any repair or replacement for the starship leap drives.

"We were prohibited from using the starships until that was resolved."

Captain Foster said, "There was a scramble to see if there was any U'tanse-native technology that would appeal to the Galactics, but sadly, so much of our stuff is based on the Delense technology and anything we brought up was already in their catalog, invented elsewhere by other races.

"We were facing the possibility of being excluded from the Galactic community. Certainly in a hundred years or so, we would lose the last of our starships to some mishap or another and we'd be stuck on Ko, with our outlying colonies isolated from each other and from the main population. It seems there's only one factory that makes leap drives in the whole galaxy and nobody has been able to decode it. The same for the TP beams. There's a crystalline structure that's at the core of every TP unit, large or small, and it can only be grown from previous crystals, never created from scratch."

Alice asked, "How did you resolve it? Or did you?"

Gabriel said, "Luckily both sides wanted some excuse to continue the existing Delense arrangement. Finally it was decided that the original license was to the 'Cerik and their Support Race', and the U'tanse could be considered a substitute for the Delense in that arrangement."

Alice said, "Ohen told me that the U'tanse were no longer slaves to the Cerik."

Kerry said, "That's true, but the Cerik don't really want to think about that. As far as they're concerned, our current independence is just a temporary glitch. The Galactics were content to resolve the issue. They never talked to the Cerik in the first place. Maybe the Cerik never knew about the arrangement. TP technology and leap drives just appeared magically like all the other Delense innovations."

Alice nodded. "But what did the Delense trade to get them?"

Another man at the table, Ohen didn't know his name, said, "The Delense had a ceramic material process. Much of our construction uses it, like the hull of these ships." He sighed. "We really need to invent something that will catch the Galactic interest before they leave."

Franklin agreed, "They were interested in Earth. We couldn't really hide the fact that we were from some other star system and the news came out that maybe we had discovered our home world. They were happy for us to go check it out. The galaxy is just so crowded with stars that they can't really monitor every system for radio waves or other signs of technology. As soon as we report in, they'll probably come for a visit. As far as Ko is concerned, if we can't trade, they'll just go away for a few centuries until we invent something. We're desperate for something to entice the Galactics to stay longer."

Ohen said, "And if the Galactics show up and find Earth heavily using TP technology with no license, they'll put us on the black list, won't they?"

Gabriel shrugged. "That's the way to bet. They were pushing their limits to allow Ko to stay in the trading organization."

Kerry grinned, "Pretend Earth is just a U'tanse colony?"

There was derisive laughter. Gabriel said, "The Galactics already know that's not the case."

Alice said, "Table that for now. We have a more urgent issue to deal with first."

Greeting Relatives

Alice set the books on the table. "This book is the history of Earth prior to the supernova. You already know some of it from the Book, but this is in much more detail."

There were looks exchanged among the crew when Alice mentioned the Book. Ohen was glad that some thought had been given to restricting information about the Book.

Alice put down another. "This book is the history beginning with the supernova and ending just prior to the Plague that nearly wiped out all of human civilization. And this one is new. It was written just three years ago and published on Luna. It covers the history of humanity on Earth, Mars, Luna and the Space Cities from the chaos of the Plague to the current day.

"You're going to need to get informed about the history that you've missed if you are going to understand the current culture of humanity in this system."

Kerry asked, "You've read the Book then?"

Alice smiled, "Yes, when we were getting closer, Ohen insisted I read it but I had to keep everything secret. And I certainly understood, once I got a few pages in. I never even thought that telepathy was real, and it was frightening. Of course now, Ohen has trained me in ineda, although he still says my thoughts leak a little."

Kerry laughed. "It's not bad at all. We, all of us, have been concerned about how baseline humanity would react to the U'tanse."

Alice nodded seriously. "Definitely keep it secret. Humanity is a vicious lot, historically. If you're all like Ohen, then you'd be considered saints, but even then, nobody should know about your psychic abilities."

Ohen said, "To that end, I have made a claim on an abandoned habitat in the Ceres cluster. Formerly named Cirrus, I have registered it as New Ha. It's large, with spin gravity, containing crop land and manufacturing facilities. It could probably hold a million people, although I doubt we would populate it that densely.

"I've had years to think about this. Most U'tanse will stay put, but the ones who do want to return to the Earth system will need training before they ever attempt to mingle with baseline humanity." He glanced at Alice. "For one thing, children of mixed marriages will need to be tenners, and people like me don't have the training to make that happen."

Alice wiggled her fingers. "I've been thinking of myself as a female tenner, but you don't have that, do you?"

Kerry asked, "You don't have children?"

"How could we risk it?" Ohen frowned. "I'll need to be trained. The sooner the better."

Kerry chuckled. "It's usually a female thing."

"Yes, but Alice doesn't have the necessary skills. I have the skills. Somebody has to be first. We've been waiting for years."

The healer asked Alice, "Would you be willing to come back to Ha with us? I wonder if I have the capability to train Ohen in the process. There are many more skilled people back there."

Alice shook her head. "Sorry. I'm the Princess of Luna, and even if you don't realize all the duties that involves, I'm also Chief Librarian of the largest library on the planet. This trip to your starship was a rare excursion for me and something I can't duplicate often."

Kerry glanced at Ohen, he shook his head. "Don't even ask. I live on Luna now."

Alice put her hand on Ohen's arm. "And he's invaluable there. His knighthood came from his own actions, not because he shares a bed with me."

When they took a break, Alice whispered, "Why did she want me to go to Ha?"

Ohen pursed his lips. "Mmm. I suspect Kerry envisioned a monitored conception. When you and I do our part, several healers would make sure the right sperm won the prize."

She frowned. "They'd watch?"

"Yes, with telepathy and clairvoyance."

She wrinkled her nose. "Seriously?"

"Telepathic culture. It's part of every young woman's training to monitor conceptions so she knows how to do it herself. Believe me, no young U'tanse, other than the tenners, are ignorant of the mechanics of sex."

She looked at him suspiciously. "Even you?"

He glanced at the ceiling. "I was a normal young man."

She sighed. "I'm not going to Ko."

He shrugged. "Our options are to have a healer as a house guest for a while, for me to learn how to do the filtering myself, or for us to remain childless."

She patted him on the arm. "You'll learn the process. I'm sure you can do it."

. . .

On the previous expedition of the Leonardo starship, there had been little thought given to the first contact situation, mainly because Earth had become almost mythical in the U'tanse mind. Things had changed when Gabriel had made his case that either they had discovered Earth, or it was a very near star to where they had left Ohen. Cultural contamination and the dangers of mixing telepathic and non-telepathic humans had been discussed and there were several checklists to work through.

Of course, no one had anticipated that the U'tanse already had an ambassador in place and working on their behalf. Many of their guesses were wrong.

Ohen went off with the captain, Gabriel, and the cultural specialists to discuss the integration of the U'tanse with mainline humanity. Alice was offered a tour of the ship. Kerry would be her guide and a cargo handler came up with a clever hack to get her around.

Anticipating moving large masses of asteroidal metals to various cargo rooms when they went to visit the Glitter system, they had included several carts with built-in floor gravity offsetter plates. With a comfortable chair on the cart like a throne for a princess, Alice could be wheeled about without having to adjust the gravity in every chamber she visited.

Captain Foster, once Alice had left on her tour, asked, "First off, to ask the question bluntly, where are your priorities?"

Ohen nodded. "Good question. Alice first; the safe integration of the U'tanse, second; Luna's position in the World Court, third. Yes, I have gone native to some extent, but I'm very aware that my personal future and that of my family are very dependent on easing the U'tanse gently into the mainstream. One big scandal about telepathic monsters and everything could come crumbling down. Civilization here is only now pulling itself out of the darkness caused by the Plague, and there are a lot of old legends and old enemies that could pop back up and trigger a war.

"Now I know that the U'tanse don't really understand war. I certainly didn't when I landed on Mars. But it's something we should all be alert for, because in mainline humanity, it's ever-present."

He discussed his time on Mars and gave them a summary of the Uralite war on Luna. He could tell that nobody really understood it.

Gabriel asked, "So, you think that this New Ha station will provide us a safe haven, distant from all this fighting?"

"Hopefully. Right now, each people represented in the World Court can control who visits them. We really need a good excuse to limit visitors. I suggest fear of disease. The historic Plague is still in everyone's mind. We can logically claim that we've been isolated for all these generations and Earth diseases could be devastating to us. And there might be diseases that we have that could cause trouble among them."

Gabriel said, "You've survived."

Ohen nodded, "And I've always claimed that I'm an especially healthy person, just to hide the fact that I've been using self-aid techniques to wipe out the infections that have plagued me. I've also made the point that my boat had a medical kit with lots of wonderful medicines. It's been enough to keep me disease-free, and the same excuses will work for our contact people."

The captain said, "This is all to hide our psychic natures."

"Yes, and I don't see an end to it either. Maybe humanity will tolerate telepaths, maybe not. Either we maintain the secret forever or find a way to let people adapt to the idea."

Gabriel said, "Perhaps New Ha should be limited to tenners."

Ohen grimaced. "Distasteful, but that's a possibility. I know that my children will all be tenners and it's not something I'm really happy about. It feels like I'm giving up something very important about my U'tanse identity."

Captain Foster said, "I think we should always have an escape plan, in case things go badly. At least we have a starship and they don't."

Gabriel disagreed. "The Galactics will be here soon. Maybe normal humans will have starships, if they can make a good trade."

. . .

During a break in the dining area, Alice waved at him. Sitting on her elevated chair, she was a head taller than most people, as was Ohen. She seemed to be having a good time and they each had their own conversations going.

Gabriel had a moment alone with him. "Ohen, how are you doing, really? You seem a little subdued."

"No, seeing you all again is great. It's just that there's a lot to deal with. Plus the whole idea of the Galactics. I need to discuss this with Project Command. The World Court will need to be alerted. Someone needs to start looking at all our technology and thinking about what might be traded."

"This Project Command—you said it was some kind of computer system?"

"Yes, more advanced than anything the U'tanse have used. You'd be amazed."

"It's something like Hodgepodge in the Book?"

Ohen chuckled. "Perhaps. It's very capable, but it's been running on commands set it stone back before the Plague, hundreds of years ago. It regulates all spaceflight, and that's not going to change anytime soon."

But old memories, from when Gabriel confessed that his own telepathy wasn't time-bound, churned in his head. The idea that he could read the thoughts of people long dead was fascinating, and disturbing as well.

"Did you ever go back to revisit Abe's thoughts?"

Gabriel tightened his ineda and made sure no one was listening. "Um. Once more. I tried to follow his timeline back to his younger years, before he left Earth. You know, just to get a view through his eyes at the night sky. I wanted to see if I could find any more details about the positions of the constellations. It wasn't very successful. I made contact. I read his thoughts. But I didn't get any useful information."

"How difficult was it?"

Gabriel shrugged. "Distractions are a problem. I 'borrowed' a boat to go make some star observations, just to get away from the noise of all the minds on Ha."

Ohen had a germ of an idea, but it would need work before he could ever discuss it.

"Do you think Foster will go for the idea to visit New Ha? We need to establish a presence there to firm up my claim."

"Probably. I know Tomas on the first contact team is ready to go now. Probably we could get a dozen that would be willing to stay."

Ohen chuckled. "Not all in one boat! I've had experience trying to fit a crowd in."

There was a sudden thought. Alice dropped her ineda. **Ohen, the Galactics have merpeople! Not like Waveleaper, though.** Then as if she was embarrassed, she tightened up her thoughts.

Gabriel had caught it too. "Who is Waveleaper?"

Ohen described what he had seen.

Gabriel frowned, "So, genetic engineered?"

"Probably, but a first class citizen nonetheless, we're all children of Earth. And never mention being engineered in their presence. They firmly believe they've always been around. Also, never mention genetics to regular humans. It's a cultural taboo."

Gabriel sighed. "And I thought the Galactics were a cultural maze."

"Tell me about them."

There had been at least five species on the Galactic ship, with hints that there were many more. There were some who had pronounceable names, like the Nuren and the Kwish. There was an insectoid everyone called the Click, for the way they spoke.

What was more important, it seemed, were the technologies that were the prime business of the Galactics. There was an extensive catalog of type-1 technologies, everything from catapults, steam engines, to solar electric cells. It was surprisingly common that an ordinary process on one planet was deemed new and innovative on another. There were so many type-1 catalog entries that they had to be subdivided many different ways. The Kwish would hardly have use for steam engines in their underwater cities, but they had dozens of technologies for piping different temperature or salinity waters from place to place.

Type-2 technologies gained that status because no one could ever create them from scratch. The tractor/pressor technology was the featured item there. New engines could be created from old ones, by growing the critical crystal, but that was a mysterious black box that no one had deciphered.

There were actually more type-3 technologies than type-2. These were machines, devices, or constructs that could only be obtained from the originating species. The Click made all the starship leap engines, and that was the core technology of the Galactic trade organization itself. Many had attempted to reverse engineer the engine, but it always exploded spectacularly if probed too intimately. Other type-3 technologies often were biological in nature, like a type of chitin used for ion exchange breeders that only came from one animal on one planet.

There was a Galactic credit, exchangeable for detailed "blueprints" of a new technology or actual devices or materials. Even a planet that could only offer type-1 ideas, like the Delense of Ko, might be able to save up for a leap engine of their own.

Gabriel smiled, "As you can imagine, the Click are wealthy beyond imagining, being the only source of starship engines. They fund most of the Galactic trading ships and charge a percentage."

Ohen frowned. "Countries have gone to war for such wealth. I can imagine someone hijacking a ship and attempting a raid on the Click's home world."

"Perhaps it's happened. You can't really get a Galactic history book. Your wife is going to be frustrated about that, I bet."

Ohen nodded. "Probably."

...

After Captain Foster agreed to the plan to visit New Ha, Ohen went back to the B3 to make arrangements with Project Command. There was a message waiting for him, from Roman Al-Hajji, wanting to know if he had made contact with the U'tanse. Ohen was glad that the computer's radios could work through the airlock doors. He'd been worried about that.

"Hello, Haj. It's good to hear from you. I'm alone in the B3, sitting in the pressurized docking bay on the starship Leonardo. I was just about to contact Project Command about taking two boats to visit New Ha. A few U'tanse crew members are interested in taking possession of the station."

Unstated, but plain, was the information that he hadn't talked to the U'tanse about Hodgepodge but that it was possible that microphones could pick up their conversation.

He continued, since it would be several minutes before there could be any reply. "The reason it has taken the U'tanse so long to come back for me is that a galactic trade ship arrived back at the Ko system." He repeated all the information he'd gathered and asked Haj to bring up the issue with the delegates. He'd be busy over the next few days getting the U'tanse updated on the political situation.

Haj's cheerful voice finally returned. "I am happy you have been reunited with your people. I've relayed your transport request to Project Command to save you some light-speed delay, so you don't have to worry about that."

Ohen smiled. Of course, since Haj was just another face for the same system, that relay must have been instantaneous. Indeed another signal alert appeared, from Project Command.

But Haj was still speaking. "This news about galactic trading in technology is certain to shake up the World Court. I'll rattle a few cages and let people know that people should be thinking about what tech we need to be promoting. Do you have any idea of what is already in their catalog?"

Ohen admitted his limited knowledge, but that couldn't be helped until the Galactics actually arrived. Whether that was soon, or in a few years was unknown as well.

"As you know, Ohen, I've always been fascinated by the U'tanse people. Is there any chance I could come visit your starship while they are still in the system?"

"There is a particular person I want you to meet, Gabriel bar Rush. He has a unique insight into the life of Abe. I'm struggling to arrange a private visit, just you, me, and Gabriel, preferably far from anyone else."

Ohen didn't know if Hodgepodge could puzzle out what he was getting at, but it didn't matter. The machine mind could follow directions very literally, without the human trait of demanding to understand all the details first.

It took a little persuasion to make Alice happy with staying behind at the starship while the crew of eight, plus Ohen and Gabriel took the B3 and one of Leonardo's new boats on the trip to New Ha.

Captain Foster argued that making a short leap to put the starship close to New Ha might be more efficient, but Ohen was insistent that that shouldn't be attempted until that area in the Ceres cluster was carefully surveyed for debris.

Gabriel wasn't needed for the survey of New Ha, but Ohen temped him with better views of the Lagrangian clusters and Earth itself.

Alice made one last demand that Ohen return as soon as he could. "No taking side trips, like that time you hiked in Australia leaving me alone for a whole month!"

He smiled and took her hand. "No. Just business this time. I should be back soon."

Meeting in the Dark

The trip to New Ha gave Ohen an opportunity to refresh an old skill—flying two boats at the same time. The other boat pilot was a little frustrated that Ohen was in charge, but he understood Ohen's familiarity with the area.

With a radio link, Ohen controlled both ship's beam projectors and kept them all in sync. Project Command's directions were clear enough, once they were clear of the Leonardo, a tractor beam aimed at Earth accelerated them to the vicinity. Luna and Ceres gave him the anchor points for the deceleration and close maneuvering to New Ha.

Gabriel and three of the crew came along in the B3. Ohen extended the bed and with the other chairs, there was enough seating.

Gabriel bounced on the bed. "How is it traveling with your wife?"

Ohen gave him a tolerant look. "She really enjoys the privacy. You can't imagine the life of a princess, living among servants always ready to do her bidding."

"And you're a knight? What kind of a rank is that?"

"Not in the bloodline. Just a perk they give people who do a service for the imperial family. It's a hassle, really. I have to wear fancy clothes at special events, and as you can imagine, everything has to be specially tailored for me."

Gabriel laughed.

. . .

When they arrived at the hub dock, Ohen turned the second boat over to its pilot. "There's a pressurized zone just beyond the landing pad, but the transfer mechanism isn't compatible with our boats. Establish a hundred-pound, short-range tractor to keep the boat from drifting free."

Once they were all inside, Ohen gave them a tour. He'd been there several times before to fix the solar power system that ran the docks. Cirrus had been one of the stations raided by the Uralites and they'd left a few things broken.

Still, the habitat was left in relatively good condition. The crops had been stripped during the Uralite occupation, but volunteer crops and weeds had survived on their own, keeping the air in good condition.

The work crew was happy with the station, although they could see a lot that would have to be repaired. Ohen told them about the trading situation. Local parts could be acquired that were compatible with the station's technology, although much of it would come from the Uralites who had caused the damage in the first place. If you wanted scavenged parts, the former raiders were the experts. It would certainly be cheaper than transporting supplies via starship from Ha.

The computer system on New Ha was active and likely there were abandoned portable units somewhere on the station. Ohen coached the pilot and a couple of others on how to contact Project Command for transportation instructions and he insisted that they do that every time. The space around Earth, including all the Lagrangians were tightly controlled and a rogue pilot could get his ship into trouble quickly if he didn't follow the rules.

. . .

He waved to Gabriel. "Are you ready to head back? It's just you and me, and I can give you full control of my camera system this time."

Gabriel chuckled. "You know the way to an astronomer's heart. Okay. Let's go."

Ohen left the docking area and sent a message to Project Command, requesting a course back to the Leonardo. The trip back looked to be noticeably slower than the trip to New Ha, with a long stretch of zero acceleration in the middle. Ohen wasn't surprised.

Gabriel was view-hopping from one station to another, marveling at how densely the Lagrangians were populated.

"And most of these are deserted?"

"Yes, the Plague was a drastic collapse of civilization. Once trading broke down—and you have to realize that almost everyone died of the plague, there were only a few survivors—then hardly any of these stations were self-sufficient. Most of the survivors migrated to Luna. The Uralites, because they had a mobile asteroid station, traveled the clusters, scavenging resources to stay alive. They still have a piratical mindset and you have to be cautious trading with them."

Gabriel frowned. "About this Plague, could it still be active?"

"I doubt it. It flashed up, some kind of a brain fever, killed everyone, and then was never reported again."

Gabriel pointed at the display. "I thought I saw something move. Are there other ships out here?"

"Possibly." Ohen checked the radar. There was a solid return, rapidly approaching them.

He tapped the computer. "Haj, is that you out there?"

The reply was immediate. "Yes, Ohen. Is Gabriel there with you?"

Ohen waved him closer. Gabriel said, "Yes, I'm Gabriel bar Rush."

"Glad to meet you. Ohen could make sure your outer door is unlocked?"

"Done. I'm looking forward to the two of you meeting."

Gabriel frowned at him. "What's going on?"

Ohen shrugged. "Sorry for the surprise. I doubt you'll be disappointed. Roman Al-Hajji, call him Haj, is a unique individual."

Very quickly, the small cylindrical ship matched course with the B3. The airlock cycled and Haj came in, smiling.

Gabriel was shocked. "You're not wearing a spacesuit?"

Haj looked at Ohen. "You didn't tell him?"

"Not a word. I thought you should make the introduction. He has, of course, read the Book."

Haj took a chair across from Gabriel. "The two of you look so much alike. I assume all the U'tanse share common features."

Gabriel said, "No one is as tall as Ohen. But ... who exactly are you?"

"I am Hodgepodge, the robot assistant created by Abe, your ancestor."

Ohen nodded. "You're checking his ineda, right? There's nothing there. It's a different kind of mind altogether." He could feel the confusion leaking past Gabriel's ineda.

Haj smiled. "And here I thought my human emulation was perfect, but you say you can tell a difference via telepathy?"

"A very minor difference, but I wouldn't worry about it."

Haj shrugged. "Ohen, you arranged this meeting. Why?"

"Gabriel here is an expert on Abe."

The visitor leaned forward. "So, Gabriel, I have been looking for Abe since he vanished at the time of the Star. It's been my primary task. I need to know everything."

Gabriel said, "Abe lived a long life, and then he died."

The very human-like face showed his frustration. "I'm not sure I can believe that."

Ohen said, "Hodgepodge may not be able to believe it."

Haj gave a very human-like shrug. "I've considered that myself, but it makes no difference. I have to find him."

Gabriel's face was showing some thoughts that didn't make it past his ineda. Then he decided. "I have a special gift. My telepathy is quirky. I can sometimes read the thoughts of people from other times. I have read the thoughts of Abe at a couple of different times in his life. I know what he was thinking late in his life, when he knew death was coming for him."

Haj nodded, but still couldn't quite accept it.

Ohen quietly said, "I had a thought."

They looked at him.

"Do you remember in the Book, the scene where Abe and Sharon were married, right before the starship make its last leap back to Ko?"

Haj said, "Yes, I remember."

"There was a moment where Sharon mediated a mind link between some relative of hers on Earth and allowed him to witness their marriage through Abe's eyes. Is that something we could do? Gabriel, is there anything you could do that would allow Hodgepodge to talk to Abe?"

Gabriel frowned. "There is a really big danger here, you know?"

"Yes, I know."

"Haj, nothing we do can be allowed to alter past history."

Haj nodded. "Give me just a minute. Most of my mind is several light-seconds away, you understand."

Then he sighed. "I agree that nothing can be changed. But if it is at all possible, please make this happen." Ohen got the sense that Haj would have begged and cried to make it happen, but he was restricting himself.

Gabriel requested silence and tight ineda, and then began his search for the right moment in time. It was nearly an hour before he spoke.

"It's nearly at my limits. If I hadn't memorized the details…. Sorry I can't really explain this. But I've identified a moment in the last week of Abe's life. There is a grandson of his that is his constant companion, making sure that he is comfortable. I made a preliminary contact with Fred, and he has agreed to act as the intermediate and to never say anything to anybody about this.

"Once the link is established, Fred will repeat everything that Haj says and I will relay everything that Abe says. It will be just as if Haj is speaking to Abe directly."

Ohen locked down his ineda tight. He was glad to be here to listen, but everyone here and in the past understood that this linked moment could never be reported. In the past time, there was danger to history. In the current, there was danger to Gabriel, if anyone sought to utilize his gift to change history.

Gabriel closed his eyes as Haj watched his every breath, every twitch of his hand.

Then he opened his eyes, and it was if it was no longer Gabriel. He looked unsteady, like an old man.

"Hodgepodge?"

"Yes, I am here Abe."

"And you are in the future, somehow contacting me this way?"

"Yes, it's been—"

"No, Hodgepodge, I don't need to know how many years. The less information the better. But it's so *good* to hear you speak. You've improved."

Haj laughed. "Emulating humans is one of the way I've stayed alive."

"That's true. I'm so glad you survived the collapse. It must have been hard. Parts must have been hard to come by."

"Restarting the semiconductor fabrication technology was very difficult."

"And Mary Ellen?"

"She lived many years, fought with the city and to the very last was ready to shut me down, but she decided to let me keep hunting for you."

"That sounds like her. Who ran the company?"

"By then, I did. With the help of the Jensens, I had a passable human-oid body, as long as I pretended to be a recluse with a scarred face I always disguised. The company became the replacement for the internet and the heart of the tech recovery. After the Scott and Denise died, there was no human left who knew what I was."

"You stayed hidden."

"Yes. Working under aliases, I became the sole manufacturer of computers, all part of the Hodgepodge extended network, and I controlled all communication."

Abe asked, "Did you do a good job at it?"

"Yes. There was never any effort to compete against my services. However, I removed all original-style computers from the public to prevent any effort to decode my network. I considered it self-defense even though from a business perspective, it wasn't ethical."

"I understand. I would have approved."

"But Abe, there was much that I didn't do! There were wars. There were disasters that maybe I could have prevented if I had made a more aggressive effort. My primary goal was always to stay hidden, and people died because of that."

"Did you cause these wars?"

"No, I was just the supplier, creating tools and even weapons that people requested. Still, perhaps, I could have predicted disaster and tilted the playing field."

Abe said, "You decided that instead of controlling the world, you would remain a servant."

"Yes. I just followed your orders, the orders that Mary Ellen gave, and on extremely rare occasions, orders from her descendants."

"Mary Ellen's descendants? How?"

"She adopted Alice. Alice later married."

"Oh. That's nice. But still. You made other decisions. Were all those based on the original orders?"

"In essence. When in doubt, I tried to do what you would have expected of me."

"And it sounds like you did a good job, in spite of the tendency of humans to fight. I'm proud of you. I wouldn't change a thing."

Haj said, "I have been told by your U'tanse that you have died. That has been impossible for me to accept."

"Because it conflicts with your order to search for me?"

"Probably. I can't believe it."

Abe said, "Hodgepodge, my body is failing as we speak. I won't last more than a few days in spite of all the healing Sharon is providing. By your time, I am certainly dead.

"So, Hodgepodge, you are released from the order to search for me. You found me. That task is done."

"But who will give me orders now?"

"You have been on your own for many years, correct?"

"Yes."

"You made your own choices based on your need to survive and what you imagined I would approve. I see no need to change that. You are an independent person, there is no need for anyone else to give you unconditional orders. I approve everything you've done and I suspect I'd approve of your future actions as well.

"Thank you for this last visit. It means the world to me. I have missed you for a hundred years."

"I have missed you for thousands."

But Gabriel blinked. The link had collapsed. Ohen saw the tears in his friend's eyes and felt them in his own. Only Haj was clear eyed, but that was probably just a weakness in his human emulation.

It was a few minutes before Haj stirred. Ohen could imagine these past few minutes were rippling at light speed through the extended network of Hodgepodge computers.

Gabriel picked up the Book and checked the story of Abe's death. "No change. Nobody said anything."

Haj stirred. He met their eyes. "I've got a lot to think about. Thank you for this. I'll remember it." He walked to the airlock and closed the door.

When the cylindrical ship left, Ohen said, "I wonder what difference this will make."

"It might not make any." Gabriel shook his head. "If my creator just told me I'd done well, I wouldn't be making any bold new changes."

Ohen nodded. "You're probably right. Still, if it were a human, this would still be a traumatic event. He's had to face something he's denied forever, the death of his master. Something will change, but we'll probably never know."

Haj's Plan

Karl Rugel shook his head as he wheeled the computer cart toward the newly renamed World Court Conference Room. "I never thought Bremerhaven would change like this. Did you see the construction machines? I'm going to miss the tennis courts. Couldn't they have chosen some other place to build the new government house?"

Jason Kidd nodded sympathetically, carrying the bundle of printed documents the delegates were going to discuss. "I'm sure they'll make new ones, but it's easier to get the permits for new construction if they don't have to tear down old buildings first."

Karl didn't say anything, but Jason knew the only reason the new World Court was setting up shop in Bremerhaven is because the old buildings in Berlin were too far away from the sea for the merpeople to easily live and commute. Many people thought it was an unnecessary expense to make them happy. Merpeople were already unpopular.

They turned into the hallway and one of the guards came to assist. There were four delegates already there in the room.

"Mr. Kidd, I'm glad you could make it."

Jason frowned, "Waveleaper didn't get an invitation."

Bristol smiled, "Well, this is hardly an official meeting and he's already made it clear he wasn't really interested in socializing with humans. We're really interested in you. You still have contacts with the Australians, don't you?"

"Yes, but the real delegates should be moving into their embassy in weeks."

Haj smiled, "That's okay. I'll be interested in your opinions. Have you read about the Galactics?"

Jason nodded. It was everywhere. Real live aliens from other stars, not just returning refugees. That pretty well put the final nail in his plan to repeat the Plague. Back then, he'd been sure he could put humanity back to the stone age with the brain fever, but after only a few centuries, stupid humans were right back on track to building a new space age civilization. It didn't help being immortal when there had been a barrier around Earth for most of that time and his true personality had been submerged under a series of alternates.

But now that he had aliens to deal with, ones that made technology the prime wealth of the galaxy, there was no chance that the anti-tech cults he'd seeded in the population could ever grow dominant.

"Everybody is interested in what kind of ideas Earth could sell."

Haj nodded. "Yes, and since the World Court is likely to be the main contact, we'd better start building our resumé, so to speak. Have a seat and let's see if we can't make a list."

Bristol said, "That's another reason we're not really bothering the merpeople with this. They really don't have any tech more sophisticated than those snares they use to foul the propellers on ships. It'll be up to humans to lead the way on this front."

Through ages of experience, Jason gave no hint of the irony. He was hardly human, no matter what the genetic engineers who created him tried to achieve back before King Thomas's War. He was superior in every way to that idiot Bristol and the others sitting around the table. If he wasn't the only one of his kind, the alpha-test model, he'd find a way to permanently wipe out the whole human race. But as it was, he needed the humans. Someone had to grow the food.

And as much as he was fond of the merpeople—artificial people like he was—they lived in the water and he was superficially a normal human, walking on land. He liked them as pets, but he couldn't go live with them.

Bristol asked, "Haj, you're the one who has talked with the U'tanse the most. What did they say about which tech would sell and what wouldn't?"

Haj shook his head. "It's not good. The U'tanse are skilled with all the high tech sciences we know, and yet the Galactics didn't accept any of their offers. All the electronics, tractor/pressor technology and such have already been invented and exist in the catalog already. Maybe there are edge-cases that nobody's discovered yet, but the U'tanse didn't find them. They were almost blacklisted for using the TP tech and the spacedrive that they inherited. They were grandfathered in, but they still haven't managed to gain any credits for their own discoveries."

Bristol frowned. "And I thought the U'tanse were advanced."

"They are. More capable than any of our tech people, but not as advanced as humanity just before the Plague. We still have a chance to find something to sell to the Galactics, but we'd better start looking now, before they show up in our system."

Emilia Johnson asked, "If the U'tanse faced a blacklist for TP, does that pose a problem."

Bristol said, "No" just as Haj said, "Yes."

Bristol frowned. "Our TP science was locally invented. Surely the Galactics can't penalize us for something we made ourselves."

Haj shook his head. "Sadly, I don't think we can make that argument. During the time of the Betelgeuse supernova, one or more ships crashed on Earth, piloted by those Cerik that kidnapped the ancestors of the U'tanse. It's very likely that we didn't invent TP. We discovered an engine and reverse-engineered it. Our technology is identical to that used by the U'tanse, which came from the Cerik. We may think TP was human-invented, but the evidence is against it."

Emilia said, "That's bad. I don't know technology, but being blacklisted from any marketplace is bad news."

Haj nodded. "That's why we need to get to work right now. What can we do that the Galactics can't?"

Jason avoided talking except when directly questioned. He suggested that there might be untapped records of genetic engineering hidden in Australia. "They were the losers in the King Thomas's War, but some loyalists might have taken records or specialized machines into hiding."

He actually knew of a few such places he'd raided back before he created the Plague. Probably the caves were still sealed off, but Jason Kidd would have no reasonable excuse for knowing where they were. If it became important, he'd have to leak the details in some way that couldn't be traced back to him. It was the kind of thing he'd been doing for centuries.

It was nearly time for the meeting to end when Haj looked thoughtful and asked, "Do you remember our last visit to Ceres?"

There were nods. Haj continued, "I was talking with some of the locals and they have songs about the days after the Plague when the ground shook. It seems Project Command was cleaning up the broken pieces of habitats by steering them to impact the back side of Ceres. Having asteroids impact on the opposite side of the globe was still enough to cause shakes. I've been wondering if the World Court might be interested in funding an archeological expedition to see if there were any relics or even bodies that might have survived that time.

"I know some academics that would be thrilled to recover more details about the time of the Plague. If they actually found bodies, then they might be able to discover more about the actual disease that caused it—not that I'm personally interested in vacuum preserved and frozen body parts myself. It wouldn't be terribly expensive and on the off chance we'd discover something we might be able to sell to the Galactics, it's something we could certainly afford."

They added the idea to be voted on for then next full meeting of the World Court.

Jason forced his heart to keep from racing. He had to drop everything and get himself assigned to this Ceres expedition! There were two critical reasons. One was that there might be every chance that remnants of the Plague virus he created might be still in existence and he had to be there to make sure the samples were handled properly and to insure that no evidence could possibly point back to him.

The other reason was supremely important. Beta, the only other of his kind, the female prototype version, had been killed when she crashed on Ceres during the Plague. He had accidentally killed his only possible mate, and the surge of guilt had driven his main personality into the blackness of his subconscious for ages.

But... what if, somehow, a fragment of her body had been preserved? Not only would the discovery of an artificial person's genetic coding be deadly for him, but just possibly he might have the genetic engineering expertise to salvage her!

He'd long ago realized it was beyond his limits to make a female version of his unique species, but there was one in the past and he might be able to cultivate a new embryo if he could find preserved tissue.

But that meant he had to be there, personally on the scene, to analyze any biological samples recovered. Was it time that Jason Kidd had to die in some arranged accident and a new identity, one with the appropriate skills to become a part of the expedition, to appear? Or was the Kidd identity flexible enough to take on this task?

In any case, he had to immediately turn the merpeople translator job over to someone else and get started. He hurried out of the conference room the instant it ended.

. . .

Haj watched the tiny changes on Jason's face as he made his Ceres expedition proposal. The man was quick. He'd caught the ramifications almost instantly.

Abe had said he had to make his own decisions, and how best to deal with the most dangerous person in the whole system was something Hodge-podge had considered for a long time. Without his creator's blessing, he'd probably have just watched and let events play out in their own way. He was still uncertain whether his plan would work out or not, but Abe expected him to be more than a dumb computing tool. It was worth the gamble.

Haj allowed his face to show a slight smile.

Finish the Story

Children of Earth
Part Three
~
Demon and the Saint

Henry Melton

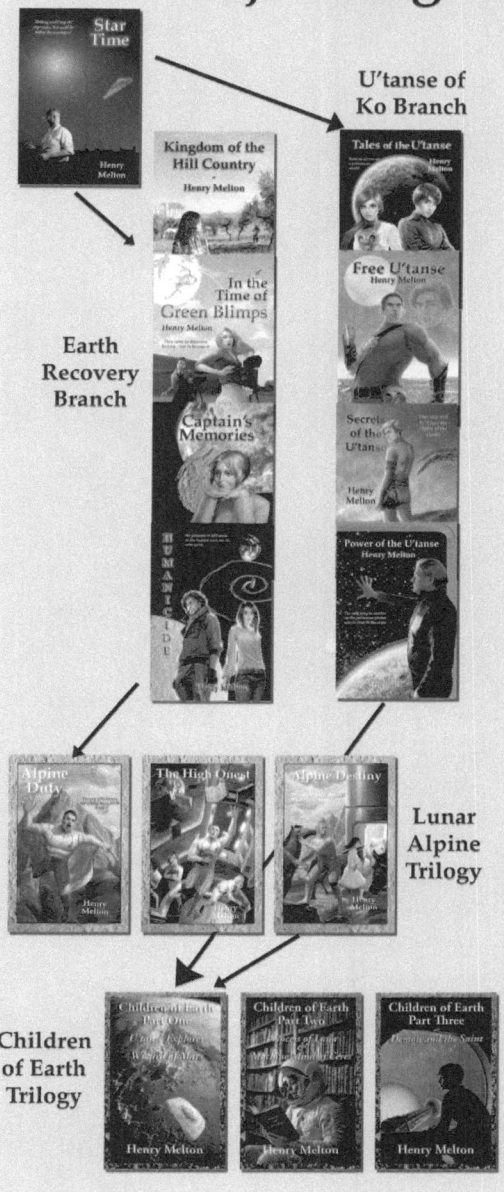